PRAISE FOR
AUDREY CARLAN

"FIVE STAR REVIEW! I recommend this book to anyone looking for a sweet, fierce love story. It takes a lot to write an original story that takes twists and turns you won't see coming."

~Abibliophobia Anonymous Book Reviews Blog

"Damn Audrey did it again! Made me smile, made me laugh & made me cry with her beautiful words! I am in love with these books."

~Hooks & Books Book Blog

"I have a new addiction. I count down the days until the next Audrey Carlan's Calendar Girl book releases as soon as I am finished with the current one. I am loving the journey that Mia is on. It's seductive and powerful - captivating."

~Maine Book Mama Book Blog

Resisting Roots

A LOTUS HOUSE NOVEL: BOOK ONE

This book is an original publication of Audrey Carlan

Cover Design by Waterhouse Press, LLC

Cover Photographs: Shutterstock

Paperback ISBN: 978-1-943893-10-2
PRINTED IN THE UNITED STATES OF AMERICA

Resisting Roots

A LOTUS HOUSE NOVEL: BOOK ONE

AUDREY CARLAN

DEDICATION

Debbie Wolski

I'm dedicating this novel to you,
an angel among us mere mortals.
You taught me everything I know about yoga,
the chakras, and more importantly,
you helped me find my balance.

I'm not sure where I'd be today
without your support and spiritual guidance.
I love you with my entire being.
Thank you for being such a gift to me
and the rest of the world.

Forever your student.

Namaste

NOTE TO THE READER

Everything in the Lotus House series has been gleaned from years of personal practice and the study of yoga. The yoga positions and chakra teachings were part of my official schooling with The Art of Yoga through Village Yoga Center in Northern California. Every chakra fact and position description has been personally written by me and comes from my perspective as a Registered Yoga Teacher, following the guidelines as set forth by the National Yoga Alliance and the Art of Yoga.

If you want to attempt any of the positions within this book or detailed in any of the Lotus House novels, please consult a Registered Yoga Teacher.

I suggest everyone take a yoga class. Through my yoga schooling and teaching the gift of yoga to my students, I have learned that yoga is for everybody and every body. Be kind to yours, for you only get one in this lifetime.

Love and light,

Audrey

CHAPTER ONE

Lotus or Accomplished Pose

(Sanskrit: Siddhasana)

To enjoy lotus pose, sit down on your mat with your legs crisscrossed and seat bones grounded into the floor. Straighten your spine, level your head, and place your hands on each knee with thumb and forefinger touching. This is one of the most basic yoga poses that calms and centers one with his body, mind, and surroundings.

TRENT

"Wake up, you sorry piece of shit!"

A growling sound accompanied by a searing pain in my leg had me blinking against the too-bright light. My mouth felt like dust bunnies had crawled into it and grown roots.

Smacking my chops, I blinked a few times and gripped the top of my good leg for leverage. A knot that had wormed its way into my neck protested as I rose to a seated position.

"Ross?" I shook my head and looked at the gray-haired ticking time bomb who was my agent. His large form blocked some of the light streaming through from the windows behind him—windows I had closed tight in fear of this very moment when I'd have to open them, wake to another day of pain, therapy, and more goddamned therapy. "What are you doing here?" I asked around the furry friends in my mouth. Reaching for the first thing I could wrap my fingers around, I tipped the bottle of orange Gatorade back and almost spit the offending liquid across the room the second the rancid flavor hit my tongue. I regarded the inside of the bottle and gagged. The sight of the black flecks floating around made the previous night's booze overload swirl and churn unpleasantly in my gut.

Food. That's what I needed. Load up on some greasy shit to absorb the night's activities. Patting the table, I searched for the stack of takeout menus.

Ross slapped my hand away along with everything on the coffee table, including the orange drink that, apparently, I'd been using last night to flick my cigar ash in. Would have been good to remember that *before* I'd I chugged back a huge swallow.

"So this is what it's come to? Six weeks of recuperation, and what do you have to show for it?" He slapped his thighs as he looked around. "You're living in filth. Drinking? Smoking?"

"Only cigars, Ross."

He took his cap off, smoothed back his hair, and put it back on. Not a good sign. He was beyond frustrated and about to blow his lid. After five years on the Oakland Ports, I knew when my agent was going to lose his shit.

"Fox, you're the best hitter on the team. Hell, you rank in the top three hitters in the American *and* the National Leagues. So you got hurt. Big frickin' deal! Get over yourself, and get your head back in the game." Ross paced the room.

I sat up straighter. Sitting up was a bad idea. The pounding in my head matched the sound of a bat cracking in half upon contact with the ball. I gripped my temples and squeezed, my hammy aching as I readjusted my leg to rest on top of the table.

"Have you even been to therapy?"

Snide son of a bitch. I gritted my teeth and clenched my hands into fists. "Of course I have, Ross. Three times a week. Three other days, I hit the gym and lift weights with Clay."

He widened his eyes. "Are you supposed to be lifting?"

Shrugging, I peered out the window. "I'm also using the treadmill." Even I could hear the childlike, defensive tone as I spoke. Ross could bring me right back to the time when I was a lowly rookie again itching for the big time.

He scoffed, "And what about the strengthening, flexibility, stretching? Who are you working with on that? The last report I got from your sports doc recommended you take a daily yoga class." He sat down in the chair across from where I'd made a bed on the couch.

Once again, Ross took off his cap. This time, he held it loosely by the brim between his knees. Once he relaxed, I took a load off, allowing the tension to seep out my pores. Not even my own father had the power to control my emotions like Ross did. If I didn't know any better, I'd swear he'd served in the military. The way he got all of his athletes in line proved how much he cared. Agents didn't have to make house calls to check in on their clients, but hidden beneath the rough and tumble act was a bit of a softie. Only I hadn't been in line with my team in over six weeks—since the day it had all gone to hell in a handbasket.

The crowd roared. Standing next to home plate, waiting for the pitch was nothing short of a religious experience. Every. Damn. Time. My spine tingled and the hairs on the back of my neck stood at attention as if God himself stood over my shoulder, waiting for the play. The pitcher pulled back his arm, and everything went dead silent. The crowd, the announcer, my team, everything stopped. It was me and the ball. I swore I could see the pitcher's fingers tighten around the ball, knuckles turning white...and then it would rush forward like a high-speed train. The ball rocketed through the air, subtly swaying in its path as it arched slightly before its descent. Right down the middle. I didn't see that coming. Usually a pitcher avoided the middle with me at all cost. With good reason. It was my sweet spot.

I pulled back both my arms, and a tiny pinch at my shoulder blades told me I was in perfect position. As the ball came closer, its path edged toward the strike zone. With my feet planted, I twisted my entire upper half, used every ounce of strength I possessed, and smashed that ball with my bat. The crack as the ball met solid oak echoed around me. Instantly, the ball changed direction and flew into the air. For half a second, I watched that ball fly, pride filling my pores with power and energy. Then I let the bat fall, twisted my leg, and jolted into a run.

All hell broke loose. Pain seared through my hamstring like a hot knife through butter. I clutched at the ravaged limb, a few steps into running toward first base, and I went down, down, down. Crashing onto the red clay below, my uniform streaked with dirt as if I were a warrior downed in battle.

The only silver lining was that I'd hit a home run. Even though my hammy had snapped like a broken rubber band, that single hit allowed the guys on second and third to run home, and the San Francisco Stingers went home the losers. I left in an ambulance and ended up in surgery for a torn hamstring.

"Snap out of it, kid!" Ross gripped my shoulder and shook me hard. He stood and rummaged through all the pill and liquor bottles on the side table next to the couch. "This is what you're doing with your time." His mouth was twisted into a disgusted frown. "Surprised there isn't a groupie here warming your bed right now."

While seated, effectively preventing the couch from levitating, I thought back to last night. Huh? Where was that chick anyway? Tiffany, Kristy, Stephanie... What was her name? She'd ridden my cock for a while, but then I blacked out right in the middle. I snorted. Maybe she left when I wasn't able to get her off. Usually, I prided myself on being a generous lover, but I could barely string together enough words to make a sentence last night, let alone make a groupie sing my praises.

Ross spun around, groaned, raked his fingers through his hair, and put the cap back on. "Christ. Pills, liquor, women? What else?"

"Look, I don't owe you any explanations. I'm on medical leave—"

"The hell you don't!" He came over to me fast, much faster than a man with two blown out knees and a heart condition should have been able to, and pushed his finger into my chest. "You've got two choices. Get your shit together, or lose your contract. Don't you realize you're up for renewal? You may not have blown through that thirty mil in the last three years, but you're risking your five-year contract. The numbers are staggering, kid. With the way you've been hitting, you're looking at an offer for upwards of a hundred mil for five years. All that"—his eyes blazed—"gone!" He snapped his fingers. "In the blink of an eye."

I closed my eyes and swallowed. My agent hadn't put the prospective numbers into any real terms. We'd been hoping for the same deal of at least thirty million for three more years. If what Ross said was true, I was worth twenty million a year.

"Jesus," I whispered, my heart pumping hard. My mouth went dry as the foothills during a California drought.

Ross set his hands on the back of the chair, hunched his shoulders over, and shook his head. "You have to get back into the game. The team needs you. They've already lost the playoffs and the pennant this year. Coach wants you there for spring training. That means you've got until the third week of February to recuperate and show the suits what you're made of. You need to be ready to train in three months."

His tone held a hint of uncertainty. "Are you telling me if I can't play at full capacity by spring training, I could get cut from the team?"

Ross ran his hand under his chin a few times. I could almost hear the sound of his palm grating along the scruff there. "I don't know. Depends on how well you heal up. In the meantime, what's the plan?"

With the potential loss of my contract on the table, including losing more money than I'd spend in my lifetime, I exhaled long and slow until all the air was gone and only a burning sensation remained. "I'll lay off the booze and late nights."

"And do the therapy and yoga?" He tipped his head to the

side.

I shook my head and wrung my hands, loosening the tension. What I needed right now was my boxing bag. “Yoga? Really? Look, I can’t touch my toes to save my life, and all that bending and twisting sounds downright boring. Nuh-uh, I’ll leave the granola crunching to the vegans I date and figure something out.”

Ross was next to me in a flash. He whacked me upside the head just like my old man used to. My old man did it in jest. Ross meant to rattle my brain. Irritation filled me, burning white-hot. I ground my teeth and held onto my anger by a thread. If I struck him, I’d sever a tie. He could be an asshole, but he meant well and cared about me. Kind of. Okay, probably. Either that, or he liked the fat wad of cash he scored for representing one of the best players in Major League Baseball.

“Don’t be a blowhard, kid. You go to that class, or I swear on all things holy I will drag you there like a sack of potatoes and throw you at the feet of those Gumby tree huggers, pour honey all over you, and let the Stingers do their worst!”

Damn. He was referring to the San Francisco Stingers. The rival’s coach had already made several house calls, trying to get my attention. They were after my hide because, even if I wasn’t at my best right now, I would heal. A typical hamstring tear healed six weeks after surgery, followed by another couple months of physical therapy and rehab. I’d been blowing off a lot of my therapy and not doing the extra work, thinking I could heal it with walking, weights, and the treadmill. Unfortunately, all that had done was land me in the hot tub working out the kinks.

“Fine, I’ll go.”

“When?”

Taking a breath, I looked around my place. A sour, funky odor emanated from a spot in the corner. A greasy pizza box sat there, surrounded by other various food cartons. I couldn't even remember when I'd last had pizza. Maybe a few days ago? When was the cleaning lady due, anyway? I shook my head and rubbed my chin. Ross waited for me, hands on hips.

"Tomorrow!" I waved a hand in the air. "I'll go tomorrow."

"You promise?" He took a few steps toward the door.

"I'm a man of my word."

"Yeah, you always were." His shoulders slumped, and he looked down. "Prove it." He slammed the door hard enough that the Big Gulp cup perched precariously close to the edge on a nearby table toppled over in a deluge of cherry-colored liquid.

I closed my eyes and rubbed my aching forehead. "What next?"

GENEVIEVE

"Not happening, Row. I said no, and I meant it." My voice had taken on a scary timbre that eerily reminded me of Mom. If she were here, she'd know what to do.

Rowan backed up, crossed his arms over his widening chest, and gave me the stink eye. "Seriously? I'm sixteen, not five." He glanced at our baby sister, Mary, who was happily munching on her Cheerios.

Sighing, I slapped peanut butter on two pieces of bread. "I'm sorry. I don't know these kids, and besides, I need you Friday night to take Mary to dance class and pick her up. I have two clients coming over for a color and cut."

Rowan's voice rose almost to a yell. "You always have

clients coming over. Every flippin' weekend!"

The butter knife clanged as I slammed it on the kitchen counter. "Yeah, and how do you think I came up with the money for your baseball uniform? You think money grows on trees? Because if it did, don't think I wouldn't be planting an orchard full of them in the backyard!" I winced. Now that definitely sounded like Mom. "The uniform alone took me two months to save up for!"

Rowan curved his shoulders in and down as he let out a long breath. He shook his head. "Fine! I'll just be the laughingstock of all the juniors!"

He pushed at the chair defiantly and grabbed the sack lunch I'd made him. I cuffed his wrist and waited until he lifted his gaze to mine.

"I'm sorry. We need the money," I whispered low enough so Mary would stay blissfully ignorant.

My little brother closed his eyes and inhaled. All the anger had seeped out of his form when he opened them again. "No, I'm sorry. It's a stupid party anyway."

I found it strange that he'd even asked to go. Usually, he stayed close to home on the weekends and invited friends over to have video game wars on the Xbox I'd scrimped and saved for. Giving him that Xbox and the two games he'd coveted for months had been worth all the extra yoga classes I'd taught and all the hair I'd done at half price. Since I cut hair out of my garage, I couldn't exactly charge what the average salon charged, especially since I didn't have my cosmetology license. One day, maybe. Although with the way the bills were piling up, that dream was going to remain on the back burner for a lot longer than I'd planned.

"It's not stupid to want to hang out with your friends.

Maybe I could change the appointments to later in the week, so we wouldn't lose the money—"

He stopped me by pulling me into a full-body hug. My brother was good for big bear hugs, especially when he knew I was worried or needed that connection to another person who understood our situation as deeply as I did. Only this time, it was different.

"Thank you, Vivvie, but no."

For as long as I could remember, my family had shortened Genevieve to Viv or Vivvie. I'd cursed Mother for naming Mary and me after our grandmothers. Here I was, a twenty-four-year-old woman with a name that suited a woman fifty years my senior.

"Don't worry about it," Rowan added. "Honestly, it's not that big a deal. I know better. Besides, I've been applying for jobs in the area, too. You know, to help out."

I shook my head and waved my hands in the air like a crazy person swatting at invisible flies. "No. No, you don't. You are focusing on your studies and baseball. Your job is to keep that straight-A average and get into a good college on scholarship, because you know there's no way I'll be able to afford that."

If I couldn't even finish cosmetology school, I'd be damned if my brother was going to miss out on getting into a good school. Our parents would have wanted that and made sure he got it. A pang of sadness filled my heart as it tightened painfully. It would pass...eventually. Always did. If Mom and Dad were around, our lives would be totally different. Easier. More peaceful. Regardless, I did the best I could to keep the family together and under the roof where we'd lived all our lives.

"Vivvie, I have to. You can't keep working yourself to the

bone like this."

"I'm fine." I put together Mary's lunch and tossed in an extra cookie to brighten her day. "We've been going strong for three years now. Why change it?"

"Maybe because you haven't gone out with a friend or been on a date in..." He lifted his gaze to the kitchen ceiling while he tapped his chin. "I don't even remember the last time I saw you with a guy."

I braced myself against the tile counter. "That is none of your business. Besides, I see guys all the time."

He snorted and chuckled. "Yeah, in your yoga class. And cutting their hair doesn't count, either."

I scowled. Forcibly turning him around, I led him toward the front of the house. Our family home was located in the heart of Berkeley, California. The house had been my parents' pride and joy. Mom had always been a homemaker, and Dad was a lawyer and worked in downtown Oakland. The house was paid off, thank God, or I'd never have been able to keep it. Even so, the property taxes and home repairs were piling up. Shaking off the worry that always came with wondering what would break next and take the little bit of extra money I'd saved, I nudged Rowan toward his backpack.

The wood floors throughout the house had seen better days, but I kept them clean and waxed as often as I could. The kids helped, of course. We all had our chores. The house hadn't changed much over the three years since Mom and Dad passed. We'd kept as much of them alive within it as we could, like our own personal shrine to them. All the pictures they'd hung, their books, even the figurines they'd treasured all stayed where they'd been lovingly placed over the years. That was one thing I was determined to preserve. My brother and sister would always have this home to come back to when they left the house each day.

Rowan picked up his backpack and slung it over his shoulder. His shaggy dark-blond hair fell into his brown eyes. I lifted my arm and moved the stubborn strand away before caressing his cheek. All three of us had our father's brown eyes, though Row and Mary's were more of a caramel brown, and mine were so dark they looked almost black.

"Take care of yourself out there, okay? Come back home safe," I said.

"You can count on it." Rowan smiled and saluted before walking out the door.

Mary shuffled into the living room, her shirt on backward.

I laughed. "Honey, your shirt's on the wrong way."

She held her hand out. "I know! It's backward day at school. Everyone has to wear their clothes like this." She rolled down the front of her skirt. "See, the tag's in the front." Her eyes sparkled, and her white-blond hair fell in a flat sheet down her back.

"Well, that's silly, but okay. You got the brush?"

Mary held up Mom's old hairbrush. The paint around the handle was chipped and flaked off in tiny specks. I didn't say anything. If Mary wanted to use Mom's brush until there were no more bristles left, that's what she'd do. Far be it from me to take away something that made her comfortable. Mary and I had our own little morning routine. She sat on the ottoman, and I sat in the cushy lounge chair that had been Dad's favorite reading spot, and I brushed her hair every morning and each night, the same way Mom had done for me.

"Braid today or ponytail?" I asked.

Her pink lips puckered. "Two braids, tied together at the

back."

"Oooh, I see we're getting fancy. Have you been looking at my books again?" I'd received the hairstyle books when I signed up for cosmetology school before our parents got into the accident. When they passed, I had only three months left. Only problem—besides the fact that I was a grieving—I was twenty-one and suddenly head of the household. The insurance money paid off the house and got us through the first year, but we'd been struggling ever since.

She smiled and nodded. "Yep. You can do it, right?"

"Of course I can. I'm the hair master, remember?" I tickled her ribs.

Mary giggled and wiggled, smiling wide. That smile and the pink in her cheeks were enough to make any day a good one.

All things considered, we were doing okay.

Once I finished her hair, I ran to my room and pulled on a clean pair of yoga pants, a sports bra, and a ribbed black tank. Every day, I rocked cool yoga pants, the one little splurge I allowed myself every couple of months. Today's were a marbled mixture of hot pink and black that stopped just past the knee. I added the quartz crystal necklace my yoga guru, Crystal—a lady very aptly named—had given me. After I tucked it down into my shirt to ward off any negativity, I slipped on a simple pair or flip-flops.

I pulled my own platinum-blond, shoulder-length hair into a tight bun at the nape of my neck. Then I layered on bright pink lipstick and added a thin black line of liquid eyeliner to each eye to create the cat-eye look that worked best with my features. Finishing up with a few strokes of mascara, I was ready to take on the day and teach a slew of clients how to find peace on the mat.

CHAPTER TWO

ROOT CHAKRA

A chakra is often described as a spinning vortex of energy created within ourselves through the connection of the physical body and consciousness. When combined, chakras become the center of activity for our internal life force or "prana." When the primary seven chakras are aligned and open, you experience your best self.

TRENT

I parked my Maserati GranTurismo Sport—lovingly referred to as the silver bullet—at the curb in front of the Lotus House Yoga Center. My sports doc had scheduled me for "hatha yoga." I had about ten minutes before the class started, so after I stuffed the meter with enough for two hours, I took a look around.

This particular street was right out of the seventies with its wild array of psychedelic colors and textures in the midst of an old humdrum neighborhood. The area offered an inviting feel with its hanging flower baskets, colorful flags, and quaint outside seating.

Taking small strides, I gripped the upper part of my hammy, waiting for the pain to dissipate as I took in the bizarre area. In front of me was the Rainy Day Café. The people milling along the sidewalks and in the café sported twisted braids, afros, tie dye, Birkenstocks, and comfortable threads. A definite hippie vibe controlled the local scene.

I passed the Tattered Pages Used Bookstore, definitely not the garden-variety big bookstore. No, this one looked more like a long-forgotten tomb with its dark wood facade and minimal decoration. I stopped and peered inside one of the large windows. Shelves of used books lined the walls from floor to ceiling, along with cramped enclosures where books were carelessly stuffed every which way. Like the café, this place was packed. People leisurely came in and out of the store, carrying armfuls and bags of books. A sign on the door said *Save a Tree—Bring Your Own Bag.*

I continued down this street that had been lost in a time warp. Next to the bookstore was the Sunflower Bakery. I rolled my eyes at the silly name, but that did not prevent my mouth from watering at the deluge of cinnamon-sugary goodness that poured out the door as a delivery driver exited. After the bendy break-my-back-class, I'd be hitting up this bakery. That scent...damn, it followed me as I kept walking.

The front of the yoga center was white with teal trim. Heavy glass double doors stood, tall and inviting. Each door had a flower with a person in some sort of yoga pose etched into its surface.

When I entered, the scent of sage and eucalyptus assaulted me. My nose tickled at the foreign smell. Several women stood at a long counter, yoga mats strapped to their backs and wearing zip-up hoodies paired with long pants. I was eyeballing their asses when my name was called.

"Can I help you, sir?" a fiery redhead with big blue eyes asked. Her skin was pale and seemed to glow against the teal-blue tank that had the center's logo on the front. A set of pert breasts bounced as she moved around the table, helping regulars while waiting for me to respond.

"Yeah. I'm Trent Fox, and I believe I'm scheduled for a class that starts soon."

The redhead typed a few things into a computer and nodded. "Yep, you're set for a three month unlimited membership."

With efficiency and speed, she pulled out a card shaped like a flower. No shit. A flower. On the back was a bar code. She ran it in front of the scanner that matched the ones I saw patrons using on another set of doors that must have led deeper into the building.

"You'll use this card by just waving the bar code against the scanner right there." She pointed to the other set of doors. "It will get you into the building during normal business hours. Since you have unlimited access, you don't have to check in. In three months, you can renew again or end your membership." She lowered her voice, forcing me to lean closer to hear her. It also gave me a great view of her sweet rack. "We're not pushy around here, so if you decide yoga isn't your thing, we won't hunt you down."

I smiled my panty-melting grin. "Good to know. Will you

be teaching the class?"

Her cheeks pinked up in a lovely blush. The color looked good on her. She shook her head. "Nope. There are two classes going right now. A vinyasa flow with Mila that's already in session, and hatha yoga, which is designed more for beginners and intermediate yogis. It's taught by Genevieve Harper every morning at nine."

"Works for me. And your name, sweetheart?"

"I'm Luna Marigold, the daughter of one of the owners."

Of course she was. "Look forward to seeing you around." I tapped the counter and winked.

She blushed a fine crimson. "You, too, Mr. Fox. Thanks for joining Lotus House. *Namaste*."

Using my new flower-shaped plastic key card, I entered the belly of the converted warehouse. Directly in front of me was a long hallway. To the right, two signs said *Yoginis Sanctuary* and *Yogi Sanctuary*. Based on the last letter, I figured the left was the men's locker room, and the right was the women's. I headed down the center hallway. The walls were painted in an ongoing mural of a meadow. As I made my way to the end of the hall where an open door was, the tall grass in the image seemed to sway along, moving with me. I knew it wasn't possible, but it was so lifelike that it tricked the eyes. Damn good artist, indeed.

To the left was a door through which I could hear the Beatles blasting. Odd, as this was a yoga studio. Next to the door was an indoor window so that patrons in the hall could see the class in session. At least thirty people had their hands and feet on their own mat, asses in the air. Together they were a sea of triangle shapes, and then as if choreographed, they all popped a leg high into the sky. Some were a little shakier than others, and some seemed to have scissor legs that naturally separated at the hip.

A Hispanic woman with a hot little body and curly hair bouncing along her shoulders called out something that I swore was, "flip your dog." And the entire room dropped the leg they held up, only not down. No, they twisted their entire bodies so that their fronts were now facing the ceiling, the leg that had been up was on the ground facing the other direction, and an arm was in the air.

"Holy shit." I made a mental note never to take whatever they called *vinyasa flow*.

As the instructor clapped, the entire room twisted back around so the single leg was back in the air and everyone was in a triangle shape again. *If this is yoga, I'm screwed.*

Afraid to see any more, I took a calming breath, shifted my head, and glanced at the open doorway another ten feet ahead. Soft classical music filtered out from the room. As I approached, the lights were dimmed to a muted glow. Mats crisscrossed like multicolored puzzle pieces against the dark carpeted floor. Several women were chatting in a huddle in a corner. Abruptly, all four women stopped speaking, and four sets of eyes zeroed in on me. I was used to open admiration of the female variety and let it roll off me.

The entire room was devoid of pictures or art because from floor to ceiling the room was art itself. This time, a forest. Trees graced each massive wall. At the back of the room were painted mountains so lifelike I wanted to keep walking, maybe hike up their peaked surface. Another wall boasted a serene rushing waterfall so meticulously done, I could imagine the spray as it hit the jagged rocks below.

As I stood blocking the center of the doorway, a few

women squeaked by. I stumbled out of the way and leaned against the wall, waiting to see what I was supposed to do. Maybe I should have brought a yoga mat? All of the women and the few men scattered around were flapping out their mats. A raised platform stood at the front of the room. A speck of a woman bustled around, adjusting things and setting up her space.

Her blond hair was pulled back tight into a bun. The track lighting above glinted off her head, making her hair shine like spun gold. She stood gracefully from a kneeling position. From her movements, the woman was obviously comfortable in her body...and hot damn, what a body. I'd thought the Hispanic yoga teacher and the gal at the front were attractive. They were nothing compared to this woman. When she turned around, I actually lost my breath, a completely new sensation for me. An unusual warmth started in my chest and expanded as I took in her profile while she chatted with another patron. Her lips were a bubblegum pink and stark against her alabaster skin. She placed her hands on her hips, nodded, and smiled, showing a set of beautiful, even teeth.

I stood against the wall like a creeper and watched her, my gaze glued to the only woman who had ever stolen my breath with her beauty. The woman was small, probably barely reached my chin at around five feet five. What she lacked in height she made up for in toned curves and an hourglass shape. Her hips swelled out from a tiny nipped-in waist. The black tank she wore stretched across a pair of incredible tits. A full handful for sure, and I had pretty large hands. I opened and closed my fists as I imagined taking her breasts in both hands and giving a firm squeeze.

"Jesus Christ!" I mumbled, in awe of the woman before

me. With the tank that left nothing to the imagination, she wore a splotchy pair of hot pink and black knee-length pants that could have been painted on, they fit so well. Licking my lips, I kept my gaze on her, silently hoping she'd look my way. Finally, blondie's eyes squinted against the lighting above, and eyes as black as night met mine.

Seeing her full frontal made my knees tremble and my dick twitch. She turned to the person she was speaking to and laid a hand on his arm before gesturing to an open section of floor. He clutched his mat and moseyed over to his spot. Then she addressed the class.

"Class starts in a few minutes. Feel free to go into child's pose and start deep breathing." After she spoke, she walked over to me.

I watched the subtle sway of her hips as if it were the last thing I would ever see. She padded my way in bare feet and stopped in front of me. Her toes matched her lipstick—a bright pink that suggested those lips might taste as sweet as they looked.

She lifted her head, gaze assessing me from tip to toe. The top of her head barely reached my shoulder.

"I'm Genevieve, or Viv." Her brown eyes were perfectly placed within her oval face. Every blink seemed to mesmerize me. "Are you new here? Is this your first time?"

I shook off the lust daze and held out my hand. "Trent Fox."

Her eyes widened but not enough to be alarming, just enough to indicate she recognized the name. My hand swallowed her small one, and it felt good there, locked within the safety of my larger one.

"I'm here for the rehabilitation aspects of the exercise," I said lamely.

Genevieve's eyebrows furrowed, and she inclined her head and pulled her hand away. I missed its solid weight instantly. That was a new response for me to women. Any woman.

"You have a pulled hamstring, right?" she said.

My head shot back as if it weren't connected to my neck. "Torn. How did you know?"

She laughed pleasantly, the sound creating a pleasant squeezing sensation in my chest. For some reason, I had the ridiculous desire to say something funny so I could hear it again and again.

"My little brother is a Ports fan." She shook her head. "I can't believe you're here. Rowan's going to flip."

The sound of another man's name coming from lips that I had every intention of claiming—soon—caused me to stand straighter, and I clenched my jaw. "Who's Rowan, gumdrop?"

Her head jolted back at my brusque tone. "Huh? Oh, my brother...the Ports fan."

I let out a grunt. "Sorry." Spreading my arms wide, I pointed to the room. "What do I do here?"

Genevieve blinked rapidly, as if she'd just woken up. "Oh! Yes. Over here, we'll get you set up with a mat."

I gritted my teeth and followed her as she turned around and presented the most perfect ass. It was the kind of ass men wrote love poems about—heart-shaped and fuller on the bottom, which would give a man a nice handle to grip while plowing into her heat from any direction. She led me to the right side of the room where I could easily see the platform but would still have room to maneuver my six-foot-plus frame. Moving efficiently, she scooped up a mat from a nearby basket. She licked those pink lips again, which instantly gave me a semi.

While she set up a few items around my space, I shucked off my hoodie, toed off my shoes and socks, and waited for her to speak. Eventually, she finished setting me up with some yoga props, turned, and looked at me from the tips of my bare feet, up my sweats, to my white tank where she settled her gaze for longer than was appropriate, before flicking up to my face. I grinned, raising one of my eyebrows.

Genevieve laid out a bright orange mat that was at least seven feet long. "I grabbed the extended length since you're so"—she seemed to trace my figure again—"hard." She bit her lip, and then her eyes bulged. "I mean big! Tall!" She let out an exasperated breath.

"I think that means you like what you see." I ran my hand down my abs, adjusting the elastic waistband on my sweats where they hung low.

She bit down on that lip, her gaze riveted to where I rested my hands on my hips. The sound of the door slamming made her jump, and she scanned the room. Her blush made her cheeks rosy. What else could make her blush?

"Just...sit here and follow along. I'll call out the cues, and if anything puts too much pressure on the hamstring, back off from doing it. I need to start class, but we can talk more about your injury and rehabilitation after class if you'd like."

"I think I'd like that very much, gumdrop."

"Gumdrop?" An eyebrow slightly darker than her hair color rose.

Leaning deep into her personal space, I got closer to her ear. Her body trembled the closer I got. Oh, I liked that response in a woman. Too much. She laid a tentative hand on my bicep, and I flexed. With a woman like this, I'd use every trick in the book to get her attention. She probably had men beating down her door. Hell, she probably had a boyfriend. Just the thought of another man touching her, made me grind my teeth.

"Your lips are pretty and pink and look as sweet as candy. Reminds me of a pink sugarcoated cherry gumdrop. My favorite."

"Oh."

There were two kinds of women. The kind that love any type of nick name, endearment or attention I might deem to lavish on them, or the feminist kind that flip out at the first hint of what they might consider chauvinism. Genevieve's simple "Oh" spoke volumes about her. I would not be able to peg her down or predict her responses. She left me as quickly as she had arrived and headed to the platform without further comment.

"All right, thank you all for coming. Please sit down on your bottoms, removing any fleshy areas aside so your seat bones can connect with the mat. Then bring your hands to heart center." She looked from person to person. "Let's start by closing our eyes and setting our intention for today's practice."

I closed my eyes as she continued to speak.

"What is it that you want to get out of your yoga practice today? What do you want to bring into your life? Perhaps you'd like to dedicate your practice to someone who needs your good intentions more than you. Free your mind and settle on that one intention. Picture it. Let it swirl around you as you breathe."

Her words were melodic and conjured an instant sense of peace and serenity. Reminded me of when I was in the zone on the field. Nothing could break my concentration.

"Now tell yourself, what is your intention today?"

I have every intention of taking this woman home. Whatever it takes. You can only win if you play the game.

GENEVIEVE

Holy hotness. Trent Fox is on a mat, sitting in my class. Don't panic, Viv. Get yourself together. You are a professional. He's here for recuperation, not to be ogled.

I instructed the clients to get up on their hands and knees, and then I led them through cat pose where they curved their spine and then reversed it, dropping the belly low into cow pose. I scanned the room, settling on him as I went through cat and cow pose paired with breathing. Watching the way he arched stiffly and then dropped his bulky chest low, tipping a bum that looked so hard I could bounce a quarter off it, made it hard for me to balance.

"Now place your palms down at a ninety-degree angle, lift your toes to the mat, and press your hips up toward the sky, going into your downward facing dog."

A pained groan echoed from his side of the room. I lifted my head. One of his legs shook as he held the pose. His eyes were closed tight and his jaw was locked, making a harsh square that wasn't there when he smiled.

"Keep your dog, and pedal it out slowly. Take your dog for a walk. I'm going to adjust some of you."

I went directly to Trent. He opened his eyes in a flash as I straddled his mat and placed my hands on the side of each hip, gripping firmly.

"Breathe in deeply," I said. "Now out."

He followed my command for two breaths as I lifted his

hips an inch and pulled them back. "Head down."

His head fell and without even thinking, I ran my hand down the side of his thigh until the tremor in his hamstring settled. I pressed into the top of his hamstring with a fist, pushing against the tension. He moaned. Not a pained groan, more like a relieved one.

"You have a long way to go," I whispered but kept him adjusted back so the ligaments would stretch. "We'll get there," I promised, not even believing my own words. For some reason, one I couldn't fathom, I really wanted to help him.

I continued to adjust others, but like a wave rolling into the shore, I kept coming back to Trent. He was struggling but giving it his all. I admired that trait in a man.

We moved through a series of poses that were less traumatic on the hamstring. Usually, I didn't tailor a class to one client, but Trent was different, and not just because he was a Major League Baseball player and insanely gorgeous. Seeing him struggle yet still put forth the effort spoke to me on a spiritual level.

Once we got to the deep relaxation portion of class, or *Savasana* as it's called in the Sanskrit teaching, I got everyone set up with a bolster under their thighs and an eye pillow. I walked around, giving each of them a drop of essential oil on their chins and the tender space between nose and upper lip to encourage deep breathing. When I got to Trent, he took in a deep breath, which zipped through me like a physical caress, working its way down to curl my toes. His hand jolted out, and he gripped my wrist before I could move away.

He sniffed my wrist and along my inner arm. I shivered, gooseflesh rising to the surface of my skin.

"You smell better than the oil." His voice was a low growl,

as if he were halfway between slumbering and awake. I'd go a long way to hear that sexy sound again.

Yikes. What was wrong with me? I didn't have time for a man in my life. Between raising Rowan and Mary and working two jobs, the last thing I needed was a distraction or a suitor. Especially one known for being a player on and off the field. No. He was just being flirty. He didn't really like me. Heck, he didn't even know me.

"Thank you," I said softly. "I'll be back to do a *Savasana* massage. Just follow my voice, and I'll let you know when to rise."

"Your class, your rules." He smirked.

Even with an eye pillow over his face, just that twinge of lips was drop-dead sexy.

I guided the class through a meditative scene and provided a head and neck massage to several attendees. Unless I had a teacher trainer in class, I couldn't get to everyone, but I made damn sure I got to Trent. An invisible tether pulled me toward his supine form. Long heavily muscled legs and arms relaxed in repose. He was so much bigger than I was. If I lay on top of him, his body would swallow me up. I clenched my thighs to stave off the lust that hummed in my system. His arms were at his sides, palms facing up. I wanted to measure the difference in size between our hands, feel the warmth from his hand chakra connected with mine. The white tank he wore did nothing to hide his magnificent chest and abdominals. The man was a brick house of sinewy muscle and bone, perfectly molded as if etched in marble by a world-renowned sculptor.

Kneeling at the top of his mat where his head rested, I caressed just his shoulders with a featherlight touch, letting him know I was there. My fingertips tingled with the moisture from his sweat. With both palms, I pressed into the upper part of his shoulders at the junction with his neck. He moaned, and that sound tunneled its way into my mind and feathered out through my entire body like an electric charge.

Taking a slow breath, I removed his eye pillow, placed my hands on both sides of his head, and lifted and held it with one hand. Carefully, I shifted his head to the right and ran my thumb down the side of his neck to those tense shoulders and back up. Then I rubbed the bones at the base of his skull. The average person carried heaps of tension there. A subtle pressure massage usually gave maximum release and helped the person delve deeper into relaxation.

Trent's lips parted, and a hint of tongue became visible. That bit of flesh held my attention. If he were my man, I'd have leaned forward and pressed my mouth to his, tasting him while breathing in the scent of the essential oil. Closing my eyes, I repeated the massage on the other side of his head and let my fantasy play out. I rubbed his head, temples, down the sides of his neck, into his shoulders, while dream Genevieve physically molested the baseball player in a private room, where I showed him another version of *deep relaxation*.

My music had stopped playing and the room had grown silent. For how long, I didn't know. Placing his head back down, I moved to the platform, picked up the singing bowl, and counted back from five in a series of instructions that would help the mind and body move from the meditative realm to the physical one.

"Please sit up and face the teacher and all things," I called out.

Numerous sleepy heads lifted, and the attendees shuffled around into a lotus position where the legs were crossed in front of the body, the spine was straight, and the hands clasped palm-to-palm at heart center.

"I want to thank you all for coming in today and sharing your yoga practice with me, as I have shared mine with you." Slowly I made eye contact with every person attending, giving them each a bit of my soul. "The light in me bows to the light in you. When I am in that place in me, and you are in that place in you, we are one. *Namaste.*" I bowed low to the ground, hand to my forehead.

I send each and every one of you light, love, and happiness.

A chorus of "*Namaste,*" a traditional respectful Eastern Indian greeting, filtered through the room, filling the space with a sense of unity and serenity.

When I sat back up, I smiled and thanked the class once more. I turned and met the hazel eyes of the first man in a long time to make me feel something other than a friendly connection. No, nothing I felt for Trent Fox was anywhere near the realm of friendship.

Trent grinned, his dark espresso colored hair a wild mess of layers against his crown. He shook his head, a lock falling into his face as he pulled together his things and approached the platform.

"Gumdrop, that was an epic experience. We must do that again...privately."

He scanned my form as if he were applying lotion all over, making me feel soft and womanly. I sucked in a jagged breath.

I answered the only way a girl could when one of the sexiest men alive was standing in front of her, all muscle, heat pouring off of him, and sweat glistening on his skin like a sprinkling of glitter.

"What did you have in mind?"

CHAPTER THREE

Cat Pose

(Sanskrit: Marjaryasana)

Cat pose loosens the tension in your spine, often giving relief to a sore back. It is especially helpful to those who have sedentary lifestyles. To get in this pose, place your knees hip distance apart, your arms straight down in front of you, shoulder width. Start with a flat, straight spine, curl spine toward the sky, tuck the tailbone, and suck in the navel.

GENEVIEVE

Trent grinned, licked his lips, and bit down on the plump flesh. I bit back a whimper as I watched, fascinated by every miniscule movement. He shrugged, brought a hand up to his chin, and rubbed a hand across it.

"I'm thinking some private lessons are in order. That class"—he huffed and put a hand to his thigh where he gripped, hard—"was no joke. As much as it hurt—and, gumdrop, it hurt more than I'd like to let on—I know I need it. If I had the one-on-one time, I'm thinking maybe you could help with the pain."

A blast of raw desire hit me. A bead of sweat trickled down my spine like a silky caress as I thought back to the fantasy I'd had at the end of class and what "helping" with the pain in a variety of other ways could entail. "How so?"

He chuckled. "By...uh...not making it painful?"

I closed my eyes and smiled. "Rebuilding the strength in that leg after a tear and surgery isn't going to be pleasant."

Thinking about this beautiful man in pain day in and day out sent a pang of guilt. My own thoughts had been far from decent. A good yoga teacher should be more worried about the client and helping him heal physically and emotionally from whatever ails him, not imagining doing the naked pretzel in a private room. I added a mental reminder to mediate on this issue later with Dara, our resident meditation guru at Lotus House. She'd be able to help me find a sense of clarity when my hormones were going wacky over one ridiculously hot male client. This couldn't be the first time a teacher had felt something for a client, and as far as I knew, dating the clientele wasn't technically against the rules.

Trent's eyes seemed to glide all over my form. "Oh, I don't know, if I had someone who looked like you, wearing what you are, while I suffered through each pose... It would definitely make the process more bearable. Heck, entertaining even." His tone was throaty and deep, like a smooth whiskey over ice.

"Smooth." I crossed my arms over my chest. Player, for sure. I shook my head, not certain what to do about Mr.

Baseball. But damn, was he sexy. I'd momentarily forgotten that in all the celebrity pics and commentary on the TV, Trent Fox, baseball's finest, usually had a new young thing on his arm every week. What could he want with me besides a quick roll in the hay?

No, I wasn't going there. I had far too much on my plate. Taking care of my brother and sister, working two jobs, a household to support, and putting food on the table. Trent Fox was ruggedly handsome, but he was a distraction. However, if he wanted to pay extra for private lessons, I could definitely use the money, and I had the time while Mary and Rowan were at school.

"So what's it gonna be, gumdrop? Can you take me on for some private lessons?"

I pretended to ponder the question for a moment, not wanting to give away that I was eager for two reasons. One, he was the sexiest man I'd ever seen. Working him out would be hard, but as he'd insinuated, the view would be mighty fine. Two, I desperately needed the money.

Setting my hands on my hips, a less defensive pose, I looked at him and nodded. "Yeah, I could do it right after this class, ten thirty to noon any day of the week. Private sessions are booked individually with the instructor and paid directly to me."

Moving quickly before the next class started, I turned to the platform and got out my mini-planner. Opening it to this week, I double-checked the dates. "The private lessons are separate from your monthly fee and cost thirty dollars a session. If that works for you, I'll schedule you in. What day would you like?"

"All of them," he said flatly.

I crunched my brows together. "Can you be more specific?"

His large paw came toward my face, and I stiffened until he swept a lock of hair behind my ear. The gesture was sweet and affectionate, something a boyfriend would do. Only this man was most certainly *not* my boyfriend. My cheeks heated as he trailed his fingertips down the side of my face. He stroked my bottom lip with his thumb. I gasped at the whisper of pressure.

"I mean, I want to own all of your time from ten thirty to noon every day of the week for the next month." He removed his hand.

Strangely, I missed its presence.

I jolted back. "I'm sorry. Every weekday? That's a lot of time and money." I regretted the comment the moment it left my mouth. How much money he spent on his recuperation or what he did with his time was none of my business.

Stupid, stupid, Vivvie. You're making it too personal. This is a business transaction, even though it feels like something more.

"Oh, somehow, I think it will be well worth the expense. Besides, the doc wants me doing yoga every weekday. I figure for the first time in my life, I'll follow the rules. Because this time, maybe I'll have something to look forward to."

I smirked and hid my face under the pretense of writing his name down in my planner every weekday. Knowing that I'd be bringing in a hundred and fifty more dollars a week made my heart sing with joy. I'd finally be able to pay the back money I owed on the electric bill. Heating and cooling a house the size of ours over the summer was a killer. The classic Berkeley home was aesthetically pleasing curbside but cost a whack to cool and heat. Unfortunately, the winter months were upon us, and we'd be turning on the heater soon. I hated being cold, and the Bay Area wind had a chill that would seep right into my bones.

"Okay, big guy, I've got you down, and we'll see you tomorrow." I slapped my planner closed and held it in front of my chest. Another item keeping the two of us apart wasn't a bad idea.

His lips quirked. "Looking forward to it, gumdrop." He turned and headed toward the exit, his gait off due to the injured leg.

I'd have to look up some specific hamstring stretches that would be best at different levels of his healing process.

"Hey!" I stopped at the doorway and leaned against the doorframe. "Seriously, why do you keep calling me gumdrop?"

He was halfway down the hallway toward the front of the building when he turned around and grinned. That grin sent a fire rushing through me, and I gripped the trim to keep from running toward him to suggest we do more than his private lessons.

"I wasn't kidding before. Your lips. From the second I saw that bubblegum-pink mouth, I wanted to eat you up. And I'll bet you taste just like candy." He winked, turned, and walked out.

The next instructor, Luna Marigold, daughter of one of the co-owners, leaned against me as I watched him go.

"Damn fine-looking man," she muttered.

"I'll say."

"Did he hit on you?" Her gray eyes sparkled with silvery tones, like two identical, perfectly clear full moons.

I shrugged. "Kind of." Laughing, I shook my head. "Maybe. I'm not exactly sure."

"Well, he's beautiful, and you've been alone far too long. If anything, he looks like the type of man who could ride a girl all night long and wake up wanting thirds, fourths, and fifths."

Shoving her through the door, I wagged a finger. "Don't you have a class to teach?"

Luna grinned. "Don't you have a man to hunt down?"

"No! Besides, I'm doing private lessons with him tomorrow."

Her eyes widened as we walked to the platform. I gathered my things while she laid hers out.

"He booked a weekly private appointment with you?"

"Technically, he booked private appointments for five days a week."

Those moons went from full to ginormous in a second flat. "Oh, my! He wants you!" Luna shimmied her shoulders and swayed from side to side in a mini victory dance.

"He does not! He wants me to help him recuperate."

"Uh-huh. Okay. That's logical. He's already paid for a three-month membership where he could come to *any* class. So instead of taking advantage of what he's already paid for—something that's not cheap, I might add—he books five appointments a week with you for an additional fee?"

I rolled my eyes. "You're reading too much into this. He liked the class but said it was hard. Wanted me to help him with the pain."

"Oh, I bet he does want your help." She snorted, but the sound was lost when she flapped out her mat. "Look, Viv, just let it be what it's gonna be. You know? If the universe wants you to have some fun with this man, have some fun with him. Goodness knows, you could use it. When was the last time you had a boyfriend, anyway?"

"He's not going to be my boyfriend," I said with absolutely no hint of laughter.

"Fine! But that doesn't mean you can't have a little fun. I'd bet money your sacral chakra is closed up so tight it will take a man of his size to knock that sucker wide open." She held her hands about nine inches apart.

I'm pretty sure my eyes were so big anyone in the vicinity could see straight through to my brain. "Naughty girl, you're terrible!" I shoved her. A wave of heat singed my cheeks as I put my head down, neck burrowing toward my chest.

She chuckled, and it sounded like a song. Her mother, Jewel, had the very same laugh. Lovely and infectious. "Just don't be so closed off to the more carnal pleasures in life. When was the last time you...you know..." She shimmied her hips from side to side in a rather vulgar display.

I placed my hands on her hips to stop them from gyrating and checked if the clients setting out their mats were watching us. They weren't, thank God.

"Cut it out," I whispered. "Jeez. I don't know. Since my parents, okay?"

"No way! Three years? You haven't gotten..." She looked around and leaned closer. "You haven't had sex in *three years*? How are you even functioning?"

I laughed hard at that. "Day by day. I know. It's such a hardship."

"Girl, that *is* a hardship. This just proves my point. If that client, Mr. Baseball Hottie himself, makes a move on you, don't pass it up. Take it, and take it good."

"But I'm not looking for a relationship. You know how much I work, and taking care of the kids..." I sighed.

"That's fine. There's nothing wrong with a little casual

sex, is there?" Her cheeks pinked, and her eyes sparked with mischief.

I shrugged and bit my bottom lip. "I wouldn't know. I've only ever been with Brian, and he couldn't handle me being unavailable due to working and raising my brother and sister."

"That's because he wasn't worthy of you. If he couldn't cut it, honey, he was the wrong man. Be glad he's gone. For now, though, you need to live a little. Will you promise me you'll think about it?"

Pulling her into my arms, I gave her a hug. The smell of fresh jasmine surrounded me. "I will. Promise. Have a good class. See you tomorrow." I waved and left her to finish prepping for her Prenatal Yoga class.

As I passed, I smiled at the glowing pregnant women and their rounded bellies. For a single moment, I allowed myself to wonder if I'd ever have that—a family of my own, one that I'd created.

Sure, I was only twenty-four, but my baby sister was eight. I had a solid ten years of raising her until she went off to college. By then I'd be closing in on thirty-five and trying to start over. Maybe then I could have the big family I'd always dreamed of. Maybe own a hair salon and teach yoga classes once or twice a week because I wanted to and loved the practice, not because I needed the money. For now, those dreams were just that—dreams.

TRENT

My poor teeth had been ground down to nothing from the amount of times I'd held back the things I wanted to say to Genevieve Harper. With her, all my usual lines sounded wrong, lacked creativity. What the hell was wrong with me?

Jesus Christ, that woman with her sexy little body, toned in all the right places, curves for days in the ultimate mouth-watering areas could bring even a priest to his knees for worship. Nothing but tits and a fine, hard ass on that one, and I'd be looking at it for seven-and-a-half hours a week for the next month. I wanted to blow on my knuckles and pat myself on the back for coming up with that. Please my agent, get on the right path to recovery, and bed a damn fine woman in the process. I could hardly wait to get her under me.

First thing on my list—those sugary sweet lips. It took inhuman self-restraint not to back her up against the wall and use some serious power of persuasion on the dynamite platinum blonde. She had this Gwen Stefani look about her—unique, pristine in her beauty, without even trying. Effortless.

With a slight spring in my otherwise busted step, I felt good about this new path to recovery. Now for some time hitting the weights, and then I'd be solid as a rock—literally and figuratively.

Once I stepped outside the Lotus House Yoga Center, the scent of cinnamon hit me again. I moseyed into Sunflower Bakery, stood in line, and inspected the options. Two large curved glass cases held a wide variety of delectable treats. One side promoted fresh loaves of bread, bagels, and muffins. The other curved into an L shape and went down the length of the store to the back where all the real fatty items were displayed—cakes, cookies, donuts, pastries, bite-size things, cupcakes, and pies. I was rather impressed with the selection. The fresh-baked cinnamon rolls were calling my name even though eating one would set me back several hundred calories. I couldn't afford to get soft during my recovery, but I'd be damned if I wasn't going to scarf back a couple of those loaded doughy swirls.

I had high hopes for the pastry. If the number of customers in the place was an indication of quality, I'd likely struck gold. Several of the people who had been in my hatha class with Genevieve sat around a table, picking at a gooey dessert. A couple of the women would glance up, flirt a little, and look away. I smiled but didn't put the effort into the act that I normally would. Probably because some white-hot blonde had my nuts in a twist. No one but her would do.

The line crawled forward at a snail's pace. I sighed, worried that I might not get a couple of the sugary treats until I saw the young man hoof it back from the kitchen carrying a full steaming-hot tray.

Once I got to the counter, I was starving. Two cinnamon rolls would no longer cut it.

"What can I get for you?" a stunning young woman asked. Her coloring matched the perfectly golden-brown loaves of rye bread in the case next to us. Her honey skin tone was not what caught my attention. It was her eyes. They were straight magical. Unlike anything I'd ever seen on a woman of her coloring. They were a tropical ocean blue. Reminded me of my time in Cancun last summer. Nothing but clear aqua-blue waters as far as the eye could see.

She assessed me calmly with no hint of irritation at my stunned silence. Yeah, I checked her out, and was hit with an instant sensation of guilt cutting through my chest as I remembered Genevieve. Definitely a new response, and not one I appreciated. I couldn't be blamed for noticing this woman. I looked down at her name tag—"Dara" in block lettering.

I cleared my throat and took a breath.

"Just finish a class? Was it Mila or Genevieve?"

The second she said my girl's name, I sucked in a sharp breath.

"Aw, Viv." Her smile widened. "She's pretty, isn't she?" Dara said as if we were old friends having a regular everyday conversation about the weather. She gave off this vibe that I wasn't the only one here that she did that with. If I were a betting man, I'd have a benji on every person who came in contact with her felt like a friend. Apparently, the ease loosened my tongue because the second she asked the question, I answered on autopilot.

"Fuckin' beautiful is more like it," I grumbled and placed my palms on the counter, taking the load off my sore leg that throbbed along with my heartbeat. After a ninety-minute class and standing in line for thirty minutes, the leg had seen better days. I needed to take a load off, badly.

She smiled huge, and if anything, got prettier in the process. "I'm Dara. I teach the meditation class every morning at seven if you ever want to connect with your higher self."

I snorted and glanced at the line behind me. She didn't rush me at all, which was probably why it had taken so damn long to get up here in the first place. When Dara served me, not only did I get baked goods, I got to chat with a hottie who baked and taught meditation.

"So what are you doing behind the counter?" I asked, making polite conversation.

"Everyone has to make a living, and my mom and dad own the bakery."

"Is it 'bring your daughter to work day' all down this block?" I thought back to Luna, the redhead chick, telling me that she was the daughter of one of the Lotus House owners.

Dara laughed with a cute little snort. "There does seem to be a theme along the block. Most of these businesses are owned by families, and a lot of us work at a couple of the places." She shrugged. "It's our home. Why not work where we're happiest?"

She made an excellent point. "Which is why I play baseball. Nothing like it. I feel at home every time I approach the plate."

"Oooh, Viv's little bro is going to love you."

Dara said it as if there would be a reason for me to meet the boy. I found it interesting that this was not the first time Genevieve's brother had been mentioned. She must be tight with the kid.

I nodded. "Okay, I'll take two cinnamon rolls and three of those baby-sized chocolate milks. Those should come in adult size, by the way."

Dara snickered, moving around to get the items. "Eating here or taking them to go?"

Looking around, I really had no reason to go to my empty apartment. The laughter was plenty, and a bunch of hot, young yoga chicks wearing tight clothing, sitting around and chatting it up, made for a nice view. "I'll stay here."

"Bet that was a hard choice." She snort-laughed again while rolling her eyes. "Anything else?"

"Yeah, how about a couple of those chocolate-dipped cookies?"

"You got it."

Dara was efficient when she wasn't talking up the patrons. After I paid, the items were all laid out along with a stack of napkins and my three tiny milks. I swore they were the same size as the milk cartons I got back in grammar school, basically a sip for a guy my size.

"Keep it real," she said.

I stepped away, and she tended to the hippie standing behind me.

"Hey, Jonas, how's the paraphernalia business treating you this fine morning?" she asked.

I glanced to the side to find a thin dude with a mop of curly brown hair wearing a tie-dye shirt, loose jeans, complete with a hole in both knees, and Birkenstocks. The outfit screamed throwback to the seventies. Since Dara mentioned paraphernalia, I'd wager a guess that he worked at or ran the smoke shop across the street.

I found a spot dead center in the bakery eatery section. It took ridiculous effort not to drool when the cinnamon aroma wafted up as I got settled.

Plowing through my first cinnamon roll was like the first dunk in a steaming hot whirlpool bath after a hellish practice—beyond heaven. Licking the sticky mess off my fingers, I checked out all the people in line and the folks that had stayed. Every single person in the entire bakery was smiling. Hell, I was smiling. The happiness surrounding the place was contagious. I huffed and pulled out my phone.

To: Ross Holmes
From: Trent Fox
Did yoga today. Signed up for private lessons to work the hamstring. Scheduled every morning from 10:30 to noon, starting tomorrow. Don't book any meetings during that slot.

While I finished my second chocolate milk, admiring the

view of the new round of yoga chicks who bustled in to get the vegan wares, my cell phone signaled I had a message.

From: Ross Holmes
To: Trent Fox
Roger that. Don't skip out.

I thought about Genevieve and her eyes as dark as night, flawless skin, and a body that wouldn't quit. Those full glossy lips... Damn, my dick started hardening. Yeah, there was no way in hell I wasn't showing up for my private time with my own personal yoga hottie.

Finishing up, I waved at Dara while limping toward the door. She tipped her chin in a quick gesture toward my bum leg.

"Don't worry about it. Nothing my new private yoga trainer, Genevieve, won't help me fix."

Her eyes widened, and she smiled so big her white teeth sparkled against the contrast of her skin tone. This street was filled with beautiful women. I needed to invite some of my brothers from other mothers on my team to this side of the Bay.

While exiting the bakery, I decided to hit the gym and burn off some of the massive calories I'd just taken in. Whistling, I thought about Genevieve, Luna, Mila, and Dara. Four fine-assed women in the span of two hours. Genevieve led the pack by a mile. In baseball terms, that chick was a grand slam. Tomorrow couldn't come soon enough.

CHAPTER FOUR

ROOT CHAKRA

The official Sanskrit name of the root or base chakra is Muladhara. It is located at the bottom of the spine at the point where you sit. This chakra symbol is the most earth-centered of all the chakras. It stands for our inherited beliefs through our formative years, self-preservation, and personal survival. Our identification with the physical world centers on this first of the seven primary chakras.

GENEVIEVE

I knew the instant Trent Fox entered the small private yoga room. All the air in the room thickened, pressing against my skin, making the already low lighting seem more intimate. The room was softly lit with several mood-altering candles, sari fabric tapestries hung from floor to ceiling, and toss pillows were strategically stacked for comfort and ease of assisting with deep relaxation. Peppermint oil misted from the spa diffuser set in one corner, adding to the serenity. I'd placed my best mats down side by side in the center of the space. The goal for this type of session was to make the client feel at home and connect with him on all levels so he'd relax, and become more at peace with the *asanas*—or poses—and yoga practice as a whole.

I'd been sitting in lotus pose, hands at heart center, running through a few meditative chants Dara had taught me to center and ground myself before teaching a class. Grounding into the earth, or in this case the yoga mat, was necessary to ensure I didn't bring in any lingering mumbo jumbo from my day-to-day life as I prepared to offer a spiritual and physical connection of my energy to each of my clients. In this instance, I'd be transferring my healing energy to man candy Trent Fox.

"Hey, gumdrop," he said, his enormous muscled body heaving through the space and breaking every ounce of concentration I'd achieved through mediation.

I opened one eye and watched as he toed off each tennis shoe. He wore a pair of loose black cotton pants, perfectly appropriate for yoga. He lifted up his T-shirt, pulled it off, tossed it on top of his shoes, and faced me with an obscenely sexy, bare chest. I opened both eyes and took in the magnificence that was Trent Fox. He stood before me, looking like the standing version of Auguste Rodin's *The Thinker*. He must spend hours in the gym to have a body that toned.

"Wow," I whispered, not realizing that I'd said it out loud.

"Now that's what I'm talking about. Finally!" He rubbed his hands together. "Was worried you might be into chicks." He chuckled.

I frowned. "Whatever would give you that impression?"

He moved over to the mat and did a hilarious series of twists and turns until he was able to sit down. I snickered but shouldn't have. His limitations were *not* funny, but the way he went about dealing with them was.

He didn't say anything about my response to his movement but did respond to the question. "Yesterday, I worked the mat like a madman in spring training, and you didn't even bat an eyelash."

A flush of heat spread across my face. "Ah, I see. Your pride got hurt a little?" I grasped his wrists and moved his hands to his heart center. "Hold them here. Allow the energy within your hands to circulate through your chest."

His eyebrow quirked, but he did what he was told. "My pride? Nah, just made me wonder if I was wasting my time. Seeing you looking at me like I was the best thing since the invention of the microwave a minute ago put that curiosity to rest." He smirked.

I wanted to kiss that smug expression right off his handsome face. My cheeks heated again. "Perhaps you just caught me off guard. It's not every day a man undresses in front of me." Total lie.

Every single day, male clients came to class wearing only pants. T-shirts were restrictive, and it was best for males to be bare-chested. Less restriction made for stronger focus on the practice and less on dangling bits of fabric.

Chancing a glance at Trent, I noticed he smiled, but didn't respond with anything other than a hum.

"Today we're going to focus on range of motion. I want to see where you are now, catalog it, and determine a routine that will loosen your limbs, give you an overall mental and physical workout, and not put too much strain on the injured hamstring."

"Sounds like a plan to me, gumdrop. And I like the red." He pursed his lips and focused on my mouth.

It took me a minute to figure out what he was talking about. My attire didn't have a speck of red. I'd worn a yellow ribbed tank and a pair of yellow-and-black checkered yoga pants. Then it dawned on me. "Oh! The lipstick." I shrugged. "It's kind of my thing."

"Yeah, mine too." His voice was a low rumble.

Tremors skittered through my body. I flung my hands out, releasing the excess energy. Getting to work right this minute would be the best approach to relieve some of this built up sexual tension.

For the first thirty minutes, I took Trent through a series of poses while seated on the floor. It was obvious by the lack of flexibility that he needed yoga in his life. The man was strung tighter than a drum.

"Okay, lie on your back and place your right ankle on your left knee."

He followed my instructions precisely.

"Now lift the leg up, bringing the leg and ankle closer to your chest."

The leg didn't budge too far before a pained expression stole across his face. I leaned toward him and placed the extended foot against my abdomen. I moved my hands to his knees and supported him while I leaned forward, putting pressure on the legs, forcing him to move them closer to his chest.

"Now lean up toward me."

Trent leaned closer, and for a few moments, we were

face-to-face. His breath wisped across my lips. I licked them reflexively, and he zeroed in on the movement.

"Genevieve, has anyone ever told you how ridiculously beautiful you are? It's almost hard to look at you without reacting inappropriately."

I leaned back, trying to hide my response while still feeling a tad shaky. Lust swirled low in my belly, and moisture pooled between my thighs at the mere hint of what he could possibly want to do to me that would be categorized as inappropriate. Just thinking about it again had my sacral chakra reacting with a fiery need to be filled.

Trent's slick back slammed to the mat when I bounced backward. Sweat pooled in the creases of his rigid abdomen, bringing additional attention to the perfect mountain range that was his cut abs.

"Other side," I said, not giving any credence to his comment and doing my best to get my libido under control. Perhaps Luna was right. Maybe I did need to have sex to take the edge off. My battery-operated boyfriend was obviously not doing the trick.

Trent inhaled a few breaths, lifted the injured leg to his ankle, and instantly winced. I placed my hand on the back of his thigh. His hand immediately covered mine, and he held it to the injury as if the double amount of pressure provided relief. He gritted his teeth and breathed through his nose.

"Here?" I pressed more firmly into the hamstring, applying a gentle pressure.

He nodded brusquely.

"Breathe with me, Trent. Inhale...two, three, four, five. Pause, holding all the air within your chest. Now exhale...two, three, four, five. Repeat."

Together we breathed through the pose called *threading the needle*. Putting my abdomen once again to his bare foot, I leaned over him but not pushing the leg as I had with the other side. With his injury, I needed to be far more cautious.

"You're doing great. Keep breathing."

His hand left mine, but instead of moving my own away, I ran the heel of my palm lightly up the length of his hamstring. Closing my eyes, I imagined the muscle and the repaired tear, focusing on sending healing energy through my hand chakras. I rubbed up the tight muscle from bum to knee and then back and forth in a consistent rhythm. He groaned, but I kept the massage going until the sound of him grunting broke my concentration. I opened my eyes and met Trent's gaze. His hazel eyes were blazing hot.

"Gumdrop, whatever you did, you're going to keep doing it. For a couple of blissful minutes, I didn't feel an ounce of pain. You're like a voodoo healer." His stare was intense, never wavering from my face. Awe and relief seeped into his features, lightening every pained line around his eyes and mouth so he looked younger, less stressed. Dropping my head, I moved back to my mat. "I don't practice magic, voodoo, or any of that nonsense. Yoga is about self-discovery, finding balance between the mental and physical world, which in turn brings you peace."

He shook his head, his dark hair fluttering into his eyes. I wanted so badly to move that hair to the side so I could see into his eyes unobstructed.

"What you did just now, with your hands and massage, was incredible. I've been to a lot of sports doctors and specialists, and not one of them could give me anything but physical therapy and a bottle of drugs for when it gets so bad I can't walk." He grasped my hand.

His hand felt solid, familiar, like it was meant to be there. But how could that be? We barely knew one another and had only met yesterday. Trent's gaze as he held my hand was clear as day. Gratitude seemed to permeate his entire being as he sat in front of me with kind eyes, ones I knew I could look into for days on end and never tire of.

"Thank you, Genevieve. Without even knowing it, you've given me hope that I'll come back from this injury. Heck, I might even come back better than ever."

I smiled huge. There was no stopping it. His words were lovely, not a pickup line, and something every yoga teacher on earth wanted to hear from their students. Knowing I'd helped just one person was enough to continue this journey of helping others find their own slice of harmony in the world. And in doing so, perhaps I'd find mine, too.

"You're welcome, Trent, but we're nowhere near done. We've got a long way to go before you start swinging a bat again. Now come up onto your knees. Let me reintroduce you to a little thing called cat and cow."

TRENT

Turned out cat and cow looked nothing like a cat or a cow. I thought about the routine the blonde with the healing hands and deep, soulful eyes had put me through.

Why was it that none of the names of the poses looked much like the animal or object they were named after? With the cat pose, I was on my hands and knees, which could loosely relate to most animals, and then when I arched my spine toward the ceiling and tucked my head under, I was contorted into the shape of a cat that was scared, or like the black one on Halloween decorations. Still, it released the knot at the base of my spine and made me feel looser than I had in years. This yoga shit was no joke. If the rest of my sessions were like today, and I could feel the tension ease from overtaxed muscles, I'd stick with it.

That's when the thought of my gumdrop entered my mind like a halo of golden light. Christ, the woman was a vision. Small yet so strong. The way her little hands pressed into the rocklike knots in my hammy belied her small stature. It felt like a grown ass man was working my leg, not some pixie of a woman with tiny hands and a sexy body. Her clothing covered more today than yesterday, but something about that red mouth had me dreaming of it wrapped around my cock, leaving an imprint of that red gloss like a mark of ownership. Thinking about it now gave me a semi.

Criminy, what the hell was wrong with me? I hadn't even kissed the woman or touched her in any way, and I was aching for it. Maybe I should just find one of my groupies, call the bimbo over to my pad, and work her over the way I wanted to work over Genevieve. Instantly, the thought put a sour taste in my mouth. This did not make sense. I'd never worried about women before, other than what I could get out of them and how quickly I could get them *under me*. Sure, I wanted that with Genevieve, but I knew from the first that once would not be enough. No, I'd need months of banging her to get her out of my system. And that thought right there was all kinds of screwed up.

This was not me.

Women were great, and I made sure they got theirs once or twice before I took mine. However, once it was over, they needed to get to steppin'. I could tell from two meetings with Genevieve that she was not that type of girl. No, seeing her soulful eyes, tight body, and calm nature, I knew that once I had her, it would take more than a quick fuck to get her out of my system.

Genevieve Harper was a game changer, and I couldn't put my finger on why. Maybe it was all the spiritual wackadoo stuff she spoke of that actually played into the connection. Maybe it was the simple fact that she was ridiculously hot and had the hands of a goddess—one that could remove pain with a single touch. That had to be it. Regardless, I was looking forward to my session tomorrow.

As I left the yoga studio, the California sun shone bright, warming my face while I inhaled the Bay Area air. My stomach growled since I'd skipped breakfast this morning. I could hit the bakery and chat up Dara if she was working the counter like yesterday, but I didn't want to have to do the extra reps at the gym that a plateful of pastries would demand.

I checked out the other businesses across the street. The New to You Thrift Store was on the opposite corner from the café. Next to it was a full-on paraphernalia and tobacco store cleverly named Up in Smoke Shop. Man, that movie was a classic.

Continuing on was Reel Antiques. The display window featured rocking chairs and dressers that held clothes for tiny people. I snickered. That dresser wouldn't hold a single pair of my folded jeans. Maybe it was children's furniture. The size of the little old lady sweeping the front walk told me otherwise. Gnarled fingers gripped a broom while she worked. A young-looking fellow interrupted her work. His apron had the same logo as the bakery. To my surprise, the young man took the broom from the old lady's hands and proceeded to sweep the entire porch as I stood in awe. When he finished, she patted his cheeks and hugged him. I had entered the land that time forgot. Were people really that nice? Not in my experience. Had to be a fluke.

I scoffed and limped along the street until I stopped in front of Rainy Day Café. Place looked as good as any. When I walked in, I maneuvered around tables where patrons were chatting and chomping away at some seriously large salads and sandwiches. Like the bakery, the place had an L-shape bar-style counter. Next to the register was a glass case with pastries that looked suspiciously like those sold at Sunflower. Instead of a long display case on the other side, it had a single wooden countertop that ran the length of the side of the building to the back. The wood looked as though a log had been flat cut in half and someone slapped some serious glaze on it. I could even see the lines from the tree's growth rings.

I felt like I had walked into the heart of a forest. The walls were covered floor to ceiling with wood panels. Potted trees were set in each corner, the branches reaching out into the open space. Vines ran along the ceiling, making me feel like I was in a cocoon. I could easily see why this place was filled with customers. Above the register area was a huge chalkboard where the day's special was written next to a listing of salads, sandwiches, and soups.

Reviewing the menu, I went up to the counter and met the eyes of a thin strawberry blonde with pale pink lips and a smattering of freckles along her nose. She wore a gold necklace that said "Corinne."

"Hi, I'm Coree. What can I get for you?" She smiled, and her soft blue eyes lit up.

I glanced at the chalkboard again. "I'm going to go with the turkey and hummus sandwich, a spinach salad, a cup of your potato soup, and a bottle of water."

She tapped some numbers into an iPad. That surprised me because everything else was so far removed from technology. I raised my eyebrows, and she pushed a strand of hair behind her ear rather shyly.

"These things are so fast, and they catalog our orders, the pricing, and do our accounting for us," she said.

I snorted. "I feel ya. Don't go anywhere without my handy dandy all-in-one." I shook my iPhone.

She laughed. "My sister Bethany was against the transition to technology at first, wanting to stick with our roots, but the fact that it does the accounting for us swayed her to the dark side." She chuckled. "Your total is twelve twenty-five."

"That's it? For a sandwich, a salad, soup, and a drink?"

Her cheeks colored. "We don't overcharge. That way people come back. We might not make as much as the guy down the street charging sixteen for the same, but our customers become regulars, and that's worth it to us." She beamed.

I shook my head. "I can see that. If your food is as good as the price, I'll be making regular visits as well."

"Even better!" The smile she gave this time was more than confident.

Sitting down at an open stool at the counter, I people-watched the way I had yesterday. Folks from all walks of life came in and out, some in yoga attire, others in suits picking up to-go orders or eating in. A short brunette with dark eyes and a constant smile worked efficiently, packing up orders.

Coree set a gargantuan turkey and hummus sandwich on thick slices of soft focaccia bread in front of me. The spinach salad filled the entire remaining half of the plate, and a steaming cup of soup sat next to it. Only the cup was more like a big bowl with a handle. How in the world did these people make any money? I ate my lunch and watched the women work.

"So did you just get out of a yoga class?" Coree glanced down past my hoodie, T-shirt, and loose pants.

"Yep, private lesson."

Her eyes widened. "Oh, yeah? Any particular reason, or are you one of those yogis who want to be able to stand on their heads and walk around on their hands?" She leaned forward, placing her elbows on the other side of the counter, and braced her chin in her hands.

"Nah, I have an injury I'm working on."

"Oh? Did you get in an accident?" Her brows furrowed, and a little line appeared above her nose.

I shook my head. "Work-related injury."

She frowned. "What kind of work do you do?"

The fact that she didn't recognize me immediately made me relax even further. I enjoyed the fame and fortune but not the loss of privacy. "Professional baseball."

She bit her lip. "Like with the Stingers?" Of course she'd choose the rival team.

Wiping my mouth after taking a bite of the world's best potato soup—including what my mother makes, and hers is damn good—I said, "No, the Oakland Ports."

"Cool," she said.

I wasn't sure if it was a placating gesture. People in the Bay Area usually only liked one team or the other and were fiercely protective over the one they chose.

"How does someone get hurt playing baseball? Did you get whacked with a bat or a ball?"

That took the cake. I sat back and laughed, a full-bellied one that felt good down to my toes. It had been a long time since I'd had something truly entertaining to laugh at. "No, I tore a hamstring. Had surgery, and I'm now doing therapy. Yoga is part of my recovery."

She nodded, went over to the pastry case, and pulled out a peanut butter cookie before plating it and setting it next to my demolished lunch. "Here, on the house. Nothing like a fresh-baked cookie to make you feel better."

"Did you make them?"

Her head popped back, and she cringed. "No way. Bethany and I stick to all the organic stuff. We make everything fresh, get our veggies every couple days at the local farmers' market, and buy our bread and treats direct from Sunflower down the way. We want our customers to have the best of everything, and they're the best. Why try to recreate what they already do perfectly?"

This street so far had boggled my mind. Everything on it was unique, yet consistent in that they all had the "do unto others vibe" about them. Seeing that guy help out the old lady yesterday, Dara at the bakery talking my ear off like I was her best friend, and now Coree and her café where they charge less yet still give more—unbelievable. I'd have to tell the guys about this. Get them to come down and give the places some fresh business. Not that they needed it. The tables were all full, almost every single seat at the bar taken, and people coming in left and right for pickups.

I'd sure make a point to come here a couple times a week after my session. Leaving a ten-dollar tip for Coree, I smacked the table and stood up. "Thanks for the food and the chat. It was rather enlightening."

"Course, see you soon."

I smiled. "Yes, I do believe you will. You've got a lot of sandwiches to try out."

"They change every week, so you'll be trying them for a long time." She grinned.

"That will not be a hardship. Catch you later."

I walked out of the café and over to my car. The silver bullet sparkled in the sunlight, its sleek lines shimmering a private hello. Tracing the hood and over its side all the way to the driver's door, I sighed. This was the life. My body felt like a million bucks compared to the last six weeks. Everything seemed brighter and more colorful. My belly was full, but not laden with the weight of a greasy burger. I'd met some really great people that were nowhere near the world of baseball, and tomorrow I'd wake up and start it all over again.

There was something to this yoga business. Day two, and I'd already started to understand why so many were committed to the practice.

CHAPTER FIVE

Downward Facing Dog
(Sanskrit: Adho Mukha Svanasana)
One of the most iconic yoga poses, the downward facing dog stretches out the hamstrings, back, arms, and neck, positively lining up your spine. Place feet and hands hip distance apart, lift the hips into the air, tuck the tailbone in, and relax the neck and shoulders down to rest level with your arms until your body forms a triangle shape.

GENEVIEVE

"Are you going to sit there and twiddle with my hair or tell me about the hotshot baseball player you've been giving *private* lessons to? Start with how *private* these lessons are." My best friend and neighbor, Amber St. James, beamed.

When Mom and Dad passed, I couldn't leave the kids for long periods of time, so a couple of my yoga buddies helped me set up a small hair salon in the garage. We only had one car, so the other two spaces were occupied by my mini-salon. The area was complete with a hair-washing bowl and vanity. I stored my hair products in Dad's shelving system and moved all the tools and things I knew nothing about to the shed out back. Rowan set the shed up as a workout and tool room, which suited me just fine.

Shaking my head, I snipped the dead ends off her thick chocolate-brown hair. Amber lived next door with her grandparents and attended UC Berkeley. She was three years younger than I but had been my best friend for as long as I could remember. We met when I was eight and she was five. Besides the age difference, we'd been inseparable. Without her help with the kids and her grandparents pitching in as much as they could with meals and babysitting, we'd have been lost when Mom and Dad died. I owed her a lot. She was in the same boat as I was. Her mother had died giving birth to her. She didn't know who her father was, and her mother either never told her grandparents or didn't know. Both Amber and I had a sneaking suspicion they knew who her father was, but he was so bad, they spared her the knowledge.

She and her grandparents were über religious. They went to church every Sunday, prayed before meals, the whole nine. Which was also why Amber lived vicariously through me. She rarely dated because she was hyperfocused on school, and as far as I knew, was still a virgin at twenty-one. Still, it worked for her. Sure, she was annoyed that she couldn't participate in the more sexy conversations during girls' night out, but she hadn't been living under a rock, and she definitely wasn't a prude.

Amber poked me in the belly as I pulled up a thick hank of hair to snip the ends. "Oomph!"

"Spill!" Her cheeks turned rosy as she grinned.

I rolled my eyes. "All right, all right. He's handsome." I thought back to our private lesson yesterday and the moment he'd removed his shirt, which was also the moment I'd swallowed my own tongue. "Built...so frickin' well." I sighed.

"And..."

I shrugged. "I don't know. He's nicer than I would have thought him to be. Cocky, but not in a jerk way, more like confident. The man has websites devoted to his body. It's no surprise that most women everywhere think he's hot."

"True. What do you think?" she asked.

"Trent Fox is definitely good-looking. Every time I'm near him, my body heats up, and I feel like a stupid girl with a crush. Honestly, it's lame. I'm supposed to be helping him find himself through yoga and heal through the practice, but half the time I can't help checking out his body." Groaning, I clipped the ends off more of her hair.

Amber, bless her heart, stayed perfectly still. This was not her first day in the chair. She got a trim every eight weeks like clockwork.

Amber pursed her lips. "So what are you going to do about it?"

I stiffened. "Nothing. He's a client. A professional baseball player. Just because I want to jump his bones doesn't mean he's relationship material. And besides, I have way too much going on between Lotus House, cutting hair, trying to make ends meet, hustling the kids to and fro..." Defeat was a wicked ugly friend of mine who'd been hanging out far too long lately. "It wouldn't work. Unless I wanted to have casual sex. Which, incidentally, is what Luna suggested."

Amber laughed. "Honey, Luna is a free spirit. I'm not going to call her a slut because I like her a lot. She's very cool, but she's a bit too free with her body, in my opinion. I wouldn't use her as an example, but she does have a point. You've not played the field at all since your ex broke up with you three years ago. Maybe it's time to put yourself out there. Live a little."

I stopped in front of her and held my hands at my hips, making sure I didn't cut open my shirt with the scissors. "This coming from the woman who won't take a minute away from her schoolwork and studies to go on a single date?" I pantomimed introductions. "Pot...meet kettle. Kettle...this is pot. You're BFFs now."

She grinned. "True, but you're not me. All I have to worry about is school. You have the entire weight of this household on your shoulders and two other living, breathing beings to take care of all by yourself. That can't be healthy. I'll bet if you talked to your yoga mentor, Crystal, she'd tell you the same thing."

Crystal Nightingale was the co-owner of Lotus House. I'd met her through my mother. My mom loved yoga and had religiously attended two of Crystal's classes every week. They were close, and when Mom passed, she knew I needed additional funds to pay the bills. For years, I'd attended yoga classes with my mother, so the practice was not something I needed to learn. Crystal put me on the fast track through the teacher training program within the center, and in six months, I had my credential and a daily spot on the schedule.

I had a suspicion, though, that Crystal wanted to keep me close now that my mom was gone. She'd taken it upon herself in the last three years to impart her often kooky wisdom that was usually dead on target. Crystal was the type of woman everyone wanted to be around. Her long golden-blond hair curled enticingly at the ends. She had blue eyes so clear they rivaled the sapphire blue of Lake Tahoe in the spring. She welcomed everyone into her life and treated all as if they were the most important people in the world.

Mom used to say that if anything ever happened to her, we should follow Crystal's teachings and she'd never lead us astray. To this day, I followed that advice, and so far, I'd done well. I was happy. Lonely when it came to men, but each new day brought me closer and closer to the larger goal. My brother and sister were happy and healthy, and my dream of owning my own salon was still fresh on the cusp of my mind.

"Do you think Crystal would have a problem with you dating a client?"

I brushed Amber's hair down her back to make sure the edges were even and rounded on the sides the way she liked. My wholesome girl-next-door bestie took few risks and was the perfect granddaughter and best friend.

Quirking my lips, I grinned. "No. Crystal would probably say it was divine intervention. That Lotus House provided the universe the opportunity to bring us together. She'd also warn me about ignoring the signs." I shook my head and snickered under my breath.

"That is true. But you know what? I think she'd be right. I mean, out of all the places a man like Trent Fox could go—someone super rich, who could have easily just hired a private yogi to come to his home—he walked into the Lotus House. He met you, took your class, and immediately hired you full time for a month. That can't be a coincidence."

I huffed. "Crystal would say there are no coincidences in

life, and everything that happens was meant to."

"Fate?"

Shrugging, I swept Amber's hair back with both hands, leaving the part down the center the way she preferred. "My guess is she'd say that life just *is*. Everything that happens around you and to you does so because it's supposed to. Then she'd tell me to go with the flow. Feel it out. If it felt right, go for it."

"And does it feel right?"

I thought about how my heart pounded when Trent came into the room. How my breathing became ragged, how hearing him groan his relief made me wonder if he made that same sound at the base of his throat at the height of sexual release. The way my fingers tingled every time I adjusted his position or leaned into his frame to offer an assist.

Inhaling full and deep, I placed my hands on Amber's shoulders and made contact with her gaze in the mirror. "It feels like something, for sure. I just don't know what. Trent Fox—"

"You've met Trent Fox?" came the startled voice of my baby brother from behind me.

He stepped down from the kitchen door into the garage. "Vivvie, tell me you did *not* just say that you met my frickin' idol?"

"Language!"

He groaned. "Vivvie...sister...Sis...my favorite woman in the whole world." Rowan got on his knees and shuffled forward with his hands clasped like he was praying.

Amber started laughing, trying but failing to hide her chuckles behind her hand.

"You *have* to introduce me. I'm begging you. Invite him to

dinner. Something. Whatever. I'll mow the lawn."

"You already mow the lawn." It was one of his weekly chores alongside taking out the trash, which he actually did with no complaint.

Rowan scowled and made his way to my knees. He hugged me around the thighs and looked up at me with his puppy-dog eyes. "Vivvie, pleeeeeeaaaaaase..."

"Row, I have no idea what his schedule is like." I ruffled his hair. He needed another haircut, but it would take an act of God to get him in the chair.

He raised his clasped hands, blinking sweetly up at me, and puffed out his bottom lip.

I blew out a harsh breath. "Fine. I'll ask him. Maybe after one of his sessions we can offer him a treat on us at the bakery, or I can comp one of his sessions. But no promises!"

Rowan hugged my legs so hard I teetered and caught the arm of the chair to keep balance. Then he jumped up and pulled me into one of his full-on Row hugs. This was worth the embarrassment of having to ask Trent to meet my little brother. He probably got tired of his celebrity status and just wanted a little peace and quiet, especially at the center.

Sighing, I moved back and swept the hair away from his eyes. "You need a haircut."

He backed up and spoke faster while shaking his head. "No, I don't! But you're the best sister ever." He started walking backward. "I'm going to think of something really cool to cook for dinner just for you."

"It's your night to cook anyway," I yelled just as the garage door slammed shut.

Amber snorted and bit down on her lip. "He so played you."

"Yeah, he did. Beautiful boys being sweet. Gets me every damn time."

"Maybe I should give that tip to Trent Fox tomorrow before you start your lesson. What are you going to teach him anyway? Downward facing dog? Then you could stare at his booty."

I'm certain my mouth dropped open and my eyes were the size of a large pizza. "Did Ms. Priss herself actually suggest I lasciviously ogle my client?"

She flushed so red it turned her chest, her neck, and her cheeks a fine crimson. "Admit it. You already ogled him."

I sighed, remembering how I helped him get into that particular pose already. "Oh, yeah." And worse, I was *not* sorry.

TRENT

Something was off. Genevieve made a concerted effort not to look at me today. And I tried my damndest to be on full display. Today, I'd shucked my shirt and worn a pair of basketball shorts. I wanted her to see every available inch of my body in hopes it would get her juices going so that when I asked her out, the answer would be a resounding yes.

My fitness buddy, Clayton, laughed his ass off when I declined a night of picking up chicks because I had an early yoga session in the morning. Called me a host of offensive pansy-assed names and agreed to come over instead and knock back a couple beers and eat some Chinese while we watched the latest football game. That's when he made a point to dig for information. Finally, under duress, I admitted I'd met a girl. He was very interested in the fact that she taught yoga. In his experience, chicks that did yoga were known to be flexible and he'd dated a yogi before who was able to bend her body in ways that the memories still made his dick hard. Only apparently that chick was a fire alarm level clinger.

With men, there was a code—at least with my friends and teammates. Some of the guys had the WAGs, which stood for wives and girlfriends. The chicks that came to every home game, some away games, and basically cheered louder than anyone in the crowd. I could dig that. Had mad respect for it. There was a definite advantage to having a woman ready and willing every night versus trolling the crowds looking for a fan who wants to bang and bolt. I'd never been the type of guy that went looking for it, so for us guys who bang and bolt, there was a system. And most of that system determined the level of clinginess a groupie had.

Fire alarm clinger meant the chick was bat-shit crazy, had graduated to stalker status, called at all hours of the day and night, even when she'd been told it was just a casual hookup. Those were the ones we had to warn our security about.

Genevieve didn't share any of those traits. If anything, she was the exact opposite of every female I'd ever met. Women fell all over themselves trying to go out with me. Everyone but the woman I wanted, the one who was currently avoiding all eye contact.

"Gumdrop, what's the matter? You've been weird. Did someone piss in your Cheerios?"

For the first time throughout the entire session, her eyes met mine. Those espresso-colored orbs seemed skittish.

"Hey, did I do something to offend? I mean, I know I crack jokes during some of the poses, but it's all in jest. Helps me get through the difficult ones."

Her shoulders slumped, and she lowered her head. "No.

Not at all. You were actually more focused today than you've been all week. It's just that I was wondering..." Her voice fell off, and she twisted her fingers. The typical strong, compelling woman had left the building, and a nervous, fragile, almost frightened one had taken her place.

The caveman in me wanted to yank her into my arms, tuck her chin into my neck, and kill anything that made her afraid. "Go ahead, gumdrop. Ask me anything."

"You can totally say no, but you see, I was wondering if I could take you for coffee or treat you to Sunflower maybe, and..."

My heart started pounding in my chest. Excitement, joy, and a downright giddy sensation worked its way through each of my sore limbs.

"Genevieve, babe, are you asking me out?"

"Huh?" She blinked a few times.

I smiled wide. I couldn't prevent the satisfaction from spreading across my face in a shit-eating grin. "You are. You're asking me out!" I thought I might hit the sky with a fist pump but held it back.

She frowned, and her nose crinkled. "No. Not exactly, it's just that..."

"You are. Come here!" I grabbed her hand and tugged her over until her curves smashed up against my harder ones. Damn, she felt good. I settled a hand low on her back, close enough to caress the upper swells of her sweet ass, but I behaved, locking down the horny, sex-starved side of me that wanted to press her up against the nearest wall and claim her.

Her face paled when I cupped the back of her neck with my other hand and used my thumb to lift her chin. "Gumdrop, I've been busting my brain trying to think of way to ask you out, and here you are looking all cute and nervous about asking me. Well, I'm going to save us a lot of time and get right to the good part of the date."

She opened her mouth, letting out a heated burst of air. I swooped in and took advantage, tipping my head and slanting my mouth over hers. She stiffened for a moment and then relaxed, melting against me as I ducked my tongue inside to dance with hers. She tasted of mint and cherries. I ate her up hungrily, moving her head from side to side. She sighed into the kiss, and her grip tightened around my neck. Eventually, I needed more. So much more. Nipping her lips, I slid a hand down over her tight ass and filled my palm with one perfectly plump cheek. She groaned and rose onto her toes, twisting my head and stealing my breath with her fervor. We groped one another like a couple of teenagers. Soft touches here, harder ones there, until I started to feel dizzy. My cock was hard as iron, and as I pressed into her lush curves, she retreated, jolting back as if zapped by lightning. Her hand flew to her mouth where that pink lipstick was smeared. Beautiful.

"Oh my... Yeah. That shouldn't have happened," she whispered.

"Gumdrop, that definitely *should* have happened, and it needs to happen again." I started to approach her.

She lifted her arms and shook her head. "No, no. You misunderstood. I wasn't asking you out on a date." Her face crumbled into one of misery. "I mean, I kind of was, but not for me." The honesty in her eyes floored me.

"Look, honey, you don't have to be worried. I'm more than happy to take you out on a date. After this week's classes and that kiss...I'm a hundred percent into you. I can hardly wait to feel you under me."

She groaned and looked up at the ceiling. "Pig," she muttered.

"What? You just hit on me, and I'm the pig?" I shot back, uncertain how this conversation had gone from her asking me out, to us kissing, to name-calling. I needed to get it back to the kissing part. There was no way in hell I wasn't going to have my lips on hers again, and soon. That was a damn fact.

"I didn't mean to ask you out. I was trying to see if you'd take a little time after your session one of these days to meet my brother."

"Your brother?" Now I was lost.

"Yes. He's your biggest fan."

Her exasperated tone was not at all what I'd hoped to hear from a woman after I'd just kissed the daylights out of her.

"Christ." I shook my head. Here I'd thought she was into me, but she was trying to set up a meeting with a fan. "Seriously? You have no interest in going out with me?"

Her mouth opened and closed several times. Ah, now I had her.

"I wouldn't say that."

Hook.

"Then you *have* thought about going out with me. Personally?" I needed to get her back where I'd had her a moment ago.

She placed her hands on her hips and looked down. Couldn't look me in the eye. Oh, yeah, I so had her.

"I may have considered it a time or two this week. When you weren't being a pig, that is."

Line.

As slow as a ninety-year-old man, I edged closer to her. She moved back with each step I took forward, until she eventually hit the wall. The patchwork fabric behind her head with all the golds, reds, and deep jewel tones set off her pale skin like the whitest marble. Placing my hands on each side of her head, I caged her against the wall. Exactly where I'd wanted her this entire time. Stuck. Completely at my mercy. The thought of having her at my mercy somewhere else made my dick hard as granite. I nudged the beast against her belly. She gasped but didn't push me away.

"I'll meet your brother, gumdrop. I would have eventually anyway."

She furrowed her brow, but I carried on, rubbing my lower region where I wanted to plunge most. I was rewarded with another gasp, this one accompanied by a soft moan.

"But this is how it's going to go. I'll meet with you and your brother tomorrow, after our session. Then, tomorrow evening, I'm taking you out. On a real date."

"I can't."

"Why not?"

"Clients."

She said the one word as if it answered the question. It didn't.

Pressing my cock harder against her, I knew I'd gotten the exact spot I was shooting for when her mouth dropped open and a little mewl slipped out. That thin fabric of her yoga getup probably provided excellent friction as I rubbed against her clit.

"What do clients have to do with anything?" I growled and brushed into her again.

She clasped her hands around my neck, moaned, and shifted her hips against my throbbing erection—by far, the most pleasurable torture I'd experienced in ages. Damn, this woman tied me up in knots of desire.

"I cut hair on Friday and Saturday nights. I have two clients tomorrow." She flexed her hips again and closed her eyes.

She licked her lips, and I brought mine close enough to smell the cherry on them.

Yoga instructor and hairdresser? "When are you free?" Moving my hands down over her ass, I cupped the sweet flesh and anchored her leg to my hip, opening her farther to my thrusts.

She panted as I smashed my cock against her sex. I increased the pace of the thrusts, and thank the good Lord above, Genevieve countered each movement with one of her own.

Her response was breathy and coated with desire when she replied. "I have to check my schedule. Oh, my word..."

I knew exactly what that meant. My gumdrop was about to go off, and if the intense concentration on her face and the mist of sweat now coating her brow was anything to go by, it would be one helluva release. Hell, yeah. I picked up the pace, pressed my pelvis forward, and rubbed my thick cock against her over and over. I lifted one hand and curved my fingers around a weighty breast. She jerked against my hand as I squeezed the globe through her tank.

"Kiss me," I demanded when her head tipped back.

The little nonsensical phrases that left her lips were constant, proving she was completely lost in the moment. Just the way I wanted her.

Genevieve opened her eyes, and I swore to Christ, I could see my future staring back at me. Her mouth was slack, her half-open eyes filled to the brim with lust, and her cheeks as pretty as any pink rose I'd ever seen.

"Trent," she whispered.

I about shot my wad in my pants. Her entire body tightened, and I couldn't wait. I laid my lips over hers and tasted her orgasm in the breath that rushed out her mouth. Tongues wild, untamed, and everywhere at once...we kissed like our lives depended on it. She clutched me and held our lower halves together as the quaking and tremors throughout her faded and eventually stopped.

Our mouths were fused together when I responded to the beauty that was Genevieve by almost blowing a load into my pants. Still, I enjoyed rutting against her like an animal, her soft curves pressed against my hardest one. "Shit!" I said, my breath coming in bursts against her moist neck as I desperately tried to get a handle on the pleasure rippling through me. I wanted to sink so deep inside her and let go. Let everything go. The pent-up tension mingled with my frustration of being so close to heaven and not getting to dive in. But this was not where I'd take her fully the first time. Instead, I licked the salty column of her neck and committed that taste to memory. Not that I needed to. I planned on having a whole lot more of it and soon. Very soon.

"So you'll check your planner and get back to me on that date," I rumbled into her ear.

Her body started shaking with laughter. "Yes. I will."

Sinker.

CHAPTER SIX

ROOT CHAKRA

The root chakra is also connected to selfishness and the ego. We use our selfishness to protect our needs, and we use our ego to protect our emotions.

GENEVIEVE

Shaking like a leaf, I entered the office where we stored our timecards. Crystal was sitting on top of the desk, not in her chair, on *top* of the desk. Piles of papers were scattered around her. She had her blond hair up in a twist held by a pencil. Her eyes were closed, and her lips moved slightly. The woman did not look her sixty years of age. She had nary a wrinkle on her face. A person off the street would probably guess Crystal was barely pushing forty. Not that she cared. She had this thing about age. Said age was nothing but a number to note the years one had been alive, not one's life experiences. I moved silently, padding on bare feet to the chest that held our cards, pulled out mine, and wrote my hours on it, as well as the hours this week I'd used the private room with Trent.

Even the mere thought of his name sent a shiver racing through my body.

"I can hear you thinking over there. What has you so twisted up, Vivvie?" Crystal asked, her eyes still closed, body comfortably in lotus pose on top of her desk, surrounded by chaos.

"Sorry I bothered your...whatever it is you're doing," I said, trying to move through my office work. In twenty minutes, I'd teach my class, have the private lessons with Trent, and then we'd meet Rowan at Sunflower Bakery. The thought of having Trent meet my brother sent a whirlwind of nervous energy scuttling in the air around me.

Crystal opened one clear blue eye. "Your energy is zapped, honey, not to mention you're putting off some tumultuous vibes. How do you expect to teach your class so depleted? Sit." She closed her eyes, put her fingers into a prayer gesture against her forehead, bowed, and then came up.

"Why are you on the desk?" I was trying not to laugh.

"Getting perspective." She shrugged, unfolded her legs, and moved to the edge. Some of the papers fell to the floor below. "You know accounting is not my strong suit, and every computer I touch fizzes out. I thought a little meditation would clear my head and provide me with the answer."

"And you had to do that on the desk?" I cocked an eyebrow and smiled.

Crystal's lips smoothed into a serene little smirk. One I knew very well. "To understand a problem to its fullest, it's best to give all of yourself. So I inserted myself into the chaos in the hopes that I could find the fix to my numbers issue."

I cringed, thinking about my own "numbers" issues. The property tax on the house was due in December, the bills were two months behind, the kids needed to be fed, clothed, and in their school activities without being overwhelmed with the financial problems of owning a giant home in Berkeley proper. Sure, if I sold it, the problems would disappear. Our family home was worth around one-and-a-half million. I'd have enough to pay off any remaining debts, go back to school, pay for Row's and Mary's college tuition, and still have start-up for my own salon one day. But it was where we grew up, where our parents lived, loved, and brought us home from the hospital for our first night's sleep. We learned how to walk, talk, and be who we are there. It would be the last bit of our parents gone. I couldn't part with it, and I'd fight tooth and nail to keep it.

Crystal assessed me with a critical all-seeing eye, the same way she approached everyone. Her talents as a yogi were something to behold, but she had other gifts, such as a keen eye for when people were hurting and great advice on how to fix it. She also had an uncanny ability to see through the sharks of the world, the untrustworthy individuals and situations most people had trouble steering clear of. Mostly though, she just knew people and had a sixth sense about relationships, business deals, and the future. Every time I'd come to her about a problem with the kids or the house, she'd offer sound advice and a token of inspiration to encourage me to figure it out on my own. Maybe she could help me with my dilemma over Trent.

"And did you find the answer to your numbers problem?"

Crystal laughed, walked over to the table that held jewelry

and bits and bobs that she made in her spare time and sold to interested patrons for a fraction of what they were worth. With a delicate hand, she lifted a stunning white crystal necklace on a long dangling silver strand and walked over to me. “I did.” She placed the necklace around my neck, the stone warm between my breasts where she’d tucked it down into my tank. “To ward off negativity.”

“What was the answer, if you don’t mind me asking?” I rubbed at the new crystal that now settled over my heart. With my own numbers problems, I could use some thinly veiled advice.

Crystal slid a lock of my hair behind my ear. “To hire an accountant.”

I’m certain my brows pinched together as she ran her thumb along the space above my nose.

“I inserted myself into the chaos, meditated on it, and found that I was not needed at all in the equation. Jewel has been on me for months to let her hire an accountant, but since it was our center and our hard-earned dollars, I didn’t want to waste them on something I thought I could do.” Crystal shrugged and walked back to her desk where she grabbed stacks of papers and piled them all neatly into one large stack on the corner. “Turns out, I’m much better at using my talents toward things that interest me rather than things that give me a headache.” She winked and sat in her chair.

“Is the center doing okay?” I asked, nervous that her money problems could also be not having enough of it. However, every class was full, which led me to believe things were going well.

“Better than ever. All of our evening classes are packed. Yours and Mila’s classes have taken off during the morning, and our private rooms are booking up. Speaking of...I heard you had a private lesson all week. Is that true?" She grinned and her entire face seemed to brighten.

The thought of Trent made my skin feel unbearably hot. That kiss, the way he'd pressed me up against the wall yesterday, had me calling out my release, his own right on the heels of mine. We'd both acted like love-sick puppies, and I couldn't help wondering what it meant. He made it clear it wasn't a one-time thing for him. He even mentioned that he wanted to take me out on a date. Problem was, he was the type of man a woman fell for...hard. I knew his history. Well, I didn't *know* know. I knew what I'd read in the smut mags and what Rowan told me about how much of a stud his idol was. Apparently, he had a girl on his arm every other week, according to star-stricken Row.

Even if we dated until he was playing baseball again, he'd be off at away games and around his people doing what they did. I had an inkling it wouldn't be hanging out in his hotel room alone, away from scantily glad groupies. No, I needed to protect myself. Sure, I was attracted to him. More than that. I *wanted* him. Wanted him like no other man I'd met. Would I be able to let him go when he was in a better position physically and playing on the team? Did it matter? Could I have a casual fling and keep my heart in check? I bit my lip.

Crystal tapped on the desk. "Honey, whatever is going on in that head of yours is torturous to watch. Please, share with me. You know that your mama left me in charge of ensuring you were looked after emotionally. Since she's not here, God bless her beautiful young soul, you've got to work with what you have."

Inhaling full and deep, the way I suggested all my clients

do throughout my classes, I straightened my shoulders and spine and looked at Crystal. "My private client is professional baseball player Trent Fox. Yesterday, I kissed him. Right here. Well, not right here"—I pointed to the floor in her office—"but in the private room. It got a little heated. Now he wants to date me, and I asked him to meet Row because he's a huge fan, and I feel like with our parents gone, if I can introduce him to his idol, even though I kissed him, and I shouldn't have, I should try to do that for my brother." I'd lost my breath by the time I finished.

Crystal lifted her hands and waved them in front of her chest. "Wait a minute. Why shouldn't you have kissed him?"

From all that, she zeroed in on to that one tiny facet of what I'd just told her? "Because he's a player. And he's my client."

She scrunched up her nose. "There are absolutely no policies regarding fraternization. We do not place rules on sexual attraction. If anything, we *encourage* it." Her eyes gleamed.

She had a solid point. The studio even had classes on the schedule for couples, tantric yoga practice, and special retreats designed to help couples find their more passionate side.

"Still, it wasn't very professional."

Crystal shrugged. "Sex, love, and passion usually aren't. Those things are not naturally confined to a perfect little box. They are messy and complicated, but the good parts feel out of this world, give our bodies and minds what they need. If this man gets your heart and root chakra heightened, why not enjoy yourself?"

I rubbed at my face. Crystal always made it sound so easy. "What if I fall in love with him?"

She snorted. “Worse things have happened to you, my dear. That would be a nice balance, wouldn’t you agree?”

Sighing, I shook my head. “No, but what if he just wants to have sex with me, not a relationship?”

She pinched her eyebrows together. “Did he tell you that?”

“Not exactly. He wants to take me out on a date and... other things.”

She smiled. “And are you interested in ‘other things’ too?”

“Oh, yeah,” I whispered breathily, thinking about how he’d made me feel up against that wall. Three long years had passed since I’d had an orgasm that wasn’t self-initiated. That one release had been better than all the self-induced ones combined, and he hadn’t even touched or seen much of me.

“Looks like you have your answer,” she said simply, going back to her stacks.

“Not at all. I’m more confused than ever,” I groaned, stood, and checked the clock. “Now I have to teach a class, and I’m going to muck up everyone’s happy place.” I wanted to stomp like a child.

Crystal stood, walked over to me, and pulled me into her arms. She held me close until I melted into her motherly embrace. For a woman who didn’t have any children of her own, she sure took on the rest of the world’s orphans as though they were from her own womb. “Listen, my dear, and listen good. You don’t have to plan this out. Not every speck of your life has to fit into a box. Right now, you have to think about you, Rowan, and Mary. However, you do not have to plan out how your relationship with this Trent fella is going to be six months down the road.” She petted my hair. “Why not take it one day at a time? If you want to have extracurricular activities with him, ones that are of the *casual* nature, go ahead. You're a grown woman. You are the only person judging you. So cut it out and live a little. Let's go through a quick chakra readjust. I can't have you mucking up our clients with your bad juju."

★★★

Crystal was right. As usual. Once she'd helped me clear the negative energy surrounding my chakras, she sent me on my way to teach my class. The class was great, completely packed, and put me in the perfect headspace I needed to be in to see Trent.

When I entered the private room, he was already sitting on a mat. A manly one at that. It was black, a full eight feet long, a special edition from a company I recognized. Top of the line, ideal for his height, with extra thick padding. That was a smart idea since he was recuperating, and a baseball player's knees needed to be in tip-top shape. His eyes were closed, but when I entered and shut the door, he opened them.

"Hey, gumdrop. I was trying the meditation shit you told me about. I kind of suck at it though. Think I'll take that hot chick Dara's class this weekend."

"Hot chick?" came from my lips before I could take it back, betraying my feelings about him mentioning the physical attributes of another woman.

He grinned and bit down on his plush bottom lip. A zap of electricity churned through my nerves. *Stupid, sexy man.*

"Yeah, you met her. Skin the color of the darkest honey, chestnut-brown hair down to her ass. Bluest eyes I've ever seen. Works in the bakery."

I flapped out my mat loudly, feeling very prickly all of a

sudden. "Yes, I know who she is."

"Then you know she's hot. Shoot, I took a look around this place after class yesterday, and the guys should come here to pick up chicks. They're all smokin' hot, bendy as all get-out, and sweet as pie."

Of course he noticed all the women who worked here. Thought they were all hot. Hmmm. Well, whatever. They were pretty. I'd give him that. But if he was trying to get on my good side and date me, he shouldn't be bringing up the hotness factor of people I considered my good friends.

"What did I do now, gumdrop?" His tone was instantly apologetic.

Holding my head high, I pretended his comment hadn't bothered me and fiddled with my props around us. Unfortunately, I failed, because in two seconds flat, Trent grabbed me around the waist and hauled me on top of him until I was straddling his thighs, my center connected to his much harder one, and our faces a scant inch from one another.

"I don't like when you ignore me. I definitely don't like you keeping your thoughts to yourself when they obviously involve me and are not heading in a good direction. Now, what's the matter?"

Pursing my lips, I raised my chin. "If you think my friends are so hot, why aren't you asking them out?" My tone was defiant and childlike. I wanted to take my response back instantly but held my ground instead, not wanting to seem weak.

He snickered. "That what this little 'tude is about? You're jealous?"

I ground my teeth together and stared hard at his hazel eyes. They were swirling with what I could only guess was mirth. "Ha! I'm not jealous. You can date whoever you want."

"That's right, gumdrop, and I choose *you*. All the chicks in this building, and they are good-looking ladies, pale in comparison to you. You hear me?" He pressed his giant paws on both of my shoulders, smoothed them up to thread his fingers into my hair where he messed with the bun at the base of my neck and unraveled it.

I was about to protest, but his hands felt so good running through my hair, I lost my train of thought.

"Jesus Christ. Look at you. No comparison at all." He moved his hands so that his thumbs were caressing both of my cheeks. "This pearly skin makes me weak. The blood-red lipstick makes me hard. And those black cat-shaped eyes make me want to hold you close and never let go. Believe me, there is no other woman I want more than you. Get that through your jaw-dropping head, will ya? And do it quick like. We have some yoga to do, and then we're gonna meet your brother."

After his spiel, he leaned close, kissed me full, deep, and so wet I wanted to hydrate on his kisses alone, and then he moved me to my mat.

"Okay, boss, put me through my paces. I've got a hot date I don't want to miss."

TRENT

"Row, why is Mary with you?" Genevieve asked as a tall young man exited the driver's side of a sweet classic 1965 Shelby GT350 in a royal blue with two fat racing stripes down the center of her.

A smaller blond-haired little girl who was a dead ringer for Genevieve busted out the passenger side, ran into her arms, and hugged her close.

"Hey, pumpkin, are you feeling okay?" she said to the little girl.

Pumpkin? Was this her kid?

The little girl skipped around her happily toward the door. "Totally fine! Minimum day," she said as she entered the bakery.

I watched the scene between Genevieve and her family play out without saying a word.

"Row, I'm sorry. I didn't check the schedule, or I would have taken you guys to school, cut it short with Trent, and picked you guys up."

Her voice was gentle but disappointed, and that disappointment was not aimed in the direction of the cool-looking teen in front of her. It was on herself, as if she'd had a giant magnifying glass and held that sucker right down over her. I didn't like how hard she was on herself. At all. People were allowed to miss things and make mistakes. Even a curvy little blonde right out of my dreams was allowed a time-out, a frickin' rain delay.

"Hey, Vivvie, no biggie. I can handle picking up our little sis. It's not an issue. We help each other out. Right?"

Oh, she was their little sister, but where were these kids' parents if Genevieve was stressed about picking them up and taking them to school? I'd be taking this up with my gumdrop after our visit with the siblings.

The man-child in front of us glanced at me, grinned, and shuffled from foot to foot. Genevieve turned around and finally noticed I was waiting patiently. I'd let her lack of interest slip... this time, and only because I didn't have the lowdown on her family situation.

"Rowan, this is my..."

I waited with bated breath to hear how she would spin our relationship to her brother. For one, we hadn't gone on a date. For two, I'd kissed her a couple of times and gotten her off against the wall where she worked. For three, I planned on getting in there fully and taking far more of her than a quick mutual rubdown, and she knew it.

"Client, Trent Fox."

"Client?" I growled into her ear, low enough that only she could hear as I stepped around her tiny form.

Genevieve's face tightened and she frowned. I played it cool. I would have plenty of time to define the parameters of what this was at a later date. For now, I had a kid to impress so I could get into his sister's panties a whole helluva lot faster. Sad but true.

In my experience with women, if I won over the friends and family, the chick would be begging for it. At least that's how it had worked for me in the past. Not that I had a lot of experience with relationships. I'd had a couple of chicks I'd gotten to the fourth date with where they wanted to introduce their friends or family. Granted, it was early on, before my fame and celebrity status, but I used to put in the time to get into their panties. Every girl under the sun put out by the fourth date. Now, however, the women I met—aside from Genevieve and her host of hot yoga chicks—put out the same night with little to no courting. Half the time, they'd have my pants around my ankles and my cock down their throats before we got up to my hotel room. With a girl like Genevieve, though, I had to put in the effort, and I was willing to do that. For now. Until the season started anyway.

"Oh my God, hi, man, I'm Rowan Harper. You're like the

best hitter in the history of baseball." The young man that couldn't have been more than sixteen held out his hand.

I shook it, and after, he stared at his hand in awe, as though he'd never wash the thing again. It took extreme effort not to laugh, because in all honesty, the kid was me about ten years ago when I'd met one of my heroes in the game.

"You play?" I asked.

His brown eyes widened. "Yeah, man. High school. Got the team record for most hits on the team."

"Any scouts at the games?"

He shrugged, and I paid close attention. His body language changed dramatically when I mentioned the scouts. Almost as if he turned inward, hiding something.

"Perhaps. I'm not worrying about it." He brushed it off like nothing.

Back in the day, I'd sat in that same hot seat. A scout watching him play was a big deal.

I glanced over at Genevieve. Her hands were on her hips, and a firm scowl marred her face. Looked like this was news to her as well.

"According to what his coach told me, he had the best batting average in the State of California," Genevieve added with pride.

"Really, that's good, Rowan. That's how I got my start."

The kid shrugged. "Yeah, well, I'm going to UC Berkeley." His tone was firm, settled.

Genevieve narrowed her eyes again. "The plan, Row, was for you to go where you wanted. Coach says lots of schools will be interested. You'll want to take the best package for your career in baseball and your schooling."

Rowan's gaze shot to mine and then back to his sister. "I'm

going to UC Berkeley. I'm getting a job, and I'm gonna help out at the house. Baseball is a long shot anyway."

She shook her head. "I don't understand."

"Sis, we'll talk about it later okay, but my mind's made up. I've already got Coach putting the word out to the scouts."

Genevieve's eyes about bugged out of her head. "You mean you've had some scouts ask about you?"

Rowan sighed, and I crossed my arms. I was an interloper in a private family conversation, but for the first time, I didn't feel out of place. Actually, I wanted to weigh in and set this kid straight about the game. If he had scouts calling, he needed to play it straight and let them battle it out for him. He was young. Had another year or two left of school, I gathered by his size and maturity.

"Yeah, okay. Can we go and get a treat? Trent's waiting." He tipped his chin at me.

I did the cool dude chin lift back.

"No, we are not going in. Trent will wait. Right, Trent?" She swiveled around to face me, the locks of golden hair flapping against her shoulders.

"Yeah, babe. Do what you gotta do."

"He called you babe." Her brother's eyes went wide as an owl's. "You his woman?"

"No!" she said.

At the same time, I said, "Yes."

I didn't know what in the world would possess me to answer that way, but when I did, it felt good. More than that, it sounded good. Right in a way I couldn't describe. It was one of those things that dug deep into my chest and planted a seed, and that seed grew roots that spread out and into my heart where it burrowed and fed, leaving me confused and off my game.

She turned to me once again. "Don't you go putting stuff in his head!" she warned and then turned back to Rowan. "How many scouts have come calling? And don't you *dare* lie to me."

The kid crossed his arms in front of his chest, taking a more adult stance than he had the balls for, but I'd give him props for trying. My gumdrop had turned into a little fireball right in front of my eyes, pacing back and forth, murmuring under her breath in a way that sounded like hissing. I caught little bits of "I can't believe this..." and "...after all they did for you..." on top of "...throwing it all away..."

Finally, she stopped pacing and poked her brother in the chest. He winced but held his ground. Weaker men would have crumbled under the weight.

"You will set up a meeting with your coach and me. Together we will discuss your options. I cannot believe you. This is your dream!"

I walked over to her and placed my hands on her shoulders. They sagged in relief or perhaps on reflex, but I hoped it was the former, my touch being the catalyst.

"How about we go order up some treats and chat about this? You can tell me what you've been told, and I can maybe give you some advice, yeah?" I said.

The kid nodded, and without a word, turned and entered the bakery. Through the window, I could see their sister, Mary, was holding the line. She had a couple people in front of her, but if Dara was at the counter, it would be a while yet.

The woman beneath my palms turned around and buried her face against my chest. Unexpected but not unwanted. I wrapped my arms around her shoulders and held her quietly for a few moments.

"I know what he's doing." She sniffed and wiped at a tear that was threatening to fall down her cheek.

I leaned forward. "What's that, gumdrop?"

She huffed. "He thinks he's doing me a favor, giving up his dream to help me. But doesn't he realize I've already given up mine? There's no reason that two Harper kids should lose everything they've ever wanted and worked for. It's not fair. I've already given mine up...for him." She pointed to the bakery and the line where her siblings stood. "And for her!"

I wiped away her tears. "Babe, where are their parents in all this? A kid like that needs his dad giving him the what for right about now."

She scoffed, "Don't I wish." She frowned and if it were possible looked even more miserable.

"They aren't in the picture?" I asked.

Her eyes were filled to the brim with sorrow when her gaze hit mine. "Our parents died in a car crash three years ago. I've been taking care of them alone ever since. And now he's going to do what I did and throw his dreams away out of some twisted alpha hero crap where you take care of your own or something." Tears poured down her cheeks.

I wiped the tears away as best I could. "Genevieve, I'm sorry. I didn't know."

Yeah, I had an awful lot to learn about Genevieve Harper, and for the first time, I looked forward to the good and the bad of it. Holding her close, allowing her to put herself back together in my arms, I wanted to be the man that made sure nothing bad happened. Because with her, I saw nothing but a bright, shining light in places where my life had only been dim.

CHAPTER SEVEN

Headstand

(Sanskrit: Sirsasana)

The headstand pose in yoga is considered an intermediate to advanced level asana and can take weeks, months, and even years to master. It takes incredible core strength to hold this position correctly with the forearms and crown of the head to the ground and legs straight up toward the sky. Inverted poses bring blood flow to the head, which is said to improve memory and thoughtfulness and to release tension and stress.

GENEVIEVE

Misery. Everyone in the Harper household avoided one another and had nothing but cold shoulders, chin lifts, and soft sighs while we sat down to eat Sunday night dinner. I'd made their favorite, turkey tacos. Even made a point to hit the garden and pull some fresh cilantro from Mom's herb garden. At least that's one piece of Mom that lived on. Her herbs. She loved gardening. The only thing I could keep alive were the herbs because I just sprayed them with water once a day, kept them out of full sun, and they did their thing. The rest of the yard, not so much. With my schedule, I could only do so much. Rowan mowed weekly, so the grass was short and green, and the bushes were somewhat in order. Every once in a while, he'd whack at some of the taller fronds, but it didn't look meticulous the way Mom had kept it. Regardless, I think she'd be proud that we were even able to keep it going this long, even though it lacked the beauty and grace of her green thumb.

I served the plates, and everyone looked at the walls, their plates, but not at each other. Once we'd left our meeting with Trent on Friday, things had deteriorated. Row and I'd been fighting ever since. He felt it was his duty as the man of the house to help provide for the family. Though I'm sure our dad would have agreed, I didn't want him to miss out on being a kid. Having fun, going to parties, hanging out with friends. Already he had to help with Mary when he should have been worrying about nothing but his baseball and schoolwork. Rowan disagreed, hence the fighting.

On top of the bad vibes in the house, Trent had texted me twice, asking for a time and day that we'd have our date. Finally, I broke down and told him we could have dinner next Friday. He was not happy he had to wait an entire week to take me out, which seemed odd to me. Didn't he have a horde of willing females at the ready? This thing between us wasn't a relationship. He was free to see whoever he wanted. I just didn't want to hear about it. Ever. I might be cool about dating a hot baseball player who saw other women, but I didn't want it thrown in my face. I also told him it was important to me to keep our date on the down-low. The last thing I needed was to have the paparazzi spreading lies or innuendo about me when I had two young, impressionable kids to take care of.

Technically, Row wasn't that young. He looked like a grown man, but I knew better. Behind all that bravado was a boy who'd lost his parents and didn't want his big sister busting her bum to cater to his needs.

I had to fix this. Subtly, I placed my hand over Rowan's. He stiffened instantly.

"Row..." I hoped he'd look at me and not his plate loaded to the edges with tacos and Mexican red rice. "Hey, bud, look at me."

Rowan lifted his gaze. The hurt I'd caused was visible through the line of tension burrowed in the skin between his brows. His expression was pained, and that simple look seared into my heart like an arrow tipped with guilt.

"I know you want to work, help out the family, and believe me, you doing what you do around the house now and helping me by taking Mary to and from school and dance class is more than any of your friends have to do."

"It's not enough. I'm a man, Vivvie. A man takes care of his family. It's what Dad would want. It's what I want."

"No, you want to be a pro ball player, and you're so close to having that. After years of hard work."

He huffed and set down his forkful of rice. "And what about you? You were almost done with school when you had to cut and run from your dream to take on me and Mary. Is it fair that you gave up everything while we get to live free and go after our dreams?"

I closed my eyes and tried desperately to find any reason I could give that would make him see it wasn't worth it for us both to lose out on an amazing life. "My dream isn't gone. Eventually I will finish my cosmetology license, and then I'll work for a while and prepare for opening my own salon. You see, my dream is still alive. It's just been postponed. And, honey"—I squeezed his hand tight—"I'd do it again in a heartbeat to see you play ball in college. Every game I get to attend means something to me. It proves that, even though Mom and Dad were lost to us too soon, we're still alive. We're fighting, and you know what, bud? Through it all, I'm happy. I think you and Mary are, too. Am I wrong?"

Mary shook her head. "I'm happy, Vivvie. I go to the same school, live in the same house, and I get to go to dance and recitals all the time."

I smiled at my little sister. "And you're a beautiful dancer. One day you may go professional with your dancing and end up on stage in a Broadway show or something. You never know. It's important to dream. More than that, it's vital to work toward them." I cast my gaze to Row. "I want to see you on the field one day playing professionally. Giving ol' Trent Fox a run for his money."

That got Rowan's attention, and he threw his head back and laughed. "Man, you dream big, Vivvie."

"And so should you. So can we please reconsider this?" I held his hand tight, wanting to imprint the seriousness of what he was considering doing straight through my heart chakras and right into his. I focused every ounce of my love and energy into this effort.

Rowan nodded. "I make no promises, but I'll set up the

meeting with Coach. And I'll also tell him I'm looking to play for UC Berkeley's team or UC Davis. That's as far from home as I'm willing to go right now. Mary will only be ten when I graduate. She can't have her bro being too far away. Nuh-uh, no way."

That was fair. Ideal, no. I'd hoped he'd be open to going wherever the best team was and with whoever would pay full tuition. But if this is what he wanted, I didn't see a way of changing his mind. At least he'd still be in the game.

"Thank you, Row. You won't regret it." I picked up my taco and took a huge bite. The cheese, turkey, cilantro, and tomato all coalesced together to make the most scrumptious burst of flavors. "God, I love tacos!"

A round of "me too" started up the normal Sunday night conversation about school, baseball, the yoga center, our friends and neighbors. Even without our parents there, we still sat around our family table and gave one another our time, the same way we had our entire lives. Only this time, two empty chairs accompanied our trio. I'd put a candle in front of each chair, and I lit them at every Sunday supper so their light would shine around us.

TRENT

She hadn't noticed me yet. I was dead silent as I stared into the open private room that had become my regular haunt since last week when I started taking the personal classes. Genevieve just lifted her legs into a precarious position, one that made my dick hard as a rock and my mouth water. Damn, she still hadn't dropped out of it. Her body was upside down, hands clasped behind her head bracing her neck. The crown of her head was to the floor, and her feet up in the sky. The pose was probably called pencil or something but I'd call it a headstand. I didn't think anyone over the age of ten could physically manage holding his own weight up like that.

In the hall, I slipped off my shoes, socks, and T-shirt and placed them near the edge of the door. Without making a sound, I pulled the door mostly shut and thanked the good Lord above that the hinges didn't squeak. I didn't let the door latch because that would have definitely pulled her out of whatever meditation or yoga-induced coma she was in, and I wanted to look at her some more.

Her ass was rounded, and the muscles in each thigh and calf flexed up to where her dainty feet were pointed. The hot pink polish on her toes matched her lips and fingernails. Christ, this woman was a wet dream incarnate. If I didn't get in there—and by *there*, I meant between those tight thighs to the promised land—I might die of blue balls. I couldn't remember the last time I went two weeks without getting my dick wet. The reason why I hadn't baffled me and put a crick in my neck I couldn't shake. This had to be a record.

Genevieve Fucking Harper.

Her legs shifted, opening into a wide V, basically offering up her sex to me. My cock paid close attention, and bolts of desire rushed through my body to settle heavily in my balls. That was it. I couldn't hold back.

I approached quietly enough that she didn't notice me until I was close enough to smell her lemon scent. Her legs faltered but before she could close them, I lightly laid my hands on each ankle.

"Now this pose, gumdrop, has some serious possibilities." I licked my lips and stared at her legs, open for me.

Her limbs twitched under my palms as I slid my hands from her spread ankles inward, toward her center. When I got to her inner thighs, about half a foot from her pussy, she started to shake.

"What are you doing?" Her voice was thick, shaky, but not scared.

Her legs twitched again as I moved my hands an inch closer, still a good five inches from where I wanted to be. Yet she hadn't attempted to close them or asked me not to touch her. If anything, my bendy girl was intrigued.

"Can you hold this pose for a long time?"

"Yeah." Her voice once again held a sultry timbre, one that spoke to me on a primal, physical level and made my dick come straight to attention.

I hummed low in my throat as I pressed my hands closer to her pussy, almost touching it. Her muscles were hard under the flowing harem-style pants. They were cinched at the ankle and made of the thinnest cotton—so thin that a dark, wet patch of fabric clung at the center of where I wanted to go most. "That's good, babe, because we're going to test that right fuckin' now."

Grabbing the yoga block that was by her mat, I sat on it, spreading my knees wide around her, almost caging her ribs with my knees. My erection was at the perfect position for her mouth if she chose to partake. And by all things holy, I hoped to hell she would. The fragile edges of my mind frayed as the wet spot in front of my face got wider and the sweet, musky smell of her sex filled the air around us. Without delay, I leaned forward and inhaled her arousal. That got her attention.

"I don't know if I can hold the pose."

"What would help? How about you put those knees on

my shoulders so I can bear the weight of your legs, but first..." I placed my fingers at her core, gripped that flimsy fabric, and tore a gaping hole right in the center. Her pink lips glistened under the track lighting above, and I thrust my hips, seeing all that wet, wanting nothing more than to delve in. "Now, knees to my shoulders, babe."

Genevieve brought her legs closed, hiding the heaven between her thighs for a moment—a moment too long, in my opinion. My mouth watered, the scent of her excitement urging me on. Then she bent her knees and shifted forward so that they were still spread, but I was bearing the brunt of the weight on my shoulders. Fine with me. It brought her wet pussy right in front of my mouth. Exactly where I wanted her.

"You light-headed, gumdrop?"

"No, not yet. I can't think straight, but I think that says more about where your head is than anything."

"Well, prepare to lose your mind, 'cause, honey, I'm about to take you in a way I've never taken any woman."

She trembled. I locked one hand around her thigh, and another at her waist to keep her steady. I couldn't image she could hold this pose for long, but I didn't expect it to take more than a couple minutes. Still, I needed to give her an out.

"Say no, and I won't. I'll count to three. You don't say no, I'm sucking on you until you come on my tongue."

She mewled, her legs tightening against my head. I held onto her legs as she adjusted her position.

"Slip your shorts down," she said.

My smaller head almost burst when I thought about those candy-coated lips covering my cock.

I did as she asked. Instantly, she licked the tip, and with that single swipe of her wet tongue, I was a goner.

"Three," I said without counting and buried my head between her thighs. Her unique flavor was sugar and spice like a cinnamon donut. Delicious. I flattened my tongue, shifted forward so my dick would penetrate her mouth, and went to town on her juicy pussy.

Her moans filled the room as I sucked, nipped, and swirled my tongue around the hard button peeking out. Damn, if there wasn't some serious merit to being with a ridiculously flexible woman. At one point, she brought those legs into wide splits, and I delved my tongue deeper inside her than I ever had in a woman. The act puffed up my ego to enormous proportions. I held on to her hips, relieving any pressure that might be on her neck.

"Lift me up. I'll brace on my arms. I can suck you better that way."

She gasped as I put the lock on her clit, sucking hard and nibbling with my teeth.

Her body trembled under my ministrations. "Oh, God, please, Trent. Now."

"Be my pleasure, gumdrop." I shifted her weight, though she hardly weighed anything. She lifted her head off the ground and braced her hands onto the mat. It made her body shift higher, so I got onto my knees. My hammy protested slightly, but this was one workout the leg absolutely needed.

The second I got her braced to me, practically holding her aloft, she sucked my cock deeply. The best part, she came at me as if I were her last meal, as if she were starved for it, licking, swirling that tongue round and round. My balls got tight, lifted, and the tension of an impending orgasm hit my lower back and traveled up my spine.

"I'm gonna come. Don't want you choking," I said around

a mouthful of the sweetest pussy. I stuck a finger in deep and stirred it around.

Her body tensed. "Me too. Sit back down, and then lie back with your knees up. I'll brace on you."

Not wanting to leave the honey between her thighs, I grumbled but figured she was the one who had been upside down and likely needed to be upright. So wrong. The second I lay down, she lifted her legs back into the pencil before she slowly lowered them until her feet landed on the mat beside my head. It was like watching an acrobatic show in slow motion. My eye was on the prize when she brought her top half down and lay over my supine form. That's when I was gifted with her pussy hovering directly over my face.

With strong fingers, I gripped her hips. "Fuckin' A!" And I pulled her down to my face.

"Oh my word..." she said, while grinding down on my face.

I loved every second of her sexual freedom. Then, as her body shook, she latched onto my raging cock, but this time took it much farther into the heat of her mouth. Way farther. Once it hit her throat, she pushed a little, but I could feel her jolt, gagging on it.

So that's what I did. I took that sweet peach of hers, pushed her ass cheeks wide, and ate her like I was eating Thanksgiving dinner. Relentless suction, two fingers pressed deep into her tight heat where I pushed against that hidden jewel inside, and her body arched. She jerked her hips down and took control of her pleasure, getting herself off while I worked her over, and she worked me over in the process. The keening sounds of her orgasm were muffled, her mouth full of cock. When her body tightened, preparing for release, I almost died and went to heaven. She fastened her mouth around the head of my cock and clamped down in a Hoover-style lock-down. Finally, she moaned, and an incredible tightness spread through my loins and out my cockhead as I shot hot cum down her throat. She took it all, sucked every drop down like she was dying of thirst.

When we both were done, she spun around on top of me as if she were the star acrobat performing in Cirque de Soleil. She was definitely shining bright.

"Holy moly, that was...wow..." Genevieve breathed against my chest, resting her head over my pounding heart.

"More like fan-fuckin-tastic. You ever do that before?"

She shook her head. "No, but I always wanted to be more adventurous with my yoga practice. My buddy Dash teaches the tantric class, and I've attended when his regular assistant couldn't help out. The stuff they do in there..." She shook her head. "Wow, doesn't cover it."

"Sign us up," I said deadpan. More sexy yoga poses that got me a mouthful of Genevieve? I was all over that like white on rice.

Genevieve giggled against my chest. Her cheeks were a softer pink, her lipstick smudged.

"Come here, gumdrop. Let me taste those sweet lips. I want to taste myself on you."

Her black eyes darkened even more, swirling with lust. I tagged her around the neck and led her to my lips. I took her bottom lip into my mouth first, licking up all her candy flavor alongside a hint of salt that hadn't been there the other times. That was me. Salt and sweet. My two favorite tastes mixed together.

We kissed softly for a few minutes, touching intimately. It was the first time I'd ever spent time just touching and kissing a woman for no other reason than getting to know her. What she liked, the sounds she made when I caressed a particularly sensitive spot were all a mystery I wanted to solve. The way she sighed when I ran my tongue between her breasts...pure heaven. Before long, it was getting late, and feet pounded down the hallway. Genevieve glanced up at the door.

"Goodness. We did all that with the door not even closed all the way." Her face turned a crimson color that looked unbelievable on her white skin.

"Relax. The door wasn't even cracked, but I agree, that was a close call." I chuckled.

She smacked my chest, hopped up, and tried to adjust her pants. Then she went over to her bag in the corner, pulled out a pair of yoga pants, and dropped the ones she was wearing. I got the most beautiful view of her half-clothed. Her legs were long for her size and toned. The thatch of blond hair between her thighs was a neat landing strip that I very much wanted to run my tongue against. Too quickly, she jumped into the new pants. I groaned, shifted my shorts over my semi, and crawled to a stand.

For some reason, between changing her pants and chucking the other ones in her bag, she got shy. Her shoulders curved, she swiped at her hair repeatedly and looked anywhere but at me. Figuring I needed to do some damage control, I limped over to where she was getting her things together. I placed a hand to the back of her neck.

"Genevieve, babe, words can't describe that experience. I'll remember it for the rest of my life."

She met my gaze, her features seeming fearful, laden with an anxiety that hadn't been there before. One I frankly didn't understand. Was she regretting what we'd done?

"You okay?" I asked, bringing both hands to cup her

cheeks.

She nodded.

I shook my head. "Words, gumdrop."

Genevieve glanced to the door. "It was wild. I've never done anything like that. Never knew I could. You bring out a side in me...a wild side that makes me lose all control. We shouldn't have done that here."

Leaning close, I brought my forehead to hers. "I get that, and you're right. We were in the moment. It was wild, but nothing we did was wrong. Just the wrong place. Next time, we'll be more private."

"Next time?" Her voice carried a slight tremble.

"Oh, yeah. There will be a next time, gumdrop. You think I can get a taste of that sweetness between your thighs and not want seconds?"

Her cheeks got hot as I held them, and I knew if I backed up, they'd be that rosy pink I loved.

"Trent, the things you say..." She sighed and leaned into my hand.

Oh, I liked that. Cuddly, like a kitten. Made me wonder what other ways I could make her purr.

I kissed her lips softly once, twice, three times, before I pulled back and let her go. Had to, otherwise I'd be pushing her up against that patchwork fabric and taking her in a whole new way. "Friday, you and me. Dinner. Then my place. Plan to stay over."

Her eyes got wide, and she shook her head. "I can't."

I frowned. "Why the hell not? You're a grown woman."

"Yeah, with two children under my care," she snapped.

"Wait a minute. You are solely responsible for your brother and baby sister?" I hadn't realized how much was truly on her plate.

Her shoulders slumped. "Yes. And they count on me to come home every night."

"Don't you have grandparents or aunts and uncles that could help out?"

I sighed and gritted my teeth. Based on the sour expression she wore, I was about to get my balls handed to me, and not in a good way.

"You've got a lot of nerve." She pointed her finger into my chest.

Ouch. Now I knew how her brother felt yesterday.

"All you see is a woman you want to bed. Well, I'm not a baggage-free floozy like the groupies you take to your bed. I have responsibilities, people who count on me to be there when they lay their heads on their pillows. If you can't handle that"—she pointed—"there's the door. Feel free to use it."

"Gumdrop, I'm sorry. I didn't know the whole story."

"Well, maybe you should ask before assuming you can just whisk me off to your bed."

She had a point, but so did I. We'd spent the past hour doing things to one another that I knew I'd never be able to repeat with another soul, and that thought made me sad as hell. My heart constricted uncomfortably. Any man would assume that the woman he'd done it with would be yippy skippy to repeat it, only horizontally with a lot fewer clothes and preferably on a bed, not a hard floor in a public yoga studio. It *had been* insanely hot, and I wasn't kidding when I'd said I wouldn't forget it. That scene was burned into the deepest recesses of my mind where I could bust it out on a whim.

"Genevieve, I'm sorry. I shouldn't have assumed. How about I take you out tomorrow like we planned? We'll talk.

You tell me all about you, and I'll tell you all about me. We'll start over," I said, not believing the words were coming directly from my mouth. It was like a case of the body snatchers. I was saying all the right words, and I meant them, but the Trent Fox I'd always been wouldn't have cared. Not a bit. This version of me was downright humbling himself to the hot yoga teacher.

It had to be the phenomenal sex.

CHAPTER EIGHT

ROOT CHAKRA

The root of our being is influenced highly by our sexual energy. A couple that is driven by their base desires are motivated by their enjoyment of each other.

GENEVIEVE

I'd agreed to start over with Trent, which was surprising. Sure he was good-looking, great body, funny, called me cute nicknames like gumdrop and babe all the time, but it was more than that. He made me feel things deeper inside, far more than I'd felt even with my ex-boyfriend, Brian, and I'd thought I was going to marry him.

It had to be the phenomenal sex.

What we'd experienced in the studio a couple days ago was right out of the yoga Kama Sutra. I looked it up. I couldn't believe I held the pose for so long. Then again, him hoisting my legs and bracing me the way he did helped. Still, I'd tapped into my super womanly sex goddess power that must have been hiding under some seriously repressed sexual tension. Just remembering his mouth on me made tingles shoot through my limbs.

I sighed and hugged my corduroy blazer tighter around my form. The air was brisk this far into October. The Bay Area wasn't known for being cold. None of California was, but it was a lot colder in the Bay Area than in the Valley. The Valley residents were still rocking shorts and tanks, but in Berkeley, we felt the chill from the Pacific Ocean.

Checking out my shoes, I tipped my foot to the side. I loved tall boots and skinny jeans. Made me feel taller, and at five-foot-five, any bit of height I could score was a good thing. Especially when I was going on a date with a man who was over six feet. What Trent saw in me I didn't know. I knew I was considered pretty. Had been mistaken for Gwen Stefani a few times, and she was beautiful, even at twice my age. I'd left my hair down, remembering how Trent had pulled it out of my usual bun this week when he kissed me. It blew behind me when I stood with my face to the wind.

I waited for Trent to arrive in front of the studio. He'd missed today's appointment because he'd had some type of marketing meeting with his agent.

"Hey, Viv!" Dara ran up to me, apron still around her waist from her time at the bakery.

She wrapped her long arms around me and brought me into a squeeze. Her body was warm, and she smelled like powdered sugar. One of the benefits of working in a bakery, she always smelled like the pastries and bread they cooked.

"So what are you doing standing out here on the street looking all sex-a-fied?"

I grinned, shuffled my feet, and looked out at the bustling street. It was early evening, and the area residents were hitting their favorite haunts such as the bakery, café, smoke shop, and running to catch their yoga class. "Waiting for my date to pick me up."

Dara's eyes got big. "Oh, yeah, and is that someone tall, as in...really tall?" She held her arm up way above her head.

I smiled and nodded.

"And does he have the thickest-looking brown hair?" One of her eyebrows rose into her forehead.

"Maybe." I bit down on my bottom lip, and a flush of heat rushed to my cheeks.

"And would he possibly be the sexiest baseball player alive with a rugged jaw, sensual hazel eyes, and a body that's worth drooling over?"

"Uh-huh," I chuckled.

Dara reached out and shoved my arm. "You suck! I so was gonna hit on him. He is scrumdidilyumptious. Great score on that one." Her eyes twinkled.

What else could a girl say? She was not wrong. "I know." I hugged myself as a sleek silver Maserati rolled up in front of me and parked in the loading zone. Total bad boy.

Trent slowly exited the car. His limbs were long and encased in a pair of dark-wash jeans. He wore a black henley that sheathed his muscles like a second skin. Dang, Trent Fox was something right out of a hot sports guy catalog. He limped over to me, but the limp was slightly less pronounced. Either he was having a good day, or the yoga was helping. I hoped it was the latter.

"Gumdrop..." He leaned right in front of me, got on my level, wrapped a hand around my neck, tipped my chin up, and took my lips in a soft all too-short kiss. "Missed you today, babe."

"Hot damn!" Dara said under her breath but loud enough for both of us to hear.

Trent did a super cool chin lift move in greeting. "Dara, how you doing, beautiful?"

I cringed at hearing him call her beautiful. As the first prick of jealousy hit my nerves, I chastised myself. Man, Luna and Amber were right. I'd been out of the game too long.

"Not as good as you two, I see. Your auras are shining so bright they're blinding me. Wow. You're gonna have some fun with that." Her lips twitched.

"With what?" Trent asked.

Not a lot of people knew that Lotus House's resident meditation specialist also read auras. And her readings were never wrong.

"The fun you're going to have tonight. With one another." She pointed to the two of us and shook her head. "Your auras are flaming red." She waved at her face as if she had caught a hot flash of her own.

Trent shifted his hands to my hips, and he brought me close. "She a kook?"

I giggled. "Yes, also dead accurate with her readings." Though it didn't take a mind reader to know Trent and I had passion sizzling between us. It was like an electrical current the moment his hand hit my neck and his lips briefly touched mine.

Trent lifted his head and turned toward Dara. "It was good seeing you, beautiful. Catch you next week for a couple pastries, yeah?"

"Sure thing, handsome," she replied. "Bye, Viv. Have fun." She waved her fingers and waggled her eyebrows.

Me? I was downright annoyed. He called her *beautiful* and she called him *handsome*. I hadn't even come up with something clever to call him, and here she was giving him a proper nickname. And it was a good one, too. I pouted.

Trent leaned close again and rubbed his forehead against mine. "What does a red aura mean, anyway?"

I grinned and lifted my face up so I could better assess his eyes. They were more of a deep green than hazel in this light. "Means passion, love, hunger, immediacy, charged energy, stuff like that." My voice had taken on a lower, more sultry timbre.

He hummed low at the back of his throat. "Then she has a gift, gumdrop. Looking at you wearing that outfit, that bright red lipstick coating your kissable lips, I was thinking a lot of those things."

I couldn't help but smile wide, rub his nose with mine, and tell him exactly where I was. "Me too."

He ran his hand down my arm and tugged. "Time to get dinner, or before long, I'll be eating you instead." As he opened my door, he blatantly adjusted his crotch.

I held back the laughter bubbling under the surface. Everything about this man made me feel light, girly, and most important...wanted. It had been so long since I'd allowed myself the affections of the opposite sex, and now that I had, the floodgates had opened and my entire body was awash with sensation. A physical heat throbbed between my legs, up my belly, over my chest, neck, and through each arm to my fingertips. I was wired, charged for anything. One single touch, even brief, could set me off. I'd never felt more alive than I did right then.

TRENT

Genevieve was quiet in the car on the way to the restaurant. I was taking her to the one at the top of my building. It had a sky lounge that I used regularly. I knew the people there and had a standard Friday night reservation. The food was good, the atmosphere business casual, and the view superb. I pegged Genevieve for a woman who hadn't spent a lot of time being wined and dined.

We pulled up to the valet for the twenty-four-story building that sat in the center of Oakland, just east of the business district. My apartment was located on the twentieth floor and had a great view of Lake Merritt, but I didn't intend to tell her that. She'd think I was planning to get her into bed. Which, incidentally, wasn't exactly untrue. I hadn't had a woman in two weeks. Sure, I'd had a single taste of the sweet Genevieve, and every last bit of her that I tasted was succulent. I wanted more. So much more.

"Wait here," I said.

Using the curves of the vehicle as leverage, I moved around the car as quickly as my injured leg would allow and opened her door. The smile on her face when she looked up and put a booted foot to the asphalt was worth the hustle. Christ, she had the most exquisite face I'd ever seen. Her skin shone like sculpted ivory. The red of her lips against her flawless skin made something in my heart tighten as well as something my jeans.

"You ever been here before?" I asked.

She shook her head. "No. I don't usually spend a lot of time in Oakland. Oddly enough, almost all of my time is spent in Berkeley. I work there, my friends live there, and my siblings go to school there." She shrugged. "Really hasn't been much reason to branch out."

"No baseball games?"

She grinned. "I haven't been to a professional game in years. The last one was when my dad took Rowan and me. I was his age then, sixteen. He was eight. We rooted for the Ports though." Her grin turned into a shy smirk.

"Is that right?" I led her up the steps to where the doorman held the door.

"It is."

"Well, we'll have to see about getting you in the stands for one of my games then, won't we?"

My entire body tightened when she stopped dead in her tracks.

She lifted her head and seemed to search every inch of my face when she looked at me. "Trent, don't say things you don't mean, okay?"

Her words were spoken in a whisper, but the emotional punch they held hit me right in the gut.

"Gumdrop, I..."

She waved her hand and walked toward the elevator, me hot on her heels. "No worries. It's just I don't want to get attached."

Again, stupidly, I scowled and responded with no fucking filter. "What if I want you to get attached?"

Genevieve spun around quickly. "Seriously, we both know what this is. Let's not make it anything more."

We stepped into the elevator.

"With your infinite yogi wisdom, what would you say this is?" I moved toward her.

She stepped back until I'd caged her in. Unable to control myself, I pressed my body into hers.

She gasped when my body came in contact with the length of hers. "Fun. Casual. Maybe more." She spoke in that sultry, low timbre that filled my mind with thoughts of fucking the hell out of her.

Trying to rein in the lust, I ran my nose along hers and then down to her neck. Inhaling her sugar-and-spice scent right at the back of her neck, I laid a kiss there. She sighed and melted against me.

Growling against her warm skin, I kissed along her neck. "Casual? Maybe." *Kiss*. "Fun? Definitely." *Kiss*. "More? Absolutely." I brought my lips to hers and claimed her mouth.

She opened to my searching tongue, instant participation. Wild, searching, passionate.

We kissed without any regard to who might have come and gone from the elevator. Eventually, the doors dinged, and someone cleared his throat. I wanted to throat punch the man that held the door open as I pulled back from her sugarcoated lips.

"I believe this is your floor."

I recognized the restaurant's host, and he had the decency to cast his gaze down.

"Restroom?" Genevieve asked immediately, wiping below her kiss-swollen lips.

A sexy smudge remained from our kiss, and by the end of the night, I planned to have the candy apple red color all over my body instead of hers. God willing.

The host showed her the way and got our table together.

When she walked back out moments later, her lips were perfectly red and glossy. Genevieve was every man's fucking dream girl. Her hair was back in place and hanging in soft curls over her shoulders.

"You're so beautiful," I said instantly.

She clucked her tongue once before responding. "You mean like Dara?" She pursed her pretty lips.

I closed my eyes with a chuckle. "I didn't take you for the jealous type, gumdrop."

"I'm not. But when the man you're going on a date with calls you beautiful after calling your friend he just saw on the street the same, it kind of waters down the impact."

"Duly noted." I led the way to my normal table by placing a hand to her lower back.

Man, this woman didn't miss a beat, and beyond that, she was a challenge. One I absolutely got off on.

Once we were seated and I ordered a beer ordered for me and a cosmo for her, I started in on the questions. Until now, the way I operated, I'd meet a chick, feed her a couple drinks, and bang the shit out of her until neither of us could walk. With Genevieve, I was actually interested in learning more.

"Please explain what's up with the siblings. Why is it that they are your responsibility alone?"

Genevieve took a sip of her drink. Seeing her wrap those ruby-red lips around a sugared rim, my dick throbbed painfully in my jeans.

"My grandparents are dead. Both Mom and Dad were only children. I don't have aunts or uncles in the conventional sense. I have my next door neighbor, Amber, who's also my best friend, and her grandmother who help out when they can, but Amber is a full-time student. And when I say full-time, I don't mean twelve credits. I mean eighteen. She's going to be a doctor."

I nodded, focusing on the way she spoke, what she was saying, and her hand movements. Graceful and direct. Everything was free and easy with Genevieve. Ask a question, she answered it. No games. No bullshit. No trying to get in my pants. That last one rather sucked. The woman had no ulterior motives. She wasn't looking to hitch herself to a wallet or ride on someone's coattails, nor did she seem the type of girl who would ever be a trophy sitting on a man's arm, although she was pretty enough. The woman defied everything I'd ever learned about women.

"So you said you were going to be a hairdresser. And that stopped because..."

A sadness swept across her features, and I wanted to take the question back immediately to save her from the obvious sorrow that appeared in her frown and the slump of her shoulders.

She looked out over the lake, which was really a man-made lagoon. "Mom and Dad had their accident when I was a few months shy of getting my license. By the time I could even consider focusing on schooling again, I'd lost time. I'd need to take an entire semester again, which would cost some serious cash."

"Did your parents leave you an inheritance?"

She snorted. "Yeah, but the house I live in is old, beautiful, and worth tons of money. What money there was covered paying off the remaining mortgage but not the property taxes or what it takes to keep it up. I sold their cars to pay the taxes the last couple years and have been working as much as I could to pay the rest, utilities, provide food for the three of us, baseball equipment and gear for Row, and dance tutus and classes for Mary." She hid her eyes, looking down and away. "There just wasn't any left. Someone had to work and keep things afloat. So I teach yoga and cut hair in my garage to make extra money."

Thinking of her working her ass off to take care of her siblings and her family home equally angered and stunned me. The woman was, by all accounts, incredible. She gave up her dream to take care of her family, worked too many hours, yet still seemed to be one of the happier people I knew. How she wasn't cowering in a corner throwing a pity party, I didn't know. Every single woman I'd known until now, aside from my mother, was the save-me-Trent and pay-my-way and buy-me-presents type of chick. Genevieve hadn't asked for anything. She'd even tried to avoid going out with me.

"Do people with money make you uncomfortable?" I asked out of the blue. The question weighed heavily on me.

She scrunched her nose in that cute way I liked, a cross between disgusted and confused. "No. Why would you think that?"

I shrugged. "No reason. You're just down to earth and not impressed by the things that other women are."

She chuckled. "You mean like your fancy car or job title?"

I grinned and cocked my head. "Something like that."

Genevieve shook her head. "Money is money. Before my parents died, you could say we were doing pretty well. My parents' home is worth a lot of money. Not baseball contract money"—she winked—"but my dad was a pretty big-time lawyer. They were young when they died, only forty, so they hadn't amassed what they'd intended for their lives."

"Your parents were only forty?"

A sad smile crossed her ruby lips. "Yeah, they had me young. Very young. Nineteen, right after school. They were high school sweethearts. Then they waited until Dad had finished law school and got set up as a lawyer. Then they had Rowan, and Mary was a surprise. Mom called her a gift. Said they were not planning to have more but were thrilled when they found out they were pregnant again."

Chuckling, I did the math. "Seems like they were on the eight-year plan. Every eight years they had a kid."

Genevieve's eyes lit up. "True. Guess they had a pattern. What about you? Do you have any siblings?"

I shook my head. "Nope. My parents wanted a house full of them. They had me, and when they were trying for another, Ma had some kind of exam that showed she had the first stages of cervical cancer. They had the option to attempt to save the uterus, but my father was adamant they remove it. Together, they decided a full hysterectomy was better. Ma's mom died of cervical cancer, and they chose not to risk it. They had me and were happy."

Genevieve listened intently, leaned her elbow on the table, and rested her chin in the palm of her hand. She seemed totally focused on me and the conversation. Definitely not the average groupie I met on the baseball circuit. Not even in the same stratosphere.

"Smart decision your folks made. It probably ensured she'd live a long time. Tell me about them."

Not one woman had ever asked about my parents. Yep, Genevieve Harper was unique. Soft spoken, a fireball sexually, and quite possibly the most devastatingly gorgeous woman I'd ever known. Being around her was like sitting in front of a fire on a cold Bay Area day. Warm, inviting, with all the comforts of home. What the hell did that mean for the future? I had no clue.

CHAPTER NINE

Camel Pose

(Sanskrit: Ustrasana)

This pose is considered an intermediate level pose. Though this pose is helpful for relieving back pain, anxiety, and fatigue, you must prepare your body to enter an extreme chest opener. Kneel with your knees hip distance apart, bend back at the waist, arching your chest forward, before reaching the arms back to rest on the heels, and then allow the neck to softly rest back. Also opens your heart chakra.

TRENT

We'd ordered our food and the waiter delivered our plates. I ordered the steak, roasted red potatoes, and vegetables. Genevieve ordered the most inexpensive item on the menu—a simple angel hair pasta in a light red sauce with chicken. No salad, no soup, and she'd eaten none of the bread provided, whereas I'd already had to ask for another basket. The woman was curvy, and she definitely dug into her pasta when it arrived, but the two times I'd taken a groupie to dinner here, they both ordered the most expensive lobster or prawns dish, flashy wine, with a salad and soup and then pecked at it. Made me insane. When I took them to my apartment, I had no problem hitting the sheets and kicking them out after.

Groupies I understood. They used me. I used them. We both got what we wanted out of the deal. In all honestly, I didn't know how the hell to act half the time around Genevieve. She threw me off my game to the point where I didn't even know where the board was anymore or how I'd gotten my pieces up and down to score any points.

As with anything else I knew very little about, I'd decided to let the cards fall where they would and wing it.

"My parents are great, amazing really. Dad owns Fox Mechanics, which my grandfather owned and still works at to this day. He doesn't do much since he's in his seventies, but he tinkers on the older cars, hangs out with my dad, and greets the customers. My father bought him out years ago, but Gramps still gets paid. Both of my dad's parents are still living. My mom's have passed."

"Tell me more about your mom."

Thinking about Ma always put a smile on my face. "Ma's the shit."

Genevieve laughed, and it sounded like a song. One I'd like to hear a whole lot more of.

"Crazy in her own way. Cooks like Betty Crocker, runs the household. She worked in the school district in Oakland for thirty years. Now she enjoys riling up my dad, painting, cooking, and tending to her garden. Basically enjoying retirement."

"That's awesome. You're lucky."

Even though it should make her sad, after having lost both of hers, Genevieve was upbeat. Happy to be talking about my family.

I nodded. "I am. And of course, they boast every chance they get about their son. Being an only child, I wanted them to be proud. Dad and Mom worked their buns off to put me into every baseball clinic, travel ball, fall, summer, and spring ball all my life. I wanted it, showed commitment, and they rewarded that."

"See, that's what I want for Row. He's good, Trent. Really good. I don't want him to miss out." She frowned.

"Did you talk to him about college ball?" I asked, nervous that it would make the mood turn a bit sour but interested nonetheless.

Genevieve's coal-colored eyes seemed to light from within. "Yes! Finally got him to agree to let me meet with his coach." She shoveled a bite of pasta into her mouth and chewed. "He said he'd consider the scouts for UC Davis and Berkeley, but he's adamant about staying in the home, being where he can keep an eye on me and Mary."

Something about a sixteen-year-old kid planning to forgo his own future to protect my woman ruffled my feathers. "You're not *his* responsibility," I said the words, and damned if I didn't mean them. I'd wanted to add "you're *my* responsibility," but didn't. Thank God. For a moment, I'd almost lost my mind.

She nodded and sipped her drink. "Right. I've told him that time and time again, but he feels like he's the man in the house, and our dad would want him to look out for his sisters."

No truer words... A good man, any good man who cared about the women in his life should protect them. Unfortunately, the kid felt the need to step up and was risking his own future to do so. I had to give it to him, even though it irked me. "It's a trait to be respected. But keep driving it home that he needs to think about himself, too. Maybe I could help, talk to him for you. You know, man to man?"

She lifted her gaze from her plate and almost choked on her meal. Once she took a sip of her water, she brought her napkin to her mouth and coughed into it. Fear swept down my spine, and I stood.

Genevieve stopped me from coming to her by holding out her hand flat in front of me. "I'm fine, I'm fine. Sorry. Your offer just took me by surprise." She took long slugs of her water and then cast her dark gaze to mine. "You'd really do that? Talk to him, that is?"

Man, she was sweet. Not only did she smell like sugar and spice, she damn well *was* sugar and spice and all things nice. Fuck. My gut twisted tight. "Yeah. For you, and for him. I like the kid. He seems like he has a good head on his shoulders, wants to take care of his family. Ain't nothing wrong with a man who has values. Especially when he's devoted to the women in his clan. If my dad goes, you'd better believe I'd be Johnny-on-the-spot to take care of Ma. Hands down."

Genevieve bit down on her lip, and her eyes went soft, more dark chocolate than espresso. The woman looked at me as if I were the sun, the moon, and the stars. Even though the warning sirens were blaring loud, I pushed them aside and enjoyed every second of a good woman looking at me as if I alone could make each day brighter. Hell, it felt damn good, too. Better than any home run, and that, more than anything else, was far too telling. I had to put the brakes on whatever the hell was happening to me. Start focusing on the prize. And that was Genevieve under me, in my bed, screaming my name at the top of her lungs. Yeah, that was where this was headed. Anything else didn't matter.

GENEVIEVE

Trent was full of surprises. He'd shared things with me that I wouldn't normally have thought went along with a casual type of date that we both knew was heading straight to the bedroom. Did I want to get to know him better? Yes. Was I scared of that? Absolutely. I knew that, once Trent was back in fighting shape, he'd be onto the next game and likely the next good-looking female within a ten-foot radius of him. We had not set any parameters for this thing between us, but I knew the score. Fun now, heartbreak later if I didn't rein it in. It was time to stop thinking of him as boyfriend material and focus on the physical benefits of a casual fling with Trent.

Sex.

Really hot, satisfying, mind-bending, body-melting sex was the only thing on the table. And it sounded delicious.

Trent paid the check and led me from the table to the elevator. Instead of hitting the lobby level, he silently pressed button number eighteen. I raised my eyebrows as he looped an arm around my shoulders. "My apartment is on twenty," he said.

"Okay," I said.

He tightened his hand around the ball of my shoulder. "Okay."

Besides the endless conversation, he'd touched me

constantly. We hadn't sat across from one another but on the sides of the square table. He touched my hand, pressed his knee into mine, swept a lock of hair away from my face. We even had a brief generous kiss after we shared a slice of Kahlúa mousse cake. I'd wanted to say no to the additional purchase. Even though the restaurant had customers in jeans and nice shirts, the price tag on every item was way over the top. My pasta was twenty-six dollars, and that was the cheapest thing on the menu. Trent had ordered a fifty-dollar steak. What I could do with fifty dollars...

I shook my head to clear the thoughts and let him lead me down the hall to his apartment. I couldn't believe I was about to see where the famous Trent Fox lived.

He opened the door and ushered me into the foyer. It was a step up from a sunken living room. The room had plain white walls with nothing but a TV hanging from them. Across from the TV were a single leather couch, a glass coffee table, and an end table with a lamp on it. No knickknacks or even magazines lying around. Trent walked to the left and turned on the lights in a sprawling kitchen.

It was beautiful. White cabinets with shiny steel handles. Black granite countertops that gleamed under the lights, and high-quality stainless steel appliances. A toaster and coffeepot were the only things visible on the counters. No canisters, spice rack, homemade trinkets, or anything that remotely gave a hint as to what type of things interested Trent. I could see through the kitchen to a dining room that had a glass table and six chairs. Nothing else. No pictures hung, no sideboard with special china dishes, or anything remotely comforting.

"Come, I'll give you the rest of the tour." He leered. Not in a gross creeper way but in a cheesy, 'I'm going to show you my room, and we're going to spend time in there' silly way.

"Lead on." I chuckled but continued to be baffled by the lack of pictures lining the hallways. "How long have you lived here?" I asked, thinking he must have just moved in.

"Five years."

I stopped right in the center of the hallway.

"What's the matter?" He lifted his hands to my biceps. "You know, babe, you don't have to do anything with me tonight. I mean, yeah, obviously I've been thinking about nothing else since we'd had some of the best oral sex in my life." He grinned and licked his lips. "But we don't have to take that last step right now."

Of course he'd think I was having reservations. I wasn't, but what I was having was a mental stutter over the lack of personality. He only had the items he needed to survive. Couch, table, lamp, television, kitchen table, toaster, coffeepot. "I'm fine, just surprised you've lived here so long."

He ran his hands up and down my biceps. "Yeah, why's that?"

I grabbed hold of his hand to remove the tension that had seeped into his form. I liked that he'd worried about my comfort and was concerned with how I felt about this step. He didn't seem like he was trying to play me, though I knew what we were about to do would mean far more to me than him. I'd only been intimate with one man, and at the time, I thought he'd end up as my husband. With Trent, I was planning to have sex with him, share my body with him, and I also knew beyond a shadow of doubt that was all it would be to him—a physical release.

He continued to walk down the hall until he reached a set of double doors. He opened them and walked in. The biggest sleigh bed I'd ever seen sat in the center of the room. Two end tables hugged each side. The wood was a fine cherry finish and chunky, not quite manly but elegant and sturdy. A midnight-blue comforter with the slightest sheen to the fabric covered the beautiful bed. In the corner was a long dresser with a mirror above it. Catty-corner to the bed was another tall dresser and above that, another wide flat-screen television hung on the wall.

This room had a bit more life. Above the bed was a beautiful picture of the Golden Gate Bridge. "That picture is beautiful." I pointed to the giant framed photograph. The red tones of the bridge seemed to escape out of the confines of the misty fog surrounding it.

"You think so?"

"Yeah, did you buy that from a local photographer?"

He shook his head. "Nah, I took it."

I let out a shocked breath. "Really?"

He exhaled, looked up at the painting, and rubbed the back of his neck. "Yeah, a little dabble into photography. I didn't frame it and hang it though. That was my ma. The bedroom set and comforter, too. They bought me the set when I got signed by the Ports. It was their gift. I get new bedding every year for Christmas, but yeah, Ma's got good taste."

I scanned the furniture, appreciating its beauty once more. A five-by-seven framed picture sat alone on the dresser. I walked over and picked it up. A tall gray-haired man stood, holding on to a very small blond woman. They both looked to be in their fifties.

"Your parents."

Trent pulled me into his embrace from behind. His chin resting on my shoulder as we both looked at the happy couple, so very obviously still in love. My parents would have been like them, too.

His chin warmed the side of my neck. "Yeah, that's Richard and Joan Fox."

"They seem happy."

Trent's breath tickled along my ear. "I think they are. They found the one they were meant to be with very young."

I nodded. "My parents, too."

Trent reached around me, took the photo, and set it back down on his dresser. "Enough about my family and the mood killer. I've got something I think you'll be very interested to meet." He thrust his hardened shaft against my bum.

Automatically, my hands went to the sides of his thick thighs where I held on. Trent swept my hair away from my neck, reached around me, and pulled back the lapels of my jacket until he got it completely open and removed. He tossed it haphazardly on the dresser.

"I've been dying to get my hands on you all night. Hell, for two weeks. Do you know what your body does to me?"

I shook my head as his hands crept under my loose tank and up to cup my breasts over my bra. I arched into his hands, the pleasure swirling around us both almost like a fog filling the room. Our breaths came in soft sighs and eager pants as he explored my curves. He'd figured out that I wore a front clasping bra and undid it expertly. I tried not to think about why he was so good at removing undergarments and instead went with the flow.

Trent growled against the side of my neck where he bit down. Simultaneously, he plucked at each hardened nipple, and I cried out. I was shocked that my body was responding so quickly and elated that he knew just how to touch me to bring the most pleasurable result.

"Baby..." I blew out a heated breath.

He hummed against my ear where he traced the shell with his tongue. Warm and wet, just like the space between my thighs, growing with intensity under every new sensation. Trent was a master at the art of seduction and I his willing subject.

"Mmm, I like hearing you call me baby. Makes me so hard." He thrust against me once more and then spun me around so we were face-to-face. "I think we should take this someplace a bit more comfortable."

I looped my arms around his neck and grinned. "Oh, yeah? Where did you have in mind?"

He leaned close, planted his hands on my bum, and lifted me. I wound my legs around his lean waist.

"Why tell you when I can show you?"

With quick steps, he planted me on the side of the bed and fell right on top of me. "Hmm, where was I?" He placed a fingertip at my ear and ran it down my cheek, along my neck and down between my breasts. "Oh yeah, right about here." He traced the tip of my erect nipple, which poked visibly against the thin fabric of my tank.

"Trent..." I gasped as he pinched the nub through my shirt. The motion sent a bolt of fiery need directly to the tight bundle of nerves that wanted nothing more than for him to relieve the pressure, relieve the ache.

"Relax. We've got time. It's still early..." He shifted my tank up.

I lifted my arms so he could remove it and the loosened bra while straddling my form.

"Jesus, gumdrop. Your tits..." He cupped them with both

hands as if lifting them in worship. "Never fucking seen better." Trent used his thumbs to play around the areola and flick at each tip.

I jerked, grabbing the comforter below as he got to know my more feminine attributes. Trent's greatest strength, his patience, was currently my biggest weakness.

Trent petted my breasts, lifting, squeezing, rubbing, plucking, elongating the nipples until I shook with unfulfilled carnal need. I wanted his mouth on me and bigger parts of him *inside* me. Now.

"Please," I whispered, my gaze locked on his face.

A lazy smirk crossed his features when he leaned forward and took one reddened peak into his mouth.

The sensation was so extreme, I almost came against the single movement of his tongue laving my nipple. "So good," I whimpered, my legs shifting.

He licked and kissed every centimeter of flesh covering my chest. Saying he was committed to his task was stating it mildly. The man was downright obsessed.

He licked and took long sucks on each nipple before trying to pull as much of each breast into his mouth at one time. Not an easy task because my breasts were huge—size D on a five-foot-five body was ginormous in my opinion, but the vote was in. Trent Fox was a serious boob man.

"They're just perfect." He leaned back, slapped each side playfully so they knocked into one another. "Babe, I could die a happy man sucking these." Again, he latched on to a breast, swirled his tongue in the same dizzying circles he'd done on my clit the other day in the yoga room, and that's when it happened.

My phone buzzed against my bum. I jolted up.

Trent backed off as if I'd been stung by a bee. "What was

that? What happened?" He looked around the room.

I laughed and, wiggling, found my phone in my back pocket and pulled it out.

It was Row. I tapped the green button and held it to my ear. Trent groaned and sat back on his haunches.

"Row?"

My brother's voice was shaky. "Vivvie, I... I heard a noise. Well, not one noise, lots of 'em. I think someone's trying to break in. Mary's in bed, but Viv, I...should I call the cops?"

I sat up, pushing Trent off me. "Is the house alarm on?" I clasped my bra and scrambled for my shirt.

"Genevieve?" Trent said.

I didn't have the time to answer. I put the phone on speaker.

"Yeah, the alarm is on," Row said. "But the light near the garage and the backyard? That motion light is still on. It hasn't gone off, Viv."

I pulled on my tank. "It's okay. If you hear or see anything, call the cops. Trent and I are on our way. Stay on the phone with me, bud."

My brother's voice sounded low and frightened. Reminded me of how he sounded when I'd told him our parents had been killed in a car accident and it was just the three of us from then on. Why the hell had I gone on a date? If I had been there, he wouldn't be scared right now. He and Mary wouldn't be at risk.

I clenched my teeth as Trent raced us through his house, down the elevator, and through the parking garage. "We'll take the Harley. It's faster."

"I'm going to be on a motorcycle, and we're ten minutes out. Please call the cops if you're that scared. Okay?"

"Okay. Vivvie?"

Rowan's voice was so low I pressed the phone so hard against my cheek it would leave a phone-shaped Imprint.

Trent put the helmet on my head and snapped it closed. Without knowing what to do, I just hopped on to the back seat. Trent readjusted my booted feet to the appropriate pegs.

"Phone off. Now," he said.

"Yeah?" I said to Rowan while nodding to Trent.

"I love you," Rowan said and hung up.

A pit the size of the Grand Canyon took position in my stomach. Trent grabbed my hands and tucked my phone into his jacket pocket. "It will be okay."

"How do you know?" My voice shook, and tears flooded my eyes as I imagined my brother home alone, scared out of his mind, and me sitting on the back of a hot guy's bike. I'd never forgive myself if anything happened to them because I was being selfish and taking time to date instead of caring for them.

"Not gonna let it happen, babe. Period," he declared in that alpha I'm-a-bad-boy way I liked so much and worried would break my heart.

"Not going to let what happen?" I asked, gripping his waist.

"Anything," he growled. With that, he gripped the throttle, revved up the engine, put the bike in gear, and raced across town, weaving in and out of traffic like a madman, blowing through yellow lights without any thought of caution.

If I hadn't been so scared of what could be happening at my house, I'd have been bone scared of the ride from hell. Instead, I thanked my lucky stars that I was with someone who could move fast and react even faster.

The house alarm was blaring as we pulled up to the house.

I hopped off the bike and took the front steps two at a time. I'd unsnapped the helmet, yanked it off my head, and left it on the ground as I fumbled to get my key. Every windup of the alarm reaching its crescendo took my heart right along with it.

"Christ, gumdrop, wait!" Trent hollered behind me.

I didn't care. Stopping this train was useless. I had to get to my family, and I'd plow through anyone, lack of weapons or protection be damned. If anything happened to my siblings, I had nothing left to lose.

The door finally opened, and I screamed through the giant open space, my voice rising against the volume of the alarm.

"Rowan! Mary! Where are you?"

CHAPTER TEN

This chakra is driven by the survival instinct, the same that motivates us to procreate and expand our lineage. The root chakra is connected to our most primitive self and controls our primal instincts. Through this chakra, we have an inherent need to protect ourselves at all costs...to survive.

TRENT

Genevieve plowed through the door of the historical-looking home like a high-speed ball thrown by an all-star pitcher. No stopping, no concerns for her own safety. I chased after her, my injury be damned. It protested with every jolt of my feet hitting the cobblestone walkway as I jogged the best I could after her.

"Rowan! Mary! Where are you?"

Just as I hit the porch, I heard a scuffling sound behind

me and caught a glimpse of two guys dressed in black hoodies running past the side of the house where I imagined the garage was. Nimble as teenagers, they both hopped over a small fence and blasted at a full run down the street until they were out of view.

"Fuck!" I turned away, wishing I were in full fighting shape so I could run after them, but then I'd be leaving Genevieve on her own. I couldn't risk the real knowledge that there could be more than the two intruders that got away.

"Genevieve!" I roared over the sirens piercing my ears. Jesus Christ, someone needed to turn off that alarm.

"Up here!" she cried out.

Cursing these old homes and their unique architecture, complete with a double set of stairs, I attempted the task of getting up them. When I reached the top, I found a door wide open. On the bed sat Genevieve, her arms wrapped around her brother and sister. Her little body shook as she held them.

Rowan's lifted his head from their huddle, his gaze meeting mine. He gave me the cool guy chin lift, and my heart filled with pride. The boy was turning into a man and needed guidance.

"Hey, gumdrop, you think we could see about turning off that alarm while I check the house?"

"The cops should be here any second," Rowan said, just as the sound of an additional higher-pitched siren screeched into the area.

Red-and-blue lights flashed against the upper floor bedroom window. I walked over to it and checked. Sure enough, the boys in blue had arrived. "Cops are here. I'll go talk to them."

I made my way down the stairs as the cops were entering,

guns drawn. I lifted my hands up. "Just got here with the owner of the house."

The cops nodded. "Anyone else here?"

"One adult female and two children. The boy called us when he heard noises out back. Haven't checked there, but I did see two males leaving the premises. Didn't bother to stop and chat as they were escaping."

"Stay here, sir. We'll check it out." The cop waved at his partner to go around the back while he proceeded through the house.

I stood at the base of the stairs, serving as sentinel. Anyone tried to hit the stairs he'd have to go through me first.

"Is it clear?" Genevieve asked from the top of the stairs, her brother and sister behind her.

I shook my head. "Nope. Cops are checking it out."

Not wanting them to be anywhere near the lower level of the house, I made my way back up and opened my arms. Genevieve's head plowed right into the center of my chest the moment I reached the top. That fright, the one that had taken up deep in my bones when she jumped off my bike, started to dissipate but didn't quite leave.

The cops both made their way back in. "You can come down. It's clear. Can one of you turn off the alarm?"

Genevieve shuffled over to the front door where a square white panel was mounted. She pressed a few buttons and the ringing stopped. Blessed silence.

"Now, can anyone here tell me what happened in detail?" one of the policeman asked.

Rowan stepped up, his spine straight, his voice timid, betraying how afraid he was when he relayed what he'd heard. He didn't call the cops until he heard the glass breaking.

When he heard the noise of someone definitely breaking in, he took his baseball bat and cornered himself and Mary in her bedroom and called the cops.

"Yeah, you've got a broken window and a tipped over garbage can out back. Might be a good idea to change out that back door with something more solid. Those old doors with the top half having the crisscrossed windows make it child's play for intruders to break in. All they have to do is break a small window, put a hand in, and unlock the door. You've got a handle lock and a bolt, but that glass doesn't prevent them from getting in. The alarm though? A great call."

Genevieve nodded. "Thank you, Officers, for coming so quickly. Is there anything more we need to do?"

The cop stood, tall and beefy—one of those guys who took working out as serious as he did his job. His hand rested on the butt of his holstered gun. "I'm sure your husband here can secure the door."

Her stunned gaze shot to mine, eyes opened wide, and her mouth moved fast. "Oh, he's not...uh...my husband."

"Well, your boyfriend then. Whatever."

Before she could correct the cop again, I weighed in. "I'll take care of the door. Thanks, Officers." I held out a hand.

The cop closest to me proceeded to shake my hand while his eyes went squinty. "Hey! I know you. You're Trent Fox. Best hitter in baseball!"

I chuckled. "Yep, that's me."

"Good to meet you, Mr. Fox. I'm a huge fan of the Ports."

"Yeah?" Seeing a golden opportunity dangling in front of my eyes, I made my play. "If you got your notebook with ya, I'd be happy to autograph it. Maybe in exchange, you could do a couple drive-bys of the neighborhood over the next few days?

Keep an eye on my girl and her family here?" I gestured to the little huddle behind me.

Genevieve was in full mama bear mode, looking over Rowan and Mary to make sure they didn't have any scratches and hugging them profusely. I had a feeling she'd be keeping them in sight all evening.

Both cops nodded. "Sure, buddy." They handed over their notepads.

I scribbled out my name and a brief greeting, thanked them again, and walked them out. Going back in, I passed by the family huddle, heading to the back. A small window in the door was broken, glass scattered on the floor. A seething burn of anger filled my chest. What kind of pimple-nosed pricks would invade the home of a woman with two kids? Meaningless pieces of shit, that's who.

I found a dustpan and broom near the door and cleaned up the glass. Last thing I wanted was my bare-footed yogi chick scarring up her dainty feet. Once I'd cleaned that up, I went out back and found a shed that housed weights and tools. Near the back, I found a sheet of plywood that would fit the entire length of the window.

"Hey, Trent, you need any help?" Rowan came up behind me, watching while I sifted through the tools haphazardly thrown in boxes.

"You know, you should really keep your tools more organized. Not only would they be easier to find, but they'll last a lifetime if you treat 'em right." Figured the kid could use some manly advice. It was something my dad had drilled into me from the time I was a baby and set booty-clad feet in his mechanic shop.

"They were...my dad's."

I looked Rowan dead in the eyes with as much conviction as I could convey. "Then you should be treating them better because of him."

Rowan looked down as if I'd shamed him.

I placed my hand on his shoulder and squeezed. "Good job tonight, kid. It could have been worse. You acted smart. Kept your head and protected your sister."

Rowan lifted his head. The hope I saw in his eyes nearly fried me.

"Proud of you."

He nodded, moved over to a box, and found the hammer I was searching for and a box of nails.

"Thanks. Now, come on and help me board up this window. Then tomorrow I'll call about a door replacement."

Rowan narrowed his eyes and tapped his lip with his thumb. "How much does something like that cost? Vivvie's gonna freak if it's expensive. We're kind of on a budget." He looked away and shuffled his feet.

I gripped him on the shoulder again. "How about you let me worry about the door, and you worry about checking in on your sisters? Yeah?"

"Okay, yeah." Rowan jogged back into the house.

On a budget. A code word for stone-cold broke. After hearing about how she'd burned through their inheritance paying off the house and was still struggling, I knew she probably wouldn't have the coin to buy a new door. A flash in the pan for my bank account. Getting her to agree to let me buy one, on the other hand, would take some serious maneuvering.

GENEVIEVE

Trent found me upstairs just as I'd gotten Mary back to sleep. The alarm and her brother barricading her room had scared the living daylights out of her. My baby girl needed the extra time with me to fall asleep. When I looked up at the doorway, Trent stood, leaning his back up against the jamb, his massive arms crossed in front of his chest. For a moment, I pouted, feeling let down that I hadn't been able to assuage the hunger for this man earlier. Instantly, a sense of guilt poured over my body like a bucket of ice water, chilling and freezing my limbs and mind.

No. Being with Trent was what had gotten me into this position in the first place. Had I not been with him, I'd have been able to scare off the would-be intruders and I wouldn't have two scared kids and a broken window. Ugh. It wasn't his fault. I just wanted someone to blame, but with things like this, there wasn't anyone. Still, it didn't change the fact that being with Trent was a bad idea.

I got up, pulled the blankets to Mary's chin, and kissed her forehead. Shutting the door most of the way, I turned off her light and proceeded to Row's room. Soft alternative rock music came from behind his door. I knocked.

A muffled "Yeah?" came through the old wooden door.

I opened it and held the knob. He sat cross-legged on his bed, tapping furiously on his phone. Probably telling all his friends about the near miss with the break-in. The single thought sent chills down my spine.

"Just hitting the hay soon and wanted to tell you how happy I am you were here and took care of your sister."

Rowan's face lit up at the praise.

Note to self—tell him more often how wonderful he is.

"Anytime, Vivvie. It's what men do. Protect their family. Just because I'm sixteen doesn't mean I'm not capable." Rowan looked directly into my eyes and then to a spot behind my shoulder.

Trent's body was close. I sensed him before I could see him. His warmth seeped into my backside as I focused my attention on Rowan.

I nodded. "No, you're right, and you definitely proved that tonight. Thank you, Row. I love you."

"Love you too. Pancakes tomorrow?" He grinned.

I couldn't turn him down after the evening we had. Emotional blackmail. Rowan was the king.

"Sure." I smiled and slid his door shut, booty bumping Trent in the process.

Trent wrapped his large paws around my hips. "Where's your room?"

I tipped my chin toward the room at the very end of the hall. It had its own small flight of stairs. "You can't stay," I said, cutting that idea off right at the quick.

Trent's hands tightened at my hips. "Excuse me?"

I shushed him. "The kids will hear you."

He pushed a hand through his hair and sighed. "Gumdrop, the kid already knows I'm here. Now, let's go into your room, or they may end up hearing a lot more than they bargained for." His lips curved delectably into a small smile.

His eyes changed color, seemed brighter, greener, fueled by the fire we'd set earlier. *Oh, boy.* Huffing, I led the way to my parents' old room. The room was pretty large and far enough away from my brother and sister that I didn't worry they'd hear us. I opened the door and let him enter. His big form in the room somehow made the large space seem far smaller, more cozy.

"Nice room." He looked around.

My parents had had great taste. The bedroom set was a chestnut color and looked great against the cucumber-green paint and thick white crown molding and baseboards. Like a lot of houses in the Berkeley hills, this one had been renovated with top-notch window dressings, furnishings, and everything one would need to make a home a home. My parents had spent a pretty penny making this a beautiful place for us to rest our heads, and I was proud of their achievement. Hoped to goodness I could hold onto it.

"Thanks, it was my parents'. I'd already moved out when they passed, so Dad had made my old bedroom into an office. It just made sense for me to move into theirs, plus it makes me feel close to them. I did change some things."

I dragged a fingertip slowly along the comforter I'd purchased. It was a shimmery taupe and gold. It had little embroidered daisies every few inches. Reminded me of happier times when I'd pick the daises in our backyard with Mom during the spring. Now, they grew wild, and Rowan hacked them down when they all burned to a crisp under the California sun. Nothing like what my mother was able to achieve with her gardening prowess.

Trent set his hands at his hips and took a leadership stance. "Look, gumdrop, the house is not secure. I'm not going anywhere until it is. You got that?"

I narrowed my eyes and focused on him. He stood in the same outfit he'd worn to our date, only he'd removed the jacket. His henley molded to his muscular frame in all the right ways.

"I don't think you want me to go, either."

I scanned his hard body from foot to face. "Of course I want you to go. I'm a big girl and can handle myself. Besides, Rowan proved he handles things well under duress."

One second he was a good ten feet away, and in the next second, he'd closed in. As in *really* close. He cuffed my neck, thumbs lifting my chin. "No way in hell I'm leaving you or those kids alone tonight. Not until that door is secure. Now, we can continue where we left off earlier"—his tone turned suggestive—"or get some shut eye. Your choice, but I'm sleeping in that bed and there's not a lot you can do about it."

His words were confident and tripped my heart with a pang and a heaping dose of pitter-patter. If I wasn't careful, I'd fall for this alpha guy and his compelling ways without even trying. And it wasn't just because he was God's gift to women when it came to sexy bodies. More, it was because the very thing he was fighting for, the reason he was using that protective tone, was because of *me*. For *my* safety. I haven't had that since my parents died, and I'd be lying if I said I didn't love that someone else cared enough to bother.

★ ★ ★

Trent took the shower as I exited in a camisole and a pair of thin cotton shorts. They were decent but still figure flattering.

As he passed by me, he hooked me with an arm around my waist, and pulled me to his side. "You smell insanely good." He inhaled deeply against the crook of my neck. With a simple, soft kiss, he let me go and moved his big body into the bathroom. He didn't even shut the door.

I got into bed but kept casting glances at the bathroom. From this position, I could see directly into the shower stall.

It was bubbled glass, but even in silhouette, Trent Fox was a magnificent example of a virile male. His quads were thick as tree trunks, his ass a nice rounded bit of muscle at the top of those wonder thighs. His waist dipped in tight, making the V-shape that all of the girls at yoga drooled over.

My entire body burned from the inside out. I tried to tell myself it was from the hot shower, but I knew better. Trent had worked me up back at his house without even touching me. Just knowing his naked body was under the spray and slicked up with my soap gave me goose bumps. When the water turned off, I grabbed the first book I found on my end table, opened it randomly, and pretended to read it as I sneaked glances at the bathroom. I'd missed the shower exit in my haste to grab a decoy...darn it.

Trent stood at the sink, running his fingers through his tousled, wet hair. Water droplets trailed down his damp torso as if they were in a race to get to the promised land. I'd had my mouth on the appendage hidden beneath the towel slung around his hips. I remembered his taste, the subtle hints of salt and man. My knees knocked together under the blanket. That sexual experience with Trent was the most unique I'd ever had. Every evening since that night, I'd dreamed about it, used my vibrator while reminiscing over and over again.

Trent turned toward the opposite vanity near the shower, dropped the towel, and reached for something. Oh, my word. Trent had the finest bum that had ever graced my vision. And surprisingly enough, it was just as tan as the rest of him. I bit down on my lip, thinking I'd rather be biting down on his firm ass cheek. Heat rose through my chest, up my neck, and I placed a hand to my flaming face. As he bent over, I stifled a moan. Instead, I closed my eyes and did some yoga breathing.

I heard the water at the sink turn on and the distinct sound of teeth being brushed. Continuing my mini-meditation, I chanted internally.

You cannot have sex with him here.

You cannot have sex with him here.

You cannot have sex with him here.

"Gumdrop, I already told you we don't have to do anything you're not ready for. And if here is a problem for you, we'll improvise." He turned off the bathroom light and walked to the empty side of the bed.

Oh, sugar! I might have said the chant out loud. Heat blazed across my skin. I continued the measured breaths, attempting to calm down. "I know."

I couldn't help checking him out as he stretched his arms over his head. Trent wore nothing but a pair of tight red boxer briefs. His package looked huge behind the thin cotton.

He pushed back the coverlet and slid into the bed. Thank God it was a California King or his large form wouldn't have fit. The man took up far more room than I did.

"I used your toothbrush." He grinned devilishly.

Of course he did. I glanced sideways. "Did you tell me that to annoy me?"

He snuffled and rubbed his warm nose into my bicep. He slung an arm around my waist and did something I wouldn't have expected from a man like Trent. He snuggled into my side. Literally wrapped his body around mine until he was comfortable. I, on the other hand, became hot, in every sense of the word. Temperature and desire were warring against one another for top bidding as he adjusted himself like a cat circling around until he'd found just the right spot. A little twitch here, a poke there, a heavy thigh covering my much smaller one there, and—*voila!*—he stopped moving. Finally. I thought I was going to have to smack him with my book to get him to settle down. Jeez, it reminded me of Mary and her fidgets.

"Comfy?" I whispered.

He hummed from where his head lay on the pillow and my arm. "Very."

I huffed and tried to inhale a few relaxing breaths. It didn't work. I was too wired up. It had been three long years since I'd had a man in my bed, holding me, finding comfort in my body. I loved it and hated it at the same time because I knew it wouldn't last.

"How's your book?" he asked, a hint of laughter in his voice.

Without even glancing at the book, I responded, "Good, good."

"Do you normally read books upside down?"

Sure enough, when I scanned the details of the black letters on white paper in front of me, they were all upside down. *Busted.*

"I just started!" I nudged him.

Trent sat up, grabbed the book, and tossed it on the end table. "Enough. I'm beat. You must be after teaching and everything else today. Now kiss me, woman, so I can go to sleep."

"What?" I shoved my face as far back as I could so he came into better focus.

He narrowed his eyes and grinned. "You heard me, gumdrop. I want my goodnight kiss. Give it up."

"Are you serious?" I held the blankets tight to my chest.

"As a heart attack. If you don't give it, I'm going to take it."

I scowled. "You wouldn't."

"Try me, babe. Try. Me."

I didn't want to try him. I wanted to kiss him goodnight. It seemed so...normal. I haven't had normal in a long time.

"Fine!" I made it sound like it was such a chore.

He didn't care about my shenanigans, and what was better, he met me halfway.

When our lips met, the fire that raged just under the surface blazed white-hot once more. The kiss was wet, deep, and blistering in its ability to take me from zero to sixty in a mere second. Trent kissed me with long flicks of his tongue, hard presses of his lips, as if he'd never stop. I never wanted him to. Before long, he was on top of me, lying between my spread thighs, his upper body braced on his elbows, one hand squeezing my breast, and the other holding my face still so he could devour me with slow, devastating kisses.

I rubbed my leg against the back of his good thigh, pressing his hardened shaft tighter to my body. That move earned me a growl and a lip nibble.

"Damn, gumdrop, want to take you right here, right now, but I respect you too much to go against your wishes."

Trent eased to my side, rolled behind me, and tugged my body to his, my back smashed flat to his front. He pinned one of my legs with his own, shoved a hand across my waist and up between my breasts. "Hold my hand, babe. Want to feel you close while I sleep."

No sweeter words had ever been said to me. I was so screwed. In that moment, as Trent kept me close within the confines of his safe embrace, I fell a little in love with him, even knowing he could never truly be mine.

CHAPTER ELEVEN

Cow Pose

(Sanskrit: Bitilasana)

This pose lengthens the spine and lifts up the chest, allowing for any kinks in the lower back and neck to release. To get into this pose, place your knees hip distance apart, your arms at a ninety-degree angle, drop the belly low toward the mat, and lift up the head, eyes, and chin toward the sky. For best results, alternate between cat pose on the exhale with back arched, and cow pose on the inhale, dropping the belly low and lifting the head.

TRENT

Watching a woman sleep was a novelty for me. Since I'd gone pro, I'd not awakened next to a woman. Sure, sometimes they fell asleep next to me, but then I'd get up and go hit the couch. I didn't want any of my one-nighters to feel as though our night of debauchery was going to be anything more than that. But here I was, cuddling against this woman in *her* bed, the morning light shining in and casting the room in a halo-like glow. Like I woke up on a bed of clouds.

I lay there quietly. I had one leg pinning down Genevieve's and my arm wrapped around her body, holding her tight to my chest. Little puffs of air tickled against my wrist in front of her, confirming she was still deep in sleep. Moving my hips, I rubbed my morning wood against her rounded ass. She sighed when I pushed my length in between her cheeks. Hot damn, I was horny as a devil. I wanted nothing more than to rub one off against her tight body as she slept, but I wouldn't. No. The next time I got off, my cock would be buried deep within her body. Christ! Remembering taking her with my mouth had me nearly drooling for it. I could easily roll her over and go to town on her. Wake her up as she screamed her release.

That wasn't what she wanted. I didn't get the impression that Genevieve was a prude, but I did catch on to the fact that she was nervous about how to act around her siblings. Probably wanted to set a good example. Me being here already went against that concept. Attempting to be chivalrous, I stealthily moved away from her warm body and got out of bed. I needed coffee, breakfast, and to call a doorman about the busted backdoor, in that order.

Casting one last look at Genevieve, I stopped where I stood. Her platinum-blond hair was fanned out over the pale sheets. The marble quality of her skin shimmered when the sun shone down on her from the window over the bed. Those bubblegum lips that caught my eye the first time I laid eyes on her were still a soft pink, only sans the glossy sheen she added to play them up, which had the immediate effect of making my dick hard. I looked at her, my chest swelling with pride. I felt different.

The beautiful woman who lay asleep had trusted me. She slept all night in a bed that I'd held her in. Me. A man who was definitely not worthy of her attention. I scowled and berated myself. What the hell was I doing here? I had no right.

When I'd first met Genevieve, the goal was clear. Same MO I used on every hot chick that made my dick hard. Hit on her. Take her out. Bed her. Leave her.

Then why the hell was I sleeping next to her? Holding her all night? Making sure she was safe? I'd known her for two weeks and had yet to fully seal the deal. I stared at her. She was, just as beautiful in sleep as awake. More so, because the worry and stress of her responsibilities weren't weighing her down. I wanted to give her this lightness all the time. Take away some of her burdens.

What. The. Fuck. Am. I. Thinking?

Scowling, I slipped on my jeans and henley before hitting the hallway. I needed coffee...stat. Then maybe my mind wouldn't be such a mess. As it stood right now, I was gone for a tiny little blonde who was wicked flexible and tasted like sugarcoated gumdrops.

Lord help me.

* * *

Something I didn't expect to deal with when wooing a woman... kids. When I got to the kitchen to go about making my wake up from la-la land juice, two children sat at the kitchen table playing cards.

Rowan looked up in my direction. His eyes widened and his brows went up into his hairline. “Hey, man. Didn’t expect to see you here.”

“Hey, Trent,” Mary said without looking away from her cards. “Go fish!” she added, biting her bottom lip.

She looked a lot like her sister. Golden-blond hair down around her shoulders, puffy pink lips, and soulful eyes. The boys would be going crazy for her in a few years. An instant sense of irritation pounded at my chest. Little pricks with dicks weren’t touching this girl. The head of my bat would make certain of that.

Fuck!

I shook my head. Again, more thoughts of being around Genevieve for the long haul slithered their wicked way into my head. Had to be the break-in. Any good guy would step up for a woman in need. Especially a kind, loving, and caring woman like my gumdrop. Yeah, that’s all it was. A man thing. Protect the woman I care for. All men did that.

Except we didn’t care for the women we played with. Was I playing with Genevieve? Initially that was the plan, but it hadn’t been since the second I inhaled her orgasm as she gave in to me against that wall in the yoga studio. Then when we went down on one another, I had every intention of more. A whole helluva lot more. Even asked her out. I hadn’t officially asked a girl out in years.

That’s when it hit me. Like a baseball bat to the face. I was *dating* Genevieve Harper. *Holy shit!*

Closing my eyes, I took a few deep breaths. Dating. I was dating a woman. I didn’t date women. I fucked women. In my experience, women only wanted bullshit things—my body, my money, and status. Genevieve wasn't like those harlots who tried to ride my cock for their own selfish reasons. Heck, I'd be thrilled if she'd ride my cock. I'd had blue balls for the past two weeks, wanting to get in there. Only the more time I spent with her, I knew once wasn't going to be enough. I wanted to take her in every way possible—make her scream with joy, pleasure, and lose her mind all over me. I wanted her hard, soft, and everything in between. Those kind of sexcapades took time. More than a night or two.

Well I'll be damned. I leaned against the counter and shook my head. My mother was going to be ecstatic. Her son was finally dating a worthy woman. I just needed to convince Genevieve that I was worthy of her.

How the hell did I do that? A tiger couldn't change its stripes. An old dog doesn't learn new tricks. Right? I needed help. Someone that could give me advice. Real honest to God dating advice.

I groaned, pulled out my phone from my back pocket, and hit a few buttons as Mary kicked Rowan's ass at Go Fish.

The phone rang a couple times, and then she picked up. "Hey, sport."

Her voice soothed my jangling nerves instantly.

"Hiya, Ma. Was thinking of hitting you up for dinner tomorrow night."

"Really?" Hope filled her voice. Man, my mom was as real as they came.

"Yeah, really, Ma. I...want to get your advice on something."

I could hear her bustling around her kitchen, probably prepping the Saturday morning big belly breakfast for my dad. "Everything all right with the leg, dear?"

"Yes, Ma." I chuckled and opened the cabinet above the

coffeepot. Bingo! The coffee filters and coffee were all laid out in neat stacks in the cabinet next to a grinder and several multicolored big-handled mugs.

"The job okay?" She was fishing. Leave it to my mom to see right through me.

"Job's fine. Working on rehabbing the leg now. It's going well. Doing yoga, if you can believe that."

"Hmm, that's nice, dear. I love yoga. It's great exercise. Always helps me put my day into perspective. So what's this advice you need, honey? The only thing you've ever been interested in is your health and baseball. That leaves only one thing—a woman." This time the hope in her voice was reaching, almost pleading for me to agree with her.

Man, I didn't know if this was the right thing to do, but I started up the coffeepot, turned, and looked at the fridge. In myriad images, there she was. Tons of pictures held to the fridge with magnets. Genevieve doing gravity-defying poses, hugging her siblings, another with a pretty brunette, some of her and the kids with two older people I guessed were her parents. All of them happy snapshots of a beautiful life. One she continued each and every day, even when it was a struggle.

I nodded to myself. "Yeah, Ma, it's about a woman."

"Oh, thank you, Jesus, Mary, and Joseph. Hallelujah! Finally my prayers have been answered! What's her name? What does she do?" The questions came rapid fire.

"Ma!" I tried to derail the crazy train, to no avail.

"Oh, my, is she pretty? Of course she's pretty. She's caught your attention. I'll bet she's stunning." She sighed loudly into the phone. "I cannot wait to tell your father."

I moved around the kitchen and located the pancake mix, griddle, and a spatula. "Don't be spreading the love just yet."

I lowered my voice to make sure the smaller ears at the table didn't catch wind. "I don't have her, Ma. That's the thing I need to talk with you about."

"Puh-leeze. No young woman who sets her eyes on you isn't interested."

I groaned. "She's not like other girls, Ma." I glanced at the table where Rowan and Mary were in a friendly battle of War. "There are other factors to consider. We'll talk about it at dinner. Tomorrow night. Okay?"

Her breathing was labored when she replied. "Sure, sure. You got it. I'll make your favorite. Roast, potatoes, carrots, and a chocolate cake."

I started to salivate, imagining eating Ma's famous roast. She slow-cooked the meat all day until it was out-of-this-world good. "Sounds amazing. And Ma?"

"Yes, sport?"

"Thanks. It's good to know I can come to you." I choked on the lump in my throat. I looked at the two kids laughing and slamming their hands down on the table. "Not everyone still has their parents. I'm just thankful. Love you, Ma."

"I love you, too, Trent. Always, sport. Always."

"See you tomorrow."

"Okay. Tomorrow."

Her voice was soft and sweet. Reminded me of the woman sleeping soundly upstairs.

I stashed my phone and clapped my hands together loud enough to get Rowan and Mary's attention. "Who said something about pancakes? My mother taught me how to make killer pancakes. Who's in?"

Rowan grinned and nodded.

Mary wiggled in her seat and raised her hand like she was

in class. "Me, me! I love pancakes!" Her smile lit up the room.

Yeah, I could get used to this family. Definitely.

GENEVIEVE

I woke to the smell of coffee and pancakes. Turning over, I opened my eyes. Trent was no longer cuddled behind me. I frowned. It would have been nice to wake up feeling his warmth.

Laugher wafted up the stairs, and I crawled out of bed, grabbed my robe, and threw it on. After slipping my feet into my mom's fuzzy slippers, I proceeded down the stairs, pushing my hair out of my eyes.

I did not expect to see what I did when I hit the kitchen. Trent, standing in jeans, his henley, and bare feet, flipping pancakes. Jesus, he was sexy. He launched a pancake into the air, and Mary screeched as he caught it midair and slapped it on the griddle.

"So cool!" she giggled.

He leaned forward and tapped her nose. Her smile was huge. Oh, no, looked like all the Harper women had been charmed.

I leaned against the doorjamb. Trent was a master at flipping pancakes. He also looked completely comfortable hanging out with my siblings. As if it were a regular occurrence.

"Can you do that with eggs?" Rowan asked.

Trent nodded. "Totally, dude." He sounded very much the Californian.

"Will you teach me?"

"'Course. You can entertain a lot of chicks with these moves. Women love a guy who can cook."

I snorted, and the three heads turned my way.

"Don't teach my brother your player moves. He's a good boy, and he's going to stay that way."

I went over to the coffeepot, poured myself a cup, and added cream and sugar. Before I took a sip, two large arms hugged me from behind. His hands were heavy against my waist, his chest warm against my back. I sighed.

He whispered, "Don't knock my moves, gumdrop. Besides, a man needs to know how to feed himself."

"Um-hum." I sipped at my coffee, allowing the smooth breakfast blend to clear away the last vestiges of sleep.

Trent's voice was warm against my neck. "You don't agree?" He nipped at my neck.

Desire rippled down my body to settle between my thighs. I bumped into him, pushing his body back a few inches, and then I spun around. Sure enough, two pairs of eyes were on every move we made.

"Trent..." I flicked my gaze to my brother and sister. "Not here," I mouthed.

He grinned. "They're going to see us together sooner or later. I'm thinking sooner is a better plan than later." On that last word, he tunneled a hand into the back of my hair, used his thumb to lift my chin, forcing me to look up. "Let's start again. Morning, gumdrop. I slept great. Better than ever," he whispered before slanting his lips over mine.

His kiss was soft, just a few presses of lips, a tiny speck of tongue, and a touch of suction as he pulled away. "Mmm, coffee kisses." He grinned.

For a moment, we stared into each other's eyes. Something I couldn't define was happening between us, and it scared the living daylights out of me.

"Um...we're starving," Row reminded from behind us.

Trent grinned. "Pancakes!" He flipped the perfect CD-size pancakes from the griddle to the plates in front of Rowan and Mary. Four of them landed on Row's and two on Mary's. "How many you want, gumdrop?"

I sipped at my coffee. "One's fine."

He frowned. "Even your baby sis is eating two. I'll make you three."

"Do you want me to be fat?" I chuckled and crossed my arms over my chest. I worked too hard to keep my figure in shape. Women with hourglass figures naturally packed on the extra pounds if they didn't work really hard at it. I was no exception. When my mother passed, she was a solid size twelve, and though she was definitely a looker, she worked her curves like no other. I didn't have that innate sense of sexiness and hadn't come into my curves until she was gone.

Trent held the spatula against the counter with one hand and lifted up his coffee with the other. Just standing there, looking casual in my home, making us breakfast, he'd never looked sexier. I definitely needed to tread lightly or my heart wouldn't survive.

"You're kidding, right?"

I shook my head. "No, I'm not. I work hard, and I don't need to ruin it with useless calories. Pancakes are nothing but carbs loaded with sugar the second you add syrup. I have to limit those things in my diet or I'll blow up like one of those Macy's Thanksgiving Parade balloons."

He rolled his eyes. "You'll work it off later."

I set a hand to my hip. "I'm not teaching yoga later."

He turned down the burner, six perfectly shaped disks cooking on low, and stalked over to me. "I've got a different way to burn off calories."

His voice was low, the timbre speaking to the inner sex vixen hiding within me. The one that had come out only twice before, when Trent and I messed around in the studio.

"Is that right?" Before he could answer, I added, "Well, I think you're wrong." I played along, feeling every bit the sex kitten. He did that. Brought out a side to me I'd buried. The sexy side. The one that wanted to wrap my legs around his waist and ride him until kingdom come.

Again, he lifted my chin and rubbed his lips along mine as he spoke. Not kissing, just speaking against them. Rivers of excitement shot through me. I wanted him. So bad, the ache was beginning to hurt.

"Babe, I'm going to show you all the ways being wrong can be *so* right."

Right before Trent's lips were about to take our little chat to a more productive place, Rowan's voice broke through our lust bubble. "Trent, your pancakes are burning!"

Trent spun around. "Fuck!" he snapped as he flipped them over. Sure enough, each disk had a shiny black burned-out bottom.

"It's okay. We can scrape it off," I said.

He made a disgusted growl with his mouth. Without speaking, he put his foot to the garbage can, lifted the lid, and slid all six into the trash. To me, it was like throwing money in the garbage.

"Babe, you're not eating burned pancakes. When you taste my famous cakes, you're going to have them done to perfection."

I frowned. "But it's a waste of food."

Trent shook his head. "No. I'll get more mix. Relax."

Relax? I fumbled with my robe string. *Let it go this once, Vivvie. He doesn't know that the mix cost ten dollars a bag, and that's only if you get it at Costco all the way across town.* He'd get more mix. I rolled my eyes. Yeah, right. Like a famous baseball player was going to make a point to get my little family more pancake mix because he'd wasted some of it.

Trent worked fast, pouring the rest of the batter onto the griddle. He had enough for six more. I pleaded with him to only give me two. Finally, I won and we sat in the two breakfast nook chairs. The kids had already finished and left the kitchen.

The pancakes were probably the best I'd ever eaten. He added something to the batter that I couldn't put my finger on. "Special ingredient?"

He grinned. "You taste the difference, yeah?"

I nodded. "What is it?"

"Secret. Ma taught it to me. I'll never tell. Family tradition."

Shoveling in another large bite, I moaned around the fluffy cake and syrupy goodness.

"You like?" he asked, pushing my hair behind my ear in a really sweet gesture. A touch I could so easily get used to.

"So good. You'll have to come over every Saturday morning and make us your famous pancakes," I joked.

He set his fork down, put his elbow on the counter, and planted his chin in the palm of his hand. Then he looked at me. Not just checked me out. No, he stared into my eyes as if he were seeing straight through to my soul. I licked my lips, and his nostrils flared. He bit his own plump lower lip and rubbed his chin, continuing to stare, unsettling me with the intensity of his gaze.

"I just may do that, Genevieve." His words were firm and

honest.

Wow. Now that, I hadn't expected. In those six words, he'd insinuated that this was more than just a fling, a casual hookup. I finished chewing, set down my fork, and grabbed his hands. They were warm, and the second our palms touched, our hand chakras activated. I sensed our energy spinning in opposite directions, as though magnetized by one another.

"Don't say things that you don't mean." I blinked, looking down at our clasped hands.

Trent lowered his head and gripped my hands tighter. "I wouldn't do that to you."

"But you have to other women." I glanced to the right. If I wanted to know what this was, I needed to be honest with him and myself. "I'm told you're a player."

He nodded and inhaled deeply. "Yeah, I'd say that sums up my experience with women pretty accurately."

I tried to pull my hands back, but he held them tight.

"Trent..." My voice shook. This was uncharted territory for me. My only other serious romance ended in a big, fat fail. Starting up something with a known ladies' man, investing my heart, knowing the result, was a bad idea. Not just bad. A colossal mistake.

"Genevieve, I'm not sure what this is between us. I've never felt anything like it before. But I promise I'm not playing you. It feels like all the rules have changed when it comes to you. Women have always used me, and in turn, I've used them. It was mutual. I'm not using you, and I know you're not using me. So can we just see where this goes? Take it one day at a time?"

One day at a time.

Pinching my lips together, I thought about it. He waited

patiently, not pushing or egging me on, just sitting quietly and holding my hands. "That sounds reasonable," I said.

A beatific smile spread across his lips. "One day at a time. Starting with today. What are your plans?"

CHAPTER TWELVE

ROOT CHAKRA

Your chakras are the energetic centers of your spiritual self. Each chakra controls different areas of your life. When you can balance your chakras, you begin to find balance and peace within your own life.

TRENT

After breakfast, we divided and conquered. Genevieve did whatever it was she did with the children on a Saturday morning, and after several calls, I found a guy who would come out to the house right away. I met him at the curb, showed him the broken door, and explained what I wanted to replace it with. Not only did I want a door, I also wanted a steel security screen door. Then when Genevieve was messing around in the garden or hanging out back, she could have the door open and let the breeze in. Of course, I didn't consult Genevieve on this. I knew she'd rack up the dollar signs and not approve it even if it did better her environment. If I left it up to her, she'd fill the broken pane with a board and be done with it. No harm, no foul. To me, it was a huge security risk, and I wasn't going to have the woman I was dating or the kids she took care of living in an unsafe home.

No way. No how.

The repairman and I picked out something more solid, as well as an artistic-looking metal screen security door with an additional deadbolt lock and handle lock. Even if a perpetrator got through the screen door by some act of God or a serious crowbar and psychotic inhuman strength, he'd then have to get through the solid wooden door that had another two locks.

The guy promised he'd be back the next day with the new doors for installation. That meant I was staying another day and needed to go home and pick up some clothes. Genevieve said she had a client she was meeting in the garage and would be busy for at least two hours. I took that time to hit up my place, pick up a couple days' worth of clothes, some workout gear, and some beat-up sneakers. The backyard looked like it had gone to hell in a handbasket and needed a man's touch.

When I got back to the house, Rowan was sitting on the couch playing video games. Mary was on the floor, kicking her legs back and forth and coloring in a book that had fairies and mystical shit in it. I glanced at the page she colored. The girl was good. Not only did she stay in the lines, she used the crayons in unique and different ways, coloring patterns into the fairy wings that weren't there, outlining different sections much darker, filling them in lighter. I didn't know much about kids or their abilities, but she seemed to be quite the little artist.

"Mary, that's some mighty fine art there. I like how you add the bit of extra to the wings."

Her little head came up, blond hair falling around all sides of her face, and she beamed up at me. "Thanks, Trent. I love coloring."

"She's really good at it too," Rowan added. "Mary is a whiz at art and dance type stuff."

"You're a dancer?" I wanted to know more about the little girl. I'd never taken even a moment of time in my past to engage a child in this manner.

Mary sat up on her ankles in that way only kids could do without breaking a bone. "Uh-huh. I have a recital in three weeks. In November, so it's right before Christmas break. We're doing the Silly Nutcracker. So it's not the regular one with ballerinas and stuffy ballet moves, it's like hip-hop and contemporary. Would you come?" She clasped her hands together in front of her. "Please, please, please..."

I chuckled and patted her on the head. "I'll check my schedule, little one, and we'll see. If I'm in town or my agent hasn't booked me for some type of ad or photo shoot, you can count on it. Fair enough?"

She nodded, spun around, and went back to her coloring.

"Hey, Row-man, I'm going to work on the yard, get your plants in shape for the winter. You want to lend me a hand?"

Rowan's eyes got big, and he stood up, hit the off button on the Xbox, and set the controller on the table. "Let me run up and change, and I'll be right there."

I smacked him on the back as he maneuvered around the couch. "Good man. See ya out back. You're gonna get dirty, so wear something you don't care about."

He did the chin lift and ran up the stairs three at a time.

Good kid, but in need of a man to take him under his wing. He was eager to help the family. Even so, he didn't seem sure what to do aside from mowing the lawn. I'd give him a solid lesson on how to take care of the yard, pull weeds, cut back the shrubs so they resembled something more aesthetically pleasing, and how to tend to the flowers and trees.

Out back in the shed, I found the yard tools all tossed in one area. They should have been hanging up along the walls, easy to get to. I'd help him set that up tomorrow once we finished the bulk of the work.

Taking the electric trimmer, I plugged it in and went gonzo on the overgrown bushes. Rowan had attempted to keep them under control, but he needed to do it more often and cut back a lot more.

"So, Trent, what do you want me to do?" Rowan asked from behind me.

I showed him what were weeds in the flower beds, around the trees, and how to use the weed killer on the cracks in the sidewalk. Then we worked together on shaping the bushes and cutting back branches off the trees that were too loaded and weighed down.

Rowan was a fast learner just like I was when Ma taught me. Dad educated me on tools, how to fix a car, put shit together, handyman type stuff. My mother schooled me on the yard work and cooking. Dad never mowed a lawn a day in his life. Ma did it until I was old enough to push a mower. Then I did it. Even now, with Ma retired, I had a neighbor kid mowing the lawns for her. She tended to the trees, her veggies, herbs, flowers, and clipped her bushes daily. It was her gig, and her yard was the best I'd seen.

After two hours, Rowan and I were hot as hell, and we'd

made a solid dent in the work but were nowhere near done. I took off my T-shirt and rubbed the sweat off my face.

"Guys!" Genevieve called from the back porch. "I've made some sandwiches and lemonade."

I grinned. My girl had made me a sandwich. Limping up the steps to the porch, I found two plates loaded to the gills with fat turkey and ham sandwiches on wheat, next to which sat fruit salad in cups and tall glasses of pink lemonade. Pink. The same color as her lips. Genevieve bustled around, setting napkins and silverware next to the plates.

"Babe..." I hooked an arm around her waist, pulling her flat against my chest.

She lifted her hands and pushed against my bare chest.

"You're sweaty." She looked into my eyes, blinking sweetly.

Christ, I could eat her up. "You're beautiful," I said before bringing her lips to mine. She tasted of the tart lemonade and her own unique flavor.

For a moment, she squeaked and tried to pull away. Probably because of Rowan, but I wasn't budging. These kids were going to get used to me being around and touching their sister, because I wasn't able to keep my hands off her delectable body for more than a few minutes at a time. I slid my tongue against her lips. She sighed, opening up for me. A few quick licks into her mouth, and she melted against me as if nobody were around.

"Get a room!" Rowan laughed.

Genevieve pulled back and placed her hand over her lips. She was flushed and gorgeous. "Behave!" she scolded playfully, casting a few glances at her brother.

Rowan didn't seem bothered at all by the public displays of affection. He probably enjoyed razzing his sister, which I imagined brothers did all the time to their siblings. Of course, I wouldn't know since I didn't have any, but it made sense. I messed with Ma all the time.

I sat down, picked up the refreshing drink, and slugged back half in one go. It hit the spot. "You make this from scratch, gumdrop?"

She nodded, her cheeks pinking again. "You know, you really didn't have to do yard work. I mean, if you have other stuff to do..." She twisted her fingers.

I looked at Row, his demeanor nervous and uncertain. "Nah, nothing beats working in the sun with one of my bros. Eh, Row-man?"

His lips curved into a huge smile as he took a gargantuan bite of his lunch. He spoke around a mouth full of food—total teen move. "We're...doin' man's...work." He swallowed. "Leave us be. We've got more to do."

Genevieve moved to pass us. I grabbed her around the waist and hauled her into my lap. Her ass made contact with my cock, and I adjusted my position and pressed it against her. I had a semi the second she'd exited the house in a pair of booty shorts and a simple tank. Her hair was up in a ponytail, and she wore silver flip-flops. Even her fingers and toes were cute, painted a bright red that I bet matched that red lipstick she rocked.

"Thanks for the sandwich, gumdrop. Delicious. Almost as tasty as you."

Her cheeks pinked up. I loved that blush. So genuine and all mine.

"Now, kiss me good-bye before you go about your business."

She looked over at Rowan. He waved a hand, gesturing

that he didn't care.

"Don't look at him, babe, look at me. Eyes on me." I turned her head with thumb and forefinger. "Thank you." I pecked her lips.

At the simple touch, her body became heavier. Just when I thought she'd back off, she placed both hands on the side of my face and went in for a deep, wet kiss that made me see stars. She took control of my lips, sucked on my tongue, giving me everything she was worth. Eventually, she nipped on my top lip, my bottom lip, and then pulled away. I followed her head as she moved, wanting more of her sweet taste.

I growled, stood her up, and whispered in her ear, "I will have you later. After that kiss, I can feel how much you need it too. No more waiting. Tonight's it."

She smirked and cocked an eyebrow. "You're on," she whispered, pecked my lips once more, and bolted before I could grab onto her.

"Damn woman." I propped my hands on my hips and shook my head.

"You are *so* into my sister. That's gross, man." Rowan shook his head, stood, and went back to the yard.

I sat down and ate an awesome turkey sandwich. It rivaled the one at the Rainy Day Café, where I'd been eating regularly. They made a damn fine sandwich, but a woman cooking for a man was something special. I imagined she was adding her love and care into every condiment and layer, building a masterpiece. Fuck. I sounded mushy as hell. I needed to go chop up some bushes, put my man pants back on, pound on my chest a few times, and remind myself I wasn't a pansy-assed, pussy-whipped male. Although if any pussy could do the whipping, all my money was on Genevieve. I couldn't wait to get my mouth all over her body tonight. For that though, I'd have to set the stage.

"So, Row-man, do you think you can hook up you and the little one spending the night at a friend's house tonight?"

Rowan stopped cutting the square shape into one of the overgrown shrubs and chuckled. "Yeah, man, I think I could work something out."

"Would be much obliged. I'll make it worth your while."

His voice was low when he said, "Nah, it's cool. You've already made it worth my while just by putting that smile on Vivvie's face. I owe you one, man."

GENEVIEVE

I let out a relieved breath when I finished styling the last bit of hair on Mrs. Turner's updo for her evening out with her husband.

"It looks perfect, Genevieve, and right on time." She looked down at her watch. "Time to meet the mister." She smiled and laid two twenties on the edge of my workstation.

"Mrs. Turner, it's only twenty."

She smiled. "Honey, you don't charge enough. I would have paid at least forty for a wash, style, and updo at a regular salon. Don't sell yourself short."

I looked down at the concrete floor and shuffled my feet. "Thank you, Mrs. Turner."

"Have a good evening, Genevieve." She gathered her coat and hustled to her car in the driveway.

I waved as she backed out. Maybe Mrs. Turner was right and I wasn't charging enough, but I couldn't risk my clients going somewhere else. A lot of people in this area didn't want to get their hair done at someone's house. They wanted to go to a professional salon. And I still needed a semester of cosmetology school before I could practice in a salon.

I huffed out a breath, cleaned up my station, and went inside.

"Hello!" Mary and Rowan rushed down the stairs just as I reached the living room. They were dressed to go out even though it was dinnertime, and they had their backpacks on.

"Hey, Vivvie, Mary and I are staying the night at Jonathan and Carrie's."

Jonathan was a baseball player on Rowan's team at Berkeley High, and his little sister Carrie was in the same class as Mary. They were all best friends, and their parents were really cool about my brother and sister staying over on the weekends. Said it kept their kids busy and out of trouble. I usually never had a problem with it. But after last night, I was feeling a little raw and selfish. I wanted them to hang out at home where I could keep an eye on them.

"Are you sure? We could watch movies, have an impromptu PJ party with popcorn. I can make some pizzas."

Both of them shook their heads.

"No way. Carrie's mom is taking us to see the new fairy movie. You know I've been dying to see it!" Mary's voice was high-pitched as if she'd just *die* if I said no.

"Okay, baby girl. That's fine. Row, you'll keep an eye out?" My voice clogged up with a wave of emotion I wasn't prepared for.

He walked down the rest of the stairs and hugged me, one of the big full-body I-love-you-big-sis ones that I adored. "You know it. Their parents are both there, okay? And besides, Trent's in the kitchen making up a meal for you. He says he's got you covered tonight, so I'm going to take the 'Stang."

The 'Stang was Dad's Mustang and our only car. We usually gave one another a heads up when we needed it so the other wasn't put out.

Before I could ask what he meant about Trent making dinner, the two of them rushed out the door with a bunch of I love yous and see you laters. I shook my head and made my way into the kitchen. Sure enough, Trent was hunched over the stove, and the most wonderful smells of garlic and other spices permeated the air.

"What are you doing?" I set my hands on my hips and looked into a pot of bubbling sauce. It was chunky, filled with veggies and meat. It was the type of spaghetti sauce we could eat without the noodles, and it smelled divine. My stomach growled.

Trent hooked his hands around me from behind. "Whoa. Looks like my girl is hungry. You ready to eat?"

I snorted and looked around the kitchen. The table was already set up with plates and silverware. He didn't set out any candles or flowers like in romantic movies, but the effect was still the same. Trent Fox, famous Major League Baseball player, had set the table and made me dinner. Me. A simple girl from Berkeley, California.

"I can't believe you did all this."

"Well, my goal is to get into your panties. Did it work?" His hands fiddled with the button on my shorts.

Spinning around, I looped my arms around his neck. "Oh, yeah. It worked."

He grinned, pecked my lips all too briefly, and smacked my bum. "Get to the table, woman. I'm dishing out some grub. Eat first, sexy time later."

He dished out ginormous servings of food. Way more than I could put away. He gave me as much as he gave himself, but I didn't say anything. This was his meal. He filled my glass with a wine from a local winery I'd been to with a friend before my parents passed.

"Thank you." I lifted the glass.

He filled his and did the same.

"What shall we drink to?"

He grinned and pursed his lips. "To fucking you silly?" He smirked.

My heartbeat picked up at imaging all of the possibilities that could make me downright silly in the bedroom. "Be serious for once."

Trent rolled his eyes. "How about we drink to new experiences, doing something crazy, and hoping for the best possible outcome?"

I smiled wide. "Now *that* I can drink to."

We both drank our wine and chatted lightly. He told me about college ball, and then the majors and how he'd survived the rookie years with hope and a prayer. He explained how his mother made sure he knew how to take care of a yard and cook a meal. Apparently, he knew only a few dishes. Spaghetti and pancakes were the top of his culinary prowess. I secretly loved that he'd shared both his bests with me right away.

Dinner was heavenly and the conversation even better. Trent seemed interested in knowing more about me, not just getting into my panties. On the other hand, I was so ready to move this party forward, I could have burst at any second. Throughout dinner, he touched me as much as possible. Each touch felt like a brand, sizzling against my skin, lighting every nerve with anticipation of what was to come.

While we did the dishes, Trent's playful side came out. He flicked droplets of water at me. I retaliated by blowing suds onto him. At one point, he got hold of the sprayer and soaked the front of my tank. The tips of my breasts poked through the lace bra underneath. His eyes blazed white-hot fire. That's when he finally made his move.

I stretched past him to put the last dish in the drainer. He turned me, pressing my back up against the sink. He looked at me with a sensual gaze that traced my form like a physical caress, zeroing in on the yellow fabric clinging to my breasts. I gripped the counter behind me, curling my fingers into the tile lip. Waiting. Expecting. He leaned forward and sucked the tip of my hardened nipple right through the cotton. I grabbed his head, tunneling my fingers into the long layers of his hair.

"Trent..." I sighed, the splinters of need spiraling out from the tug and nip of my breasts between his teeth.

He growled and laved at the peak with his tongue. The wet fabric grated along my sensitive tip, sending ribbons of heat along my skin as wetness soaked my panties.

"Please..."

He pulled away from my breast and hiked me up so my legs wrapped around his waist.

"Trent, you can't. Your leg—"

He cut me off with a kiss. Not a sweet kiss. No, this one was carnal—lips, teeth, and tongues.

Slowly, he carried me to the stairs, and even though I knew he shouldn't walk up those stairs with the extra weight, I kept my mouth shut. This was, by far, the most romantic experience of my life. A man carrying me to bed.

When we got to my room, he slid my body down his, my breasts rubbing along his chest. He tunneled his fingers through my hair, cupping my cheeks and lifting my chin. "Want you more than any woman I've ever known. You strip away everything, Genevieve, and replace it with light and goodness. I need that in my life."

I held onto the sides of his face and stroked his bottom lip with my thumbs. "Then take it. For now, it's yours. I'm yours." I swallowed. The words were heavy, and they'd likely meant a lot more to me than to him, but in that moment, I couldn't deny what I wanted. More.

More of Trent.

More of his time.

Just more.

"Christ. How long's it been for you? I need to know how you want me, because I'm barely hanging on by a thread here, babe. The animal in me wants to rip off your clothes and pound into you until you scream my name. Then start all over again." His voice was ragged and deep.

That sounded utterly fabulous, but it had been a long, long time. "Over three years."

His eyes went so wide I could see every speck of color in them as if they were glowing.

"How many men?" He clenched his teeth, his jaw firm.

"Just one," I whispered shyly. I stared into his eyes and cataloged every facet of his face. I wanted to remember this moment.

Trent's nostrils flared, and he inhaled deeply. His hazel eyes filled with lust, the pupils dilating. "Like that, babe. Like that a lot. Because right now, I'm going to make you forget that one man."

Boldly, I slid my hands to his shirt and unbuttoned each button until the shirt lay open, presenting me with his bare chest. I placed each finger near his collarbones and lightly ran my nails down the long expanse. He groaned, and the bulge in his jeans got bigger.

He grasped my waist and squeezed as I leaned forward and placed kiss after kiss over his chest. Tasting his warm skin, smelling his unique leather and musk scent, I bit down on his pec and then soothed it with my tongue. He groaned long and deep.

Finally, I looked up and took in his heated gaze. "Baby, I already have."

CHAPTER THIRTEEN

Bridge Pose

(Sanskrit: Setu Bandha Sarvangasana)

This asana helps stretch the back, releases tension in the spine and shoulders, and builds muscle in your thighs, bum, and core. Bridge pose is considered one of the most versatile backbends in yoga. Lie on the floor, feet and knees hip distance apart, roll the shoulders under the body, and clasp the hands. Lift the hips until they are above the heart.

TRENT

Genevieve Harper tore a man down to the base instincts where the primitive male took control. Looking down into her black gaze and kiss-swollen lips, I had to rein in the animal within. Standing in front of me, she was every man's fantasy, her large breasts heaving under her wet tank. Her lips glistened in the low light of the lamp next to her bed. I wanted to have her, mark her, imprint her on my mind, make her mine.

Lifting her chin, I took her lips again. I dragged my tongue across them, tasting every inch, committing the kiss to memory—the way her lips felt pressed to mine, how she sighed as I kissed her. What woman sighed? The one who put her entire body into each soulful press of our lips. She burrowed her small hands into the hair behind my neck and held on for dear life. As I lowered her down over her bed, she fell willingly, our lips never leaving each other's. Magic.

Lying over her was like notching a puzzle piece into place. Resting my pelvis against hers was utter bliss. I'd never felt content to just lie above a woman before.

That she'd not been taken care of in years made me want to tear into her. Rip off her clothes and go to town on every inch of her body. Good thing we had all night because one heated encounter this evening would not be enough. No way.

Kissing my way down her neck, I licked the indent at her throat. Just as I suspected, succulent. I hovered over her and slid my fingers into the sides of her tank, pushing the fabric up and over her head. I lifted her bra over her big tits and then over her head without even unclasping it. I wanted the offending thing off and now. If I had my way, her gorgeous tits would be free, ready for my access at all times. I took one pale pink tip into my mouth. It beaded into a tight eraser-sized nub. She gripped my hair and thrust her hips up to meet mine.

"So sensitive." I laved her tip, flicking it with my tongue.

Her eyes filled with heat.

"I love that about you. Tonight, gumdrop, I'm going to find every sensitive spot on your body and drive you insane.

How many times in a row can you come, hmm?" I pinched her other peak, plucking it into the same tight nub as the one I was licking.

Her breath was labored, and she squinted. Her hips came up again, and I pressed against them with my own, rubbing my denim-clad length against her center, creating a nice friction. It wouldn't get me off, not this time. No, I had every intention of exploding within the confines of her tiny body.

"Answer me, babe. How many times can this sweet body sing?" I began sucking her other nipple.

"Only...once."

I stopped mid lick, sucked her tip until it glistened, and then gazed at her, waiting until her eyes met mine. "That's ridiculous, gumdrop. This body was made for fucking and getting off. I'm going to show you what this body can do." I sat up and gripped her hips. "I'll shoot for three tonight and see if you can handle that. Maybe go for four. Depends on if I'm going to bust a nut by then."

The way her eyes seamed to get wider told me that she didn't believe me. Challenge accepted.

"You can't possibly be serious. Three orgasms in one session?"

I nodded, unbuttoned her shorts, and pulled them off her long legs. For a small gal, she had a decent set of gams. Starting at her foot, I lifted her leg and kissed my way from her ankle to her pussy. Her cotton panties were soaked, and the scent of her arousal sent a horde of bees buzzing along my skin.

"Your panties are sopping wet for me, babe." I rubbed my nose against the damp fabric and inhaled deep, imprinting my woman's scent in my mind. My smaller head hardened wanting to plunge in there. I adjusted my cock, giving it a bit of attention while I dragged a finger down between her breasts to the top of her panties to her clit. Zeroing in on the hard button, I pressed against it. Her hips instantly followed the motion, circling in a way that made the synapses in my brain fire and shorten.

Ripping her panties down her legs, I spread her wide. "Fuck, you're flexible. It's like I can split you in half."

Her sex opened like a flower. I stuffed my nose right between her lower lips. Then I stretched my tongue out and licked her from her pucker to her clit in one long stroke. Genevieve attempted to tighten and close her legs but I wasn't having any of it. No, I planned on hearing her lose her mind tonight, and this was only step one.

"You like that, gumdrop?"

"Yeah," she whispered and closed her eyes.

I leaned back and used my thumb and fingers to play in her wetness. "What do you like, babe? Tell me."

"Mmm," she sighed. "What you're doing."

She lifted her hand and put her red-tipped finger in her mouth, biting down on the soft flesh in a graphic display of what I wanted her to do to my dick. I easily recalled the feeling of her lips wrapped around my cock. The base of my spine tightened and tingled as she played with her finger.

"No, babe. Not good enough." I moved between her legs again and held her thighs out as if I were pushing against something heavy. It was easy to keep her wide open because she wanted me there. The wetness at her core glistened, and I licked her up the center again, focusing some attention on her clit. Wrapping my lips around the firm knot, I flicked it with my tongue. Repeatedly.

She started to tremble.

"Tell me what you like. Use your words."

She hummed deep in her throat, her head moving from side to side against the comforter. "I like your tongue."

I gave her more tongue. "Like this?"

Genevieve sighed. "Yeah. And your lips."

My dick hardened. I dragged my lips through her slit, kissing and licking every inch.

"What else do you like?" I wanted to hear her say every naughty thing I was doing to her, but in her own tender way.

She lay naked and trembling as I held her open wide and made her speak to me through her pleasure. It was one of the most erotic and beautiful experiences of my life. I'd never taken this kind of time to please a woman before, but with Genevieve, I never wanted to stop.

She gave me another sigh and a deep inhale when I plunged my tongue into the heart of her. Her entire body tightened, and I knew she was going to come.

"I like...I like when you taste me deep." She tunneled her fingers through my hair, gripping it at the roots.

"Is that right? Then I better please my woman." I stuck my tongue deep into her heat, as far as I could go, wishing I had a longer tongue. Then, I used the next best thing and plunged my index finger into her sex, gratified when she cried out, her hands clasped above her head as her body tightened like a rope being pulled taut.

Her hips and legs trembled as I fingered her deep and added my tongue, licking up her arousal and loving the musky, sweet taste of my girl. I paid attention to her body, the slight jerks and twinges, waiting until she was on the precipice of her release.

"Oh, my word," she breathed.

Holding her down, I wrapped my lips around her clit, added another finger, and took her there. She cried out, and her body convulsed, but I didn't let up. Just as she started to relax, I went for it. I pushed my fingers home, hooked them up, found the spot within that made her body tighten, and I played my girl like an instrument. I sucked her clit, nibbled on that bit of flesh, and fingered her deep, never letting up on the spot that made her shake.

"Trent, Trent, Trent, oh my God!"

Her legs shook, those big titties jiggled, and I ate my woman like I would never get another chance. She thrashed around. She pulled at my shirt, ripping it over my head. I released her juicy pussy only long enough to let the shirt go.

"Want you, want you, want you..." she chanted and tugged at my head.

I shook my head. "Want you to come on my tongue again, babe. Need it," I growled. Something happened to me when she started screaming my name through her pleasure. I *had* to make her feel good. Needed to feel her body explode under my ministrations. Wanted it more than my own release even.

"Naked, baby, please," she cried out, her voice shredded.

I lifted off her, unbuckled my jeans and shucked them, my briefs, and my shoes, and hopped on the bed. "You want this cock?" I crawled up her body, licking her pussy one more time, and then up her belly, and finally each rounded titty. I was worshiping her breasts when she grabbed my cock. It was so hard I could have pounded steel and left a gaping hole.

"Yeah, baby. Turn around. Fill me."

Hearing my polite-talking Zen yoga babe being so explicit made me even harder. I spun around on top of her, my hammy protesting. I winced, but she didn't see, thank God. She'd stop if she thought I was hurt, and I needed her lips wrapped around my cock more than I needed my next breath.

Just as I straddled her head, she took me into her hot mouth.

"Fucking hell!"

I thrust into her mouth a few times. She loved it. Got off on it. Moaned around my cock, flicking the tip, sucking on the crown like a professional dick sucker. Man, this woman was going to ruin me for all future fucks.

GENEVIEVE

Trent moaned and thrust into my mouth. His salty flavor hit my taste buds, and I nearly swooned. I loved sucking his cock. Having him above me, out of his mind with passion for me, left me feeling dizzy, drunk with feminine power. The orgasm I'd already been gifted was a solid ten out of ten, and he'd promised two more. This was new territory for me. I'd never had multiples, even with my battery-operated boyfriend. Not that I used it much. Just when the tension was beyond what I could handle between work, kids, and the house.

I shifted, adjusting our bodies. Trent's mouth landing between my thighs made me forget everything but his tongue, lips, and talented fingers. The man was a sex god, and I tried not to think how much practice he'd had to get to this point.

Having his thick member in my mouth, tiny drops of his essence leaking onto my tongue, and his mouth between my thighs started the tremors through my body again. He was going to do it. Make me come again. Holy madness. I tried to focus on his shaft and licked it up and down in long, teasing strokes. He grunted, bent my legs at ninety-degree angles, and lifted them toward my armpits. I was wide open, vulnerable, and completely at his mercy. He locked my legs so I couldn't move them an inch. I was pinned, exposed, and so turned on I sucked him as far down my throat as I could, wanting to make him as crazy with lust as he was making me.

"Oh, no, you don't." He lifted his hips up so that I couldn't suck him too far down again. "Gotta keep the reins on you, fireball."

He'd used that nickname once before in similar circumstances. I loved it. Heck, I loved all his nicknames.

With a lock on my legs, I felt every touch and lick he doled out. My body got hot, so hot that a fine mist of sweat coated my limbs as I held him close. The muscles in Trent's ass cheeks were hard as rocks as I massaged and dug my nails in at every lick. I started to pant, having trouble keeping my control over his sex. His mouth was too good. He knew exactly where to lick and add the right amount of pressure. Though when he did the combo of his finger, the lock on my legs, and his mouth sucking my clit, I thought I'd died and gone to heaven.

Waves of pleasure rippled over me. Lights flashed behind my eyes, and my entire body went tight, way tighter than before. "Oh, my word...Trent!" I screamed until my voice was scratchy.

The pleasure started at my sex and shredded through me, coating every pore with a heat so intense I could hardly withstand it. I shook above him as it rolled along my limbs, but Trent didn't let up, making the orgasm go on and on, rocking over me with the effort. His cock bobbed in front of my face with each drink he took from me. His tongue fluttered deep within as he moaned around my flesh. Amazing. Life-altering, and everything in between.

Before I could say anything, Trent spun around, put on a condom, opened my legs, and power-drove his thick shaft inside. I groaned when he bottomed out inside me and pressed on. He was huge, pressing past oversensitive tissues that gripped and clawed at his intrusion.

"Jesus! Genevieve..." His mouth came down to mine, and he whispered against my lips, "Perfect. Being inside you, babe..." His words sounded rough, splintered off, and then he shook his head. He stirred his hips. "Christ, so good."

Trent kissed me hard, and I could taste myself. Tasting myself on a man's lips was a new experience and undeniably erotic. I licked his mouth and shifted my hips, giving him the green light to move. Leaning up on his knees, he lifted my hips and pounded into me. I moved my head from side to side, my fingers digging into his back, as he pounded me. Trent did not mess around when he was banging his woman. Confident, focused and sexy—he was all of those things and more as he made love to me.

When he came low to kiss me, I wrapped my legs around his ass and pressed him home again and again. His wicked hot grin and burning gaze told me he liked that, a lot. Trent's lips twisted into a snarl, the pleasure intense as he took me. I didn't know if he was mad or taken with the madness that was happening between us. His thickness felt like a giant steel rod, invading me in the best possible way.

Slowing his thrusts, he leaned over me, a grimace marring his face.

"Baby, what's wrong?" I asked between thrusts, not recognizing the sultry sex-kitten voice as my own.

"My leg..." A pained wince swept across his face.

The guilt that slammed into me made my eyes water. I

shouldn't have sat back and let him do all the work. "Lie down. Let me take the lead," I whispered into his ear, licked the shell, and bit down on the tender cartilage.

He rewarded me with a hard thrust for that move. God, he felt like my birthday and Christmas rolled into one.

Note to self—Trent likes biting.

He rolled us over so I was on top. Instead of letting me do my thing, he shoved us up to the headboard. I cocked an eyebrow.

"Want to see your eyes."

I knew better. The moment I lifted up and slammed him home, his head fell back against the headboard, he held tight around my waist, and helped me lift up and down. His shaft was thicker, harder, and unrelenting in this position, pushing deeply against my cervix.

My body tightened, the beginning of another monster orgasm working its way through my limbs. It started between my thighs, the pleasure radiating out with each of his upward thrusts. I gripped the headboard and used my knees as leverage. I wanted this to be so good for him he'd never want to be with another woman again.

Locking my knees to his thighs, I lifted up and slammed down, my teeth rattling against the strength of my movement. Within moments, the painful thrusts turned into a pleasure so acute, I focused on nothing but his length grating along the bliss spot inside over and over. I gasped and locked eyes with him.

He grinned. "Right there, huh, babe?"

"Yeah," I moaned.

His eyes were green and swirling with lust. He raised his hands to my breasts, and with his thumb and forefinger, he rolled and plucked.

The room around me disappeared. The bed, the headboard I clung to, nothing existed but the pleasure rippling through me like rain trickling down my chest from the sky. The pleasure was alive, thick, like a fog surrounding me, as I mindlessly moved up and down his length.

"Heaven."

"Hurts good."

"More."

"Now."

"Baby."

I'd been crashing down over him, the aching bundle of nerves pinned between my body and Trent's with each downward thrust. Every meeting of our bodies set up a tantalizing pressure between us that built larger at every pass. The pleasure was excruciatingly divine as everything within me coalesced together into one powerful moment where I detonated and exploded in his arms.

"Oh my word..."

TRENT

The tension was huge as her pussy clamped down around my cock in a wicked, sensual, little fist. I was strung tight as I plunged into her body over and over, using her shoulders and waist as leverage to take her hard. She cried out, those random nonsensical words continuing as she spasmed around me.

"Love."

"God."

"Hard."

"Air."

"Tight."

"Ugh."

She kept going, little one-syllable words escaping her mouth as I spurted deep within her. She milked me like no one else ever had. Stars flitted across my vision, and darkness threatened to consume me. I couldn't hear anything. Every speck of me was focused on my dick, and all of it was damn good. Best fucking lay of my life.

No woman, my right hand, no sexual experience before now could compare to claiming Genevieve Harper from the inside out. I leaned forward, lifted a tit, and locked onto the fleshy globe just above her nipple. I sucked hard, licking and sucking until my tongue hurt and a quarter-sized cherry-colored mark appeared, proving that Trent Fox owned that body. Fuck, yeah!

When we were done, Genevieve lay limp against my chest. I played with her hair, rubbed her scalp, and soothed her until I'd have sworn to all things holy, the woman fell asleep. On my chest. With my cock still nestled inside her.

I liked putting the knockout juice on my woman via multiple orgasms. Spoke directly to the caveman in me. Trying not to move too much, I shimmied us down until we were pretty flat against the mattress. She didn't even wake, and I still had my woman draped over me like a misty blanket of naked limbs and my dick buried in her heat. Wrapping my arms around her, I held her close, closed my eyes, and fell asleep.

★ ★ ★

I woke up later feeling just as good as I had when I fell asleep. I was still with my woman, and my cock was nestled safely inside her, only this time, it was her sweet lips wrapped around my cockhead.

"You're full of surprises," I mumbled as she worked my dick. Christ, her mouth was good. Almost as good as her pussy. A definite close second. I'd just bet she had a virgin ass, too. Right then and there, I made a vow to myself—no part of Genevieve Harper would not be taken by my cock.

Thinking about taking her ass made my dick impossibly hard. The pleasure of her suction, her wet lips stroking my cock, was making me lose my head.

"You're going to make me come." I gripped her hair into my fist, wrapped the blond strands around my hand, and fucked her mouth.

She was perfectly attentive to the movements I wanted, a fastidious student who allowed me to steer and kept a diabolical amount of suck to lick ratio. I was leaking precum far faster than usual. Typically, I could hold off, have a woman suck on me for a long time before I came, but not then.

Seeing Genevieve naked, up on her knees, those big titties swaying delectably while I watched her take my cock as far down her throat as possible... Christ. Magnificent. Her mouth could only go about halfway down my length. I'm a good size, probably a bit above average and she was small. Everything but her tits and ass were, anyhow. She couldn't even cover me with her dainty hand, but she sure knew how to work her mouth.

Gripping her hair tighter, I guided her head farther down my length. "Lick upward, gumdrop. Let me see your tongue wet my dick."

She smiled coyly but did as I asked. Seeing her pink little tongue come out and drag across my length made me groan with the need to fuck, to take her hard, but I wouldn't.

I cared too much about her. I let her lead and just rested my hands on the sides of her head, wanting her to take me the way she wanted to. She doubled her efforts, sucked me down hard, wrapped both hands around my length, and alternated between sucking the wide head and jerking me off. Lights, fireworks, fucking fairy dust type of shit skittered across my closed eyes. Fuckin' magical.

"Gonna come on that tongue, babe."

She latched on and picked up the pace, sucking me down as best she could.

"I mean it," I growled, barely able to contain myself.

Genevieve took me as deep as she could go and hummed around my cockhead. That was it. I lost it. I jerked, and my release shot down her throat while she swallowed. When she was done, she licked me, ending the best blowjob of my life with a sweet kiss to the tip before crawling up my body and lying over me like my own Genevieve blanket again.

"I'm hungry," she said.

I chuckled. "You just ate."

She scrunched her nose and made an overexaggerated gesture of gagging on her finger.

"Okay, okay, bad joke. What did you have in mind?"

"Peanut butter and jelly," she said shyly.

Christ she was beautiful. We fucked like bunnies, slept, I woke up to her sucking my cock, and now my girl wanted a PB and J. I shook my head. "You want me to take care of you first?" I waggled my eyebrows.

She sat up, her big tits bouncing like two ripe melons in front of me. I wanted to latch on to them and fuck her again. I was getting hard thinking about it. Maybe she'd let me fuck her tits. *Yep, adding that to the list of things we must do.* I gripped both globes pushed them together, and tongued the tips simultaneously. She hummed, arching her back suggestively.

"Trent, I'm really hungry, and if you take care of me, we're going to have sex again, and I'll never get my sandwich." She pouted, her full bottom lip puffing out.

It almost worked. I snickered and rested my chin between her boobs. "I'll fuck you later." I kissed the tops of my favorite twins.

"Well, that's the plan." She giggled.

"Gumdrop, I was talking to your tits." I grinned.

Her face turned beet red, and she placed an arm across her chest. "What?"

"You ever been titty fucked?" I crossed my fingers behind her ass in the hope that she hadn't.

She shook her head.

I inhaled deeply, thinking about my hard cock pinned between the soft globes, her pink tips turned purple from all the sucking. "Get up." I smacked her hard on the ass.

"Ouch!" She rubbed at her reddened ass cheeks.

"You don't get up, you'll never get that sandwich."

Her stomach growled. Damn, sex must really make her hungry. Good to know.

Within seconds, she popped up and off the bed. Then my shirt was flowing around her body like a dress. Something about seeing my shirt over her naked body gave me an unusual sense of peace. Following the sexy blonde, I slipped on my boxers and went after my woman.

CHAPTER FOURTEEN

ROOT CHAKRA

The root chakra takes responsibility for your sense of safety and security. A closed root chakra will leave you feeling homeless mentally and often is responsible for a desire to always be on the go.

TRENT

Limping up to my mother and father's house with a shit-eating grin on my face could not be helped. I'd just left the most desirable woman freshly fucked and dozing on her couch before the sibs made their way home from their friend's house. I'd owe Rowan a solid for allowing me the alone time with his sister. Once we'd had dinner last night, made love the first time, and then I woke to her lips the second time, we'd taken a quick break to fuel up. Then I set about making it hard for my girl to walk today. We both had a gimpy gait by the time I left her sated on the couch. I made sure she was decent, even though I'd tipped that sweet ass over the edge of it and pounded her hard between making sandwiches and reaching the room again.

Christ, I wanted the woman constantly. When I wasn't with her, I was thinking about her. Now that I'd had her, I'd been sure the edge of desire would wear down to a tolerable level, but it hadn't. I left to come to dinner at my parents', wanting to hurry so I could get back. I didn't want Genevieve to assume anything, nor did I want her to think I was coming on too strong. All that meant I'd need to sleep at my own place. The new door and security screen had been added, so my girl and her family were safe...for now. Not as safe as I could make them, laying my head on the pillow next to hers.

Fuck. I didn't know what the hell I was doing or how to proceed with that line of thinking. I'd never had these feelings for a woman. It'd always been hit it and quit it. One and then done. Mutual satisfaction guaranteed, and...*poof*...gone. Off to the next away game and the nearest piece of ass.

I hadn't thought about another woman in the better part of three weeks. Genevieve controlled all my thoughts since the day I'd met her. Having tasted her body, kissed those candied lips, slept next to her two nights in a row, I didn't know what to think anymore. My system for dealing with the madness was all jumbled, and nothing I knew matched up.

I shook my head and gripped my leg, entering my parents' house. The hamstring throbbed and protested all the recent activity, but it was a small price to pay for the time I'd had with my girl. The smell of cooked meat, potatoes, and Ma's special au jus filled the air. My stomach growled as I made my way into the kitchen. My itty-bitty mother worked at the stove, her blond bob swaying with her as she stirred something in a pot.

"Ma, something smells terrific." I wrapped her in my arms from behind and kissed her cheek while sneaking a peek. She had mashed potatoes and was adding some garlic and sour cream.

She leaned back, her head only reaching my upper chest, and patted the arm I'd wrapped around her. "How's my sport doing today? Let me get a good look at you."

My mother spun around, masher still in hand.

I moved to the fridge to pull out a beer and popped the cap, tossing it perfectly into the metal trash bin across the room. "Score!" I fist pumped the air and leaned back against the counter.

"Someone looks happy today...and tired. I'm guessing that has something to do with the young lady you wanted to talk to me about?" Her eyebrows rose close to her hairline, and she waited to grill me.

My mother was not a stupid woman. She knew men. At least she knew me and my dad. We had a way about us. There was no coercing information out of us. If we didn't want to talk about something, we just didn't. Ma learned early on that I had the exact same system as my father when it came to talking through things. So far, she'd respected that.

I took a long pull from my beer. "I think I'm happy," I said.

"You think?"

"Yeah." I scrubbed a hand over my jaw. "She's different, Ma."

"Oh?"

I rolled my eyes. "Yeah. Genevieve is not a groupie. She's not a woman you spend an...uh...evening with and not see again." I winced.

She held her lips in a firm line as she poked at the meat in the oven. The smell assaulted my nose, and my mouth watered. Ma was the best cook I knew, and her roast was to die for.

"I see. And so far, you've only dated women you spend time with for a single evening?" Her words were soft but direct.

Nail right on the head. Perfect hit the first try. "Pretty much."

"Are you opposed to seeing this girl again?"

She hummed doing her thing, but I knew she was vested in this conversation. She'd been on me about settling down, finding the right woman, and courting her—reminding me that I wasn't getting any younger—if I wanted to have children down the road and not be ancient.

I thought about it. Heck, I'd already seen more of Genevieve Harper than I'd ever seen of any woman. "I guess, Ma, you could say I'm technically dating her."

She whipped around and focused her steely blue gaze on me. "So what's the problem?"

"Everything." I rubbed my forehead and pressed my thumbs into my temples. "I don't know how to date her, Ma. I've had nothing but one-night stands since college. Women that I'm around are not the kind of women you keep or bring home to meet your parents."

She blinked a few times and swung the utensil in a circle. "And this Genevieve is?"

Just saying her name had me thinking about her coal-black eyes twinkling as I kissed her neck, her shoulders, her lips. "Yeah," I said in awe. "I should have brought her tonight."

"Oh. My. God. You're falling in love with her!" She placed her hand on her chest as if she were having heart palpitations.

My own heart starting rocking the two-step. Was I falling

for her?

Maybe.

No.

We'd just met.

I shook my head. "Ma, it's too early. We've only gone on one official date, but I've been seeing her regularly at the studio and..." I rubbed at the back of my neck, feeling heat start at my chest and push up into my neck. "Last night we took the next step, and..." I let my words fall off, not knowing what to say without sounding like a douchebag to my own mother.

"You're not used to wanting to continue to see a woman after that physical step has been obliterated?"

My mom knew her stuff. I didn't have to pussyfoot around her. She said it like it was, only in a classier way.

"Yeah." The weight of my issue pushed my shoulders down as I sucked back the rest of the beer in one go.

"Have you asked her out again?"

"Not exactly. I'm due to see her tomorrow, though, for private yoga lessons. She's really making a difference in my recuperation after surgery. She's a miracle worker."

Her smile lit up the room, and she clapped her hands. "Perfect. Tomorrow you ask her out again. Easy peasy."

I slumped against the counter top. "It's not easy peasy, Ma. She has obligations. She's the sole provider for her sixteen-year-old brother and her eight-year-old sister. Her parents died in a car accident three years ago, so she works two jobs to support them. I tried to get her to go out with me on a whim before, and she declined. With Genevieve, I have to be two steps ahead, plan for time with her, or plan to spend that time with her siblings."

My mother's eyes turned soft. "The poor dear. Being

alone like that, taking on that breadth of responsibility. She could probably use a big, strong man like you around to help her along the way."

I shrugged. "Yeah, maybe. She tries to do everything herself. Works as a yoga instructor at Lotus House Yoga and cuts hair on the sly in her garage. Has a setup and everything."

"Oh, she cuts hair." Ma plumped her golden bob.

"Yeah, she was going to school to get her license and was almost done when her parents died. She's doing what she can to make ends meet, but can't yet afford to go back to school to finish. Does a good job according to Rowan." I tugged at my own hair. It would need a cut in the next week or so. Maybe I could get Genevieve to cut it.

"Rowan?" Ma asked.

"Her brother. Good kid. Plays ball and has college scouts already looking at him."

Ma blinked a few times. "Really? So you'd be good at helping give advice on that, too. A young man with no father around to guide him." Her chin wobbled. "Tragedy. Sounds like they definitely could use *you* around."

"Nice play, Ma."

"Sport, I'm just not sure what the problem is. You're twenty-seven, closing in on twenty-eight here in the next couple months. You have a great job, are up for a new contract, and a beautiful girl has captured a bit more of your attention than you were planning for, but so what? I say get to know her. Woo her. Enjoy yourself. See how the other half does it before you cast judgment on being in a relationship. You might just find it suits you more than you ever thought."

I nodded, went to the fridge, and grabbed two beers. I needed time to think, and Dad wouldn't talk about my current female problems.

"Dad?" I said.

"Garage. As usual." She rolled her eyes. "Dinner in T-minus twenty minutes."

I stopped in front of my mom and pulled her into a hug, nestling my nose into her neck. She smelled like lavender, the same as she always did. Some things never changed, thank God. "Thanks, Ma, for making me see that it's not unusual to feel this way."

"Honey, it's unusual to *never* feel this way." She patted my back and held me tight. "Give the process a chance. Allow yourself a moment of vulnerability. Not every woman you meet is a user and after your money, and promise me this..."

"Anything." I hugged the only woman I'd ever loved, knowing with my whole heart that she loved me back.

"Allow me to cook dinner for her and those parentless kids next Sunday. Please? I promise not to make a big deal about it."

Her voice was an inch away from throwing guilt, which was not her normal speed, but I knew she wanted this bad. The first girl I'd ever talked about dating in years. Ma was probably in hog heaven.

I leaned back, keeping my mother at arm's distance. Her blue gaze pleaded with me. She bit her lip and inhaled.

"All right. But don't make me regret it. I'll see if she can. From what I understand, they always do family dinner night on Sundays, so maybe I could convince her to share her family dinner night with ours."

Ma clasped her hands to her chest again. "Oh, I'll pray that she agrees." Then she wiggled to her own beat back to her stove where she did what she did best—feed and bless her family with her gifts.

GENEVIEVE

Trent was acting strange today. He had shifty eyes that looked everywhere around the room but at me as we worked on strengthening his core and thighs for more intense positions. I wanted that hamstring stretched taut, but didn't want to harm his recovery in the process. It was a fine line between working the muscle and overworking it.

Finally, after we moved into a forearm plank pose, I slid my hands down his ribcage, set my hand on each side of his hips, and maneuvered him into the appropriate position. Straddling his body reminded me of when I'd straddled him last night. He wasn't so timid and inhibited when we were unclothed. *Why was he acting odd now?*

An acute fear hit me straight through the heart. Now that he'd had me carnally, maybe he no longer wanted me. Maybe he was here just for the private lessons. In the past two weeks, he had made remarkable progress in range of motion, weight bearing, and strengthening. Perhaps now that he'd had his wicked way with me, he no longer wanted anything more.

Genevieve, don't be stupid. Just because you felt something deeper this weekend doesn't mean he did.

I called out for him to move into dolphin pose. In dolphin, the forearms were on the mat, legs out straight and the hips lifted to the sky. It was an advanced modification on downward facing dog. It forced him to put more effort into his upper half than his lower, which should have been easier for him. As he lifted his hips, I stood behind him, gripped his hips, and assisted him in going deeper into the pose. Since we'd been intimate already, I didn't have any qualms about lining up my pelvis or leaning against his bum. I wrapped my fingers into the indent at his hips—the indent I'd spent a lengthy time discovering just last night...with my tongue.

He groaned as I pressed my fingers deeper into the muscle. I hoped it was pleasure, not pain, forcing that response.

"Are you hurting?"

"If you call my dick getting hard hurting. Gumdrop, you touch that spot on my hips, and I'll be pushing into you so fast you won't even be able to say *Namaste*."

He shook as he held dolphin pose a little longer. I counted to five, needing the full breath as much as he did. His words shook me to my core.

"Frankly, I'm relieved. Now, bring your knees to the mat and lean forward, resting your forehead on the mat for five deep breaths, going into child's pose."

He followed my instructions to the letter, which I appreciated. Made me believe he really wanted the help and wasn't just here to hit on me. Although, I'd have welcomed that.

"What do you mean you're relieved? I'm the one with a hard-on." He chuckled and rolled over on to his back. He wasn't kidding. His shaft was tenting his soft gray sweats in a graphic display of his virility. "You press that perfect body to my ass one more time, babe, and I can't be held responsible for my actions."

My face heated as though I'd been sitting too long out in the sun on a July day—only it was closing in on November, and we were inside.

"Don't act all shy. You know what your sexy body does to me. We're supposed to be working. Playtime is later."

Playtime?

I knelt in front of his legs and positioned his ankle to the opposite knee. He grimaced as I lifted the leg, rested his bare foot against my abdomen, and pushed forward. This particular pose would work the sciatic nerve and hopefully relieve some of the tension in his hamstring. I always started with the healthy leg first. I pushed against him, leaning forward so his knee and ankle moved closer to his chest.

"Damn, that feels good, gumdrop. You wore my ass out this weekend. Need this stretch. Thinking of hitting the gym's sauna after."

I stared at his sculpted face. His chin was square and his cheekbones high as he smirked. Too beautiful for words, and he knew it. Punk.

"You! I'm the one who had the experience of a lifetime. Nothing will ever compare to that. Ever." I breathed out slowly, trying not to let his words affect me, even though it was useless.

He frowned, crinkles in his forehead appearing along the expanse. "You telling me you're planning on having someone else get in there?" He nodded down to the space between my legs.

My face was so hot I wished I had my water near me to press the metal bottle against the heat. "Hardly. I just know you'll eventually move on." My words were flat and honest.

Trent's features hardened, and he clenched his jaw as we switched legs. I had to be more careful since this one was injured and stretching it had to hurt like the dickens.

"Didn't we say we were going to take this one day at a time, gumdrop?" His voice came out strained.

I shrugged. "Yes, but then you came in, and you've been acting weird, so I just assumed you wanted to move on. Really, it's fine. If that's your thing, I get it." I looked off to the side. It was one hundred percent *not* my thing, but I'd known what I was getting into when I accepted that date.

He attempted to lift his upper body off the mat. I caught him wincing as he grabbed my hands. Before I knew it, I was sprawled on top of his supine form, and his mouth was on mine.

From nothing to everything in a half of a breath. This man would ruin me.

We kissed like teenagers necking in the back of a car. I rubbed my lower half against his and gloried in the corresponding groan. He lifted his big hands and held my head while he kissed me properly. Long swipes of his tongue played over mine. I melted into his kiss, never wanting to leave.

Eventually, we both pulled back enough to suck in some much-needed air. As our heartbeats calmed, he tunneled a hand into the hair at the nape of my neck and pecked my lips softly.

"Genevieve, this is more than one night. You know it. I know it. Hell, my *mom* knows it." He laughed.

"Your mom?"

"Yeah, I talked to her about you. That's why I was acting strange. She wants you to come to dinner this Sunday, and I didn't know how to ask you. Remember, I'm not used to the dating thing." He licked his lips and bit down on the plump flesh. The lines around his eyes softened. Nothing but genuine concern emanated from his hazel gaze as he looked at me.

A relief so strong I nearly fainted flooded my body, and a bout of laughter to bubble up in its wake. I laughed at the absurdity of freaking out about him not wanting more from me. I laughed at the ridiculousness that he was nervous about asking *me* to dinner with his parents, and I laughed at how stupid I'd been, thinking he didn't want me. The connection between us yesterday had seemed all-encompassing, yet doubt had worked its evil claws into my psyche.

I leaned forward and kissed him softly on the lips. "I'm sorry, Trent. I just thought... I mean, you're *you* and I'm *me*. Men like you don't want to be tied down by someone like me. Poor. Two kids to take care of. A giant house that needs constant work." I shook my head.

He squinted. "What are you saying?"

My voice turned soft and insecure. "We don't make sense."

I tried to maneuver away from his body, but he wrapped his hands around my waist and put me in a lock-down, gripped my neck with one hand, and rolled us so our positions were reversed. I was on the bottom. He was nestled comfortably between my splayed legs.

He thrust his hardness against my center. I moaned and gasped as he pressed down, his length crushing my need.

"Does this feel as though we don't make sense?" He moved his hips in a circular motion.

"That's biology. You're a man, and I'm a woman."

"Gumdrop, there has not been a woman yet who could keep my dick hard all through dinner. None except for you. I look at your glossy red lips, and I imagine them wrapped around my length. I see your eyes, and I imagine them filled with desire. And don't even get me started on your body. Babe, everything about you turns me on, makes feel...needed."

I groaned as he continued his ministrations. We had twenty more minutes left in the private room, which was supposed to be used for Savasana, the deep relaxation portion of the yoga practice.

"I need you, too."

Instantly his lips were on mine, my legs pushed up, and

my pants around my ankles. Before I could say a word, he'd donned a condom and was pushing into me.

He was hard, thick, and so warm as he held my legs to my chest and thrust his length deep.

"Don't try to stop this, gumdrop." He swirled his shaft inside me. "I'm not going anywhere any time soon. Does this feel like I want to be anywhere else?" He thrust hard.

I cried out. He leaned over and took my mouth with his, muffling any further screams of passion. He worked that hamstring while on his knees, pounding into me, holding my knees to my chest as he took me to the brink of pleasure and then pushed me off the edge to tumble into the abyss of sheer ecstasy.

I went willingly, and within mere moments, he followed.

CHAPTER FIFTEEN

Tree Pose

(Sanskrit: Vriksasana)

Tree pose is one of the simpler balancing poses in the yogic practice. Tree pose helps you find a sense of stability, works the core, and makes you feel more connected to the present as well as the physical earth. This pose can be achieved by standing with feet hip distance apart and raising one leg to rest at the ankle, inner thigh, or in front of the quad. When you have your balance, raise hands above head into a prayer or steeple hold.

GENEVIEVE

We spent the rest of the week behaving ourselves. Trent met me at Lotus House every day for his private session. After

Monday's debacle of having real sex in the center, I cut him off. We both agreed that not only was it risqué, it made the experience feel a bit tawdry and something I wasn't proud of. Lotus House had been my home away from home. I didn't want to disgrace it by having wild sex in the private rooms. People came to find balance, serenity, and peace. Sure, a roll in the hay made people feel all those things, but it surely wasn't meant for that, and doing it there made me feel too guilty.

Trent invited himself to the house, and I allowed it once. He came for a normal chicken and rice dinner with my siblings. To my surprise, he didn't try to make intimate contact with me outside of a steamy kiss when I walked him to his flashy car. I had expected Rowan and Mary to act differently in Trent's presence, but instead, they acted as though he'd always been there.

Row enjoyed having the baseball star in the house almost as much as I did. While I cleaned up, Trent played a card game with Mary and watched football with Rowan. Every so often, Trent would engage Rowan about school, baseball, and his college plans, and shared some of his own experiences. Trent expressed that Row should consider which ride gave him the best deal. I waited with bated breath while Rowan made it clear he had no intention of leaving his sisters and that if he was meant to play college ball, he'd do it at UC San Francisco or UC Berkeley. Apparently, he was shooting for the Berkeley team. It was closer. He could live at home if he needed to.

At one point, Trent laid a hand on Rowan's shoulder and squeezed. They stared at one another, neither saying a word. Stupid males and their silent communication. Women made everything as clear as possible. Heck, we said things over and over again until our point came across. With men, it was a fist bump, a nod of the chin, a clap on the back, or in this case, a squeeze to the shoulder, and they'd shared a pivotal moment. One I was not privy to.

Now, I sat in front of the mirror in my bedroom fussing over my hair. The shoulder-length locks, thankfully, were curling nicely into the sassy old Hollywood style I liked. Often, people thought my platinum-blond hair was dyed, but it actually grew out of my head that color. Mary and I had always been considered towheads. I thought a lot about going darker but always ended up keeping what the good Lord blessed me with.

Mary entered my room at a dead run. "Vivvie, can you do my hair?" She held up Mom's old brush, a hair tie, and a giant red bow.

She had taken extra effort with her appearance as well. Her current outfit was one of my favorites—a black-and-red plaid long-sleeved romper I'd found at Target on clearance last year.

"Of course, sweetie. What would you like? Nothing too involved. Trent is picking us up in twenty minutes, and I need to finish getting ready, too." I wanted to add that her big sister was also freaking out and needed time to breathe into a brown paper bag, but I knew better than to show weakness in front of a child. That was one thing Mom had told me about parenting when I babysat Row and Mary.

"If they see a weakness, they will exploit it, Vivvie. They don't realize they're doing it. The little buggers are programmed to test adults."

It was one of the last things she'd said to me the night they had their fatal accident. At least they'd both kissed and hugged each of us.

"Vivvie!" Mary pursed her pink lips and looked at the mirror. "High ponytail with the bow hiding the rubber band."

I smiled. "Perfect choice." And it was. She looked like a hip little girl on one of those after school Disney shows where they find all the newest talent to turn into pop stars.

Mary chewed at her thumbnail. This was a sign that she had something she wanted to talk about but was nervous about it.

Tipping up her chin while holding the brush, I looked into her eyes. "Out with it. What's up? You know you can talk to me."

She brought her hands together and smoothed the fabric of her romper. "Is Trent your boyfriend?" she asked quickly.

The question sent an additional shiver of nerves racing up and down my spine. Since I believed honesty was always the best policy, I answered her as truthfully as possible. "We're dating."

She tilted her head and scrunched her eyebrows closer together. "Does that mean he's going to move in here soon?"

I added the rubber band and wrapped it around her hair several times until I got a tight fit. Then I tugged it back a touch, loosening any pull. "Mary, I doubt it. Honey, he's a very important baseball star. I'm not sure our relationship will go that far, if ever. Plus, I don't know if that's something he would want." I shrugged and clipped the red bow into her hair.

"But he likes you. I saw him kiss you at the car, and he made us pancakes, and he stayed with us when the bad guys tried to get into our house. He even fixed the door and made our yard nice."

Did all of that mean he wanted more from me? Sure, he'd said we were taking it one day at a time, but what did that mean to someone like him? Did that mean I was his girlfriend? I shook my head. No. No it didn't.

"Yes, Trent likes me, and I like him. When a man and a woman like each other, they spend time together to see if they want to become boyfriend and girlfriend." I nodded. Yes. That sounded pretty good. I almost wanted to pat myself on the back for that one. Maneuvering through these parental-type minefields was not easy. Especially since Mary was an inquisitive, mature child for her age.

"Do you want him to be your boyfriend?"

Like that one.

I set her on the vanity and continued to work on my own makeup, adding the finishing touches. A long black line to accentuate the cat shape of my eyes, and my signature lip gloss. Tonight's was red and matched the red slacks I wore. I'd paired the slacks with a simple white blouse and a pair of red cork-wedge heels.

"Well, do you want him to be your boyfriend?" Mary asked again.

I sighed and put down the lip liner. "Honey, I don't know. Right now we're just seeing how things work out."

Her lip trembled, and she bit it. My heart sank, and I worried there was something more going on.

"I just don't understand. You should make him your boyfriend and then marry him. Then you will be happy all the time, and you won't have to work so much, and then we would be safe, and Rowan could go to any school he wants." Her words came out in a rush so quick she'd lost her breath by the end of her insistent recommendations. Without further ado, she hopped off the counter and stomped out of my room. Her little shoes clomped all the way down the double staircase.

Leaning against the counter, I stared at myself in the mirror. "What the heck just happened?"

Mary obviously had some very specific hopes pertaining to Trent, but why? I hoped I'd have a few minutes to chase her down and get to the bottom of it, but when I went down the stairs, Trent was in the doorway. Mary had her arms looped around his waist. He patted her head while she hugged him. He didn't seem put off, but he definitely wasn't used to hugging a child. The stiff way he stood and repeatedly patted her head like a dog had me snorting and failing to hold back my laughter.

Trent grinned and opened his arms out wide. "A little help here?"

"Mary, honey, get your coat."

"Can I sit shotgun?" she squealed, acting like her normal self again.

"I think shotgun is for your sister," Trent said. "But another time, I'll take you for a ride. Okay?"

"Hey, Trent!" Rowan held out a hand and did the half hug, half slap on the back man greeting.

"Gumdrop, you look beautiful. Come on over here so I can greet you properly."

Shyly, I walked over to him. When I was within arm's reach, he grasped my waist and tugged me flush against him.

"Hi, babe." He leaned forward for a soft kiss.

I glanced to the side and caught Row shaking his head and looking down. Mary, on the other hand, was holding her hands to her chest and smiling so huge it looked like her dreams were coming true.

"See! I *knew* he was your boyfriend!" She jumped up and down. "Man, I should have bet on it."

I grudgingly pulled away from Trent's kiss. "Honey, he's

not my—"

But she ran off down the hall screaming, "My sister's boyfriend is famous!"

Groaning, I turned around. "Sorry." I leaned my head against his chest and patted the space over his heart.

Trent lifted my chin. His eyes were a brilliant mixture of yellow, brown, and green. "For what?"

He couldn't be that dense. "For what she said. I never told her that you were my boyfriend."

He moved his head back. "Then what am I?"

Tilting my head, I assessed his mood.

Happy? Check.

Easygoing? Check.

Commanding? Check.

"It doesn't bother you that my sister called you my boyfriend?" I desperately wanted to know the answer.

He jerked his head back and curled his lip up. "Why should it?" Then his eyes widened. "Are you dating someone else?" This time, his voice was a straight growl, and his grip around my waist tightened.

"No! Of course not. Only you. But saying you're someone's boyfriend gives a certain stature or claim, if you will, that goes with it. I didn't know if we were there yet."

Trent moved his hands down to my bum and squeezed. "Oh, I'm claiming this ass as mine. Let it be known to the world that Genevieve Harper's ass is mine from here on out." He snickered and squeezed the cheeks again.

I smacked him lightly on the chest. "Stop kidding around. I'm serious."

"Me too!" He got close and leaned his head against my forehead. "This ass is mine."

Holy crap! I whipped my head around to see if Rowan was still in the room, but he'd left. Thank God. Probably the second Trent kissed me.

Trent slid his hands up my ribcage. "These tits...mine, too."

Oh, my. My heart started beating so fast I worried it pound right out of my chest. "Trent..."

He used his thumbs and swiped the prominent peaks through my shirt. "Everything on this body is mine, gumdrop. No other man touches it. If that means you have to call me your boyfriend to be okay with that, I'm your boyfriend."

I sighed. *He doesn't get it.*

TRENT

Ma was her usual self when we arrived. Dad took our coats and hung them on the coat tree. Immediately, Genevieve, Rowan, and Mary slipped their shoes off and set them by the door.

"Are your feet hot?" I asked the trio.

Genevieve shook her head and bit her lip, blinking that doe-eyed uncertain gaze at me.

"Oh, dear, so nice of all of you to worry about keeping our floors clean. Such good manners. Your parents must have taught you well."

"Yes, ma'am." Rowan nodded and held out his hand to my mother first and then my father. "I'm Rowan Harper, and this is my sister Mary, and my eldest sister, Genevieve."

"Lovely to meet you both. Thank you for having us." Genevieve held out her hand.

My mother quickly lost her cool. Her eyes teared up, and she pulled my girl into an emotional hug. "You have no idea how long I've waited to meet you," she said dramatically, as if Genevieve were her long lost daughter.

Genevieve's cheeks pinked, and she smiled. "It's good to meet you as well, Mrs. Fox."

I rolled my eyes and tugged my mother away from my girl before she scared her off. "Ma, relax. Everybody, this is my mother, Joan, and my dad, Richard, but you can call him Rich."

All three of them thanked him and called him sir. Their manners...top-notch. Made me want to work on my own. Maybe, but unlikely.

Once the pleasantries were out of the way, the six of us made our way into the combined kitchen-family room. My mother hustled to the stove where she was pan grilling pork chops. The entire room smelled like grilled onions and green peppers.

"Smells awesome, Mrs. Fox." Rowan patted his belly before taking a seat at the bar island where Mom cooked.

Genevieve followed, holding onto Mary's hand.

Mary was acting timid, which was unusual for the more boisterous little girl. The few times I'd been around her, she wasn't so quiet.

"Sweetheart, I brought a coloring book and crayons." Genevieve took the loot from her giant purse and offered it to the girl.

Mary's eyes lit up. She took the seat directly between her brother and sister.

My mother smiled. "Ohh, Ms. Mary, I love fairies."

"You do?" Her eyes shone and her smile beamed.

Ma nodded. "I love when they have purple-and-blue wings."

Mary's head bobbed up and down. "Totally! I'll color you

a picture."

Oh, man, there it was. My mother smiled huge, her eyes tearing up.

"I would love that, dear." She walked over to the fridge and cleared a spot. "And when you're done, I'll put it right here so I can look at it every day."

Mary radiated happiness. Mom had not lost her way with kids. An unusual feeling hit my chest, kind of like a cross between an ache and a heartbeat. I rubbed at it, went to the fridge, got myself and Dad a beer and a soda for Rowan and Mary. I set the loot down on the counter and passed out the drinks.

"Babe, you want a glass of wine or a beer?"

Genevieve glanced at my mother.

"It's okay, gumdrop. Ma's having wine. Right, Ma?"

"You betcha, sport."

Genevieve smirked. "Sport?"

I rolled my eyes.

"Oh, I like that one. Sport. Suits you."

Ma came over with an opened bottle of white wine and a glass. "It always has. My big jock." Ma hugged my side and checked on Mary's drawing. "Ms. Mary. That is stunning. You're an artist for sure!" she gushed.

Ma laid it on a little thick, in my opinion. I glanced at the image. The girl did have talent, though.

"Thank you, Mrs. Fox." Mary wiggled in her chair and bit her lip as she made sure whatever she was coloring was just right.

"How's about you call me Grandma Fox? I'm old enough to be your grandma. Do you have any grandparents, honey?"

Mary solemnly shook her head.

"Well, you do now. How does that sound?"

Mary smiled wide. "Sounds awesome. Right, Row?" She nudged her brother.

"Of course, Mare." His cheeks pinked up, and he played with his soda can.

I looked at my girl, and instead of seeing a similar smile, she was ghostly white. "Excuse me." She got up. "Where's the bathroom?" Her face was strained and her hands shook.

Taking her by the hand, I ushered her down the hall and to the bathroom. I planned to go in with her, but she slammed the door in my face. All I could hear after that was the water running in the sink.

Ma rushed down the hall. "What happened? Is she feeling ill?"

I shrugged. "I don't know. She seemed fine, and then after you told Mary to call you grandma, her face turned white and she looked like she was going to hurl."

My mother closed her eyes and leaned up against the wall. "Shoot. Way to go, Joan. I screwed up, sport."

"Why?" I had no idea what would make Ma think that Genevieve feeling unwell had anything to do with her.

She leaned her head against the wall and then let out a slow breath. "Too much, too soon," she said. "I'll handle this. Just keep the other two entertained. I already took the chops off the stove, so we're fine for now."

Frowning, I shuffled from foot to foot and looked at the closed door. Part of me wanted to storm into the bathroom and make sure she was okay. The other part wanted to run far away from any potential drama that might unfold. Women rarely made sense. In the end, I decided that if Ma was willing to take on whatever happened and smooth things over, I needed to allow her female expertise to do its thing.

GENEVIEVE

"Genevieve, dear, please open the door. I need to speak with you." The sweet voice of Trent's mother lilted through the door.

I stared at myself in the mirror and wiped at my eyes, removing any residual mascara that had tracked down my face during my mini-panic attack. They didn't come that often, but when they did, I usually needed more than a few minutes to pull myself together. Maybe she'd think I was sick and Trent could just take us home.

"Sweetheart?" She tapped at the door again.

I opened it and was about to lie when she pulled me into her arms.

"Oh, Genevieve, I'm sorry. I didn't mean to come on so strong with your brother and sister. It's just that I'm so excited to have you here."

"It's okay. Everything is so confusing right now. We don't have any family, and here you are blessing us with a meal and being so nice..." My voice cracked. "Reminds me of times with our own parents."

"Oh, sweetheart. I'm sure you miss them terribly. That's why we need to get a good home-cooked meal in you three and spend some quality time getting to know one another. How does that sound?" Her tone was straightforward yet still hopeful.

I cleared my throat and decided once again to be honest. "That sounds lovely, but I don't want Mary getting too attached." I was afraid to tell her the rest. That eventually, when Trent kicked my family and me to the curb for a newer, hotter, younger model with no baggage, we'd be left missing him *and* his family. I was already in too deep with Trent. So far that when he went his own way, I'd be crushed.

Joan narrowed her eyes. "Now why wouldn't you want Mary to get attached to me, dear?" She frowned in that disapproving way moms did.

Maybe that was one of the things they taught in Lamaze class. How to make your child feel guilty as sin. Ugh. She was going to make me say it. Pulling at my hair, I thought about how I could best say what needed to be said without making her son out to be a player, even though in the past, that's what he'd been. I was just waiting for the day that his true nature would come rushing back to the surface. I figured that would happen about the time that he left for spring training in February, if not sooner. He'd go off to play ball, and we'd be left in the lurch. Heartbroken. "Mrs. Fox. I like your son a lot. More than I should. But he's admitted he's not the settling down type—"

"In the past." Her response was firm.

I shook my head. "Right, in the past—"

Again she jumped in. "Not right now."

That made me pause. "What do you mean, not right now?"

Her steely blue eyes pierced mine as she laid a hand on my bicep. "You're different. That's how I know." Such a simple statement, but it held such weight.

"Sure, I may be different. All women are. But am I enough?" I laced my fingers together. "My life isn't roses and rainbows. I have two children who need me, count on me to provide for them. Most men would not step up to commit to someone who was already filled to the brim with other commitments."

Joan shrugged. "All I know, dear, is that you are the first woman he's brought home to meet his parents in a decade. Let me say that again. In. A. Decade." She huffed and hooked her elbow with mine. "That, to me, is more than enough. Now, I've got pork chops cooked and ready to eat. Do you like pork?"

"Yeah."

"Then prepare to be wowed."

She led me back into her beautiful kitchen that smelled wonderful, where my brother was laughing at Trent, and Mary was making art for his mom.

"I already am," I whispered.

CHAPTER SIXTEEN

ROOT CHAKRA

Opening the chakras is as important to our physical body as our mental state. Each chakra is designed to store and distribute energy and messages throughout the body that control our habits, desires, and mental health. Closed chakras can hinder mental and physical health, affecting the choices and decisions we make in our daily lives.

TRENT

Due to a meeting scheduled with my agent this morning, I arrived at Lotus House early to take Genevieve's hatha yoga class. As much as I hated to, I had to pass on our private lesson. When I got there, she was chatting animatedly with a tall, muscular man who wasn't wearing a shirt. He had a pair of loose white pants that I'd seen other yogis wear before. The lack of shirt wasn't what sent my hackles rising. It was the way he kept touching Genevieve. With *familiarity*. A caress of her arm, holding her hand, and then as if watching something in slow motion, it happened. He leaned forward, all smiles and male bravado, and put his lips on my woman.

What the *fuck*?

I stormed over to Genevieve and this random man who had his lips on *my* girlfriend. When I got to them, they'd stopped kissing and were staring sweetly at one another.

Without thinking, I reacted, shoving the man's arm and pushing him roughly into the wall. The motion was so forceful, he knocked into one of the giant Sanskrit symbols that hung beyond the platform where the instructor taught, banging it into the plaster with enough force to leave a mark.

"Get your hands off of her!" I roared at the handsy asshole.

"Trent!" Genevieve grabbed at my arm, trying to prevent the automatic swing of my right hook.

If a man traipsed over another man's territory, it was throat punch first, ask questions later.

"Don't! Oh my God! What are you doing?" Genevieve pushed past me and leaned down to the man as he grabbed at his jaw.

I'd clocked him good. His lip had a slight tinge of red where it must have split. Good reminder to keep his fucking smackers off another man's woman.

"Damn that hurt," the man said, twisting his jaw from side to side.

"Trent! What were you thinking? I'm so sorry, Dash. Oh, my, you're bleeding." Genevieve grappled for a couple tissues sitting in the corner near the eye pillows and brought them to his busted lip.

The need to rip this loser to shreds spiraled through my body like an out-of-control cyclone. "I was thinking this joker better keep his hands *and* his lips off my girlfriend," I grated through clenched teeth. My hand hurt, but I flexed it open and closed, preparing to move quickly if needed.

"Ugh. I'm not your girlfriend!" Genevieve tightened her fists and tended to the Dash fellow.

Crossing my arms, I stared down at the two. "Seriously, gumdrop. You're not playing that card. We agreed. You and I are dating."

She sighed. "Dating, yes, but we hadn't discussed anything official. God!" She blew out a breath and dabbed at his lip. "Dash, I'm so sorry."

"You're apologizing to *him*? You should be apologizing to *me*!" I growled and tugged at her bicep.

Genevieve stood and crossed her arms, her beautiful face a mask of barely contained anger. "Dash is my friend, and you just punched him!" Her voice was a sharp bite to the ego. Not even a single hint of apology lay within her words.

Fuck! I didn't understand what the hell was happening. All I knew was the woman I'd been dating, the one I thought of as mine, had allowed another man to touch and kiss her. In public!

"I'm failing to see the correlation here, babe. I thought we were exclusive."

She narrowed her eyebrows. "We are." She sighed. "But that doesn't give you the right to go all gorilla crazy on any man who gets near me."

A crowd was starting to circle around us, but I didn't care. "Who the hell is this jackass?"

"He works here. He teaches the tantric yoga class and was

asking me to assist."

All I heard was the word *tantric.* That shit involved sex of some sort. What kind of sex? I didn't know, but I'd be consulting Google here directly, and there would be no "assisting" of that class...ever.

"Over my dead body!" I huffed, my anger hitting a height I'd only experienced a few times on the field when the umpire made a bullshit call.

Genevieve scrunched up her little nose and pinched her lips, their normal pink going white. "Not that it's your decision, but I'd already told him no, that the guy I was seeing would not be pleased with me filling in for that particular class." She harrumphed loudly and slapped her spandex-covered legs. "What on earth would possess you to hit him?" She rubbed at her forehead.

I glanced at the man. Dash...what kind of stupid ass name was that anyway? He simply waited, looking completely innocent. Total bullshit.

"This man had his hands all over you and kissed you, on the mouth!" An intense heat fired down my spine and settled in my fists. I wanted to sucker-punch the pissant again.

Dash shook his head and put his arm on Genevieve's bicep...again. "Viv, honey, it's okay. He was just protecting what he clearly perceives as his. If I had a woman like you to call my own, I might have responded the same way. Trent...I apologize." The guy looked down and away. "I meant no ill will, nor was I attempting to do anything other than have our girl help me out with my class."

"Our girl?" My tone was scathing. "You mean *my* girl!" I clenched my teeth and sucked in a harsh breath.

Genevieve groaned. "This is ridiculous. I don't have time

for this male posturing baloney. Apologize to Dash, or we're through." She set her hands on her hips.

"I'm not apologizing to him. If anything, *you* owe *me* an apology. I'm not the one that had my lips all over Mr. Yoga here!"

Dash had the good grace to look away, losing eye contact. "I'm sorry, Viv. Trent, I meant no harm, man, I swear."

"Whatever, man. I'm sure you just *accidentally* kissed her on the mouth."

"He always kisses his friends on the mouth." An exasperated breath left Genevieve's lips. "He's into touch, connection. He teaches couples the art of Tantra for crying out loud!"

"And that is supposed to give him the right to put his mouth on my woman? Hell, no. Not in this lifetime."

Genevieve reached behind her and turned the music on. "Just go. Leave. I can't deal with you right now. I have enough on my plate without adding a jealous lover to the mix."

Dash, the tantric yoga guru, touched Genevieve on the arm. "Hey, Viv, I'll teach your class. Don't worry. Just go talk to him."

"Best fucking offer I've heard all day," I mumbled.

Genevieve's gaze shot to mine, seeming more like razor blades than the soulful depths I was used to. Her body jerked, and tears flooded her eyes. "I can't! I need the money."

"Don't worry about it," Dash and I said at the same time.

Dead man. Sometimes, I think people have moments in life where their path becomes crystal clear. My path was to slam my foot in this guy's ribs...repeatedly.

Dash lifted his hands in a placating gesture. "I'll teach, and you'll get the money. It's the least I can do. I'm sorry for starting something between you and your mate. The kiss... man, I'm sorry." His gaze cut to mine. "It won't happen again."

Dash's shoulders were drawn in, and he held his hands clasped in front of him in a nonthreatening gesture. Overall, his body language suggested he genuinely wanted to fix things. Maybe it was because I was huge in comparison and could kick his ass, though I tried to believe it was the former.

"Better not." I nodded.

Genevieve looked around the room. Her lip trembled, and she tipped her chin toward Dash. Grabbing her things, she hustled by me, not even sparing me a glance as she went.

"I guess that's the end of the show, folks. Carry on with your class. Sorry for the interruption," I said and followed the dust my girl left in her wake.

GENEVIEVE

The last thing I needed was a male battle over me. In public. At my workplace. I didn't have the mental capability to deal with this right now. The state was after me. I'd missed the last payment on the property taxes and the second installment was due. If I didn't pay, I'd have to sell the house or risk the state garnishing my wages. I needed a tax accountant, but I couldn't afford one. From what I gleaned online, I was in deep with the State of California. On top of that, my last two hair clients canceled, leaving me with a hundred fewer dollars this week, putting me even further behind on the electric bill.

I stopped at the curb. Trent would be hot on my heels. I stared at my dad's prized possession. It was worth about fifty grand. Selling the car that should rightfully go to Rowan was my only option. Tears filled my eyes as I stared at the one thing my dad loved more than anything besides his family—his Mustang GT. The car was in perfect condition, and I'd already had it appraised. I could easily get a used car to take us to and fro while paying the next two years' worth of property taxes as well as catching up on the house bills. I'd finally be able to breathe.

Last night, Rowan and I had sat down and discussed it at length. Of course, he wanted the car eventually, but in the end, he wanted to stay in the home we were raised in more. We also wanted to give that to Mary. We'd had our parents for a lot longer than she had. Mary only had a home to cling to, whereas Rowan and I had countless memories to dip into whenever we wanted.

"Genevieve! Hold up. Please." Trent's voice was rough, his breath coming in labored pants. A pained groan slipped from his lips as he limped over to where I stood staring at my dad's car.

"Trent, what you did in there was unacceptable." My voice sounded foreign and cold, but he'd gone over the line.

He placed his hands on his hips and looked down. "You want me to be sorry that I responded like any man who caught his woman kissing another man?"

I groaned. "You make it sound like I was sucking face with him. He's a friend. He gave me a friendly peck on the lips. He does that to *all* of us."

Trent snorted.

"He does. It's who he is. It's who he has always been. Maybe instead of overreacting, you could have taken me aside and not made a scene."

His eyes went stone cold. "I cannot believe you are trying to turn this around on me. You're kissing Mr. Yoga, and I'm the bad guy? This is ridiculous. And to think I thought you were different." He shook his head.

I huffed as tears slipped down my face. This was it. The moment I'd been expecting. We'd made it all of six weeks before it went to hell in a handbasket. "You know what, Trent? Believe whatever you want to believe, but I know the truth. Dash is nothing but a friend. A really good one at that. He was talking to me about a very hard situation and comforting me."

"Oh, yeah? About what?"

I curled my hands into fists. "My dad, okay?"

He pinched his eyebrows together, a crease forming at his brow line. He wanted to know? Well, he was about to get an earful.

"The bills are piling up. I'm behind on all the utilities and the property tax. The state has sent countless threatening letters, informing me that if I don't pay up, I will lose my parents' home. The one thing we have left of them." Tears tracked down my cheeks quickly and wet my tank. I took a ragged breath. "So Rowan and I had to make a tough choice."

"Which is?" His voice was still growly, like a grumpy old man complaining about the state of the nation.

"I've decided to sell my dad's car."

Trent's mouth dropped open, and he rubbed the scruff on his chin. Oh, how I loved that scruff. The way it felt against my lips when we kissed, against my neck, breasts, and between my thighs.

"But you and Rowan love that car."

"Yeah, well, my brother and sister need a place to lay their heads at night. On top of that, they need hot water, electricity, and a consistent home. Something you'd never understand."

He jerked his head back. "What's that supposed to mean?"

"Means you take for granted everything. Squander your money away on women and flashy cars and bikes, yet you lay your head in an apartment that's devoid of life. There are a total of two pictures in your home, and you've lived there for *years*. What does that say?"

He pursed his lips and scowled. "That I'm on the go. That I don't have the time to—"

"No! It means you don't settle down. You're as rooted here as you are on an airplane. And what's going to happen when you go back on the road? Let me tell you what I think will happen."

"Please enlighten me."

I leaned against Dad's beloved car and crossed my arms. "You'll find the next sweet little thing and hop from plane to plane. I'm not stupid, Trent. I know the second you get back in the air you're going to drop me and my family drama like a hot potato."

His head jerked back as if he'd been the one punched. He looked down and ran his hand through his hair. "You really think so little of me?"

I shrugged. "Just basing things on what I know of you."

"Yeah, but you know *me*." He pointed to his chest. "The me I want to be. The me I can be for you. The me that shows up every day for private lessons. The me that takes care of your yard, texts with your brother daily, and the me that just told Ma that you and the kids would be attending our family Thanksgiving dinner this week. Does that sound like the type of guy you can't trust?"

Each and every word hit me like a brick. One by one, they knocked the wind right out of my sails. I sucked in a harsh breath, the tears coming faster. "No," I croaked.

Instead of filleting me for being a jerk and not thinking the best of him, he surprised me. He grabbed me by the hand and tugged me to his chest. He caressed my cheek, wiping away the tears that wouldn't stop falling. "Babe, I'm going to be there for you. I'm doing everything I can to be the kind of man you'd fall for."

A choked sob left my chest. "But why?" Him trying to be with me made no sense. Not in this lifetime, not in any lifetime. Girls like me did not get guys like him to change their ways.

"Isn't it obvious?" His eyes were a brilliant green and gold when he smiled softly, his nose almost touching my own. "I'm falling all over myself for you, gumdrop."

I clenched his shoulders as I held on. "You could have anyone. Any woman in her right mind would chase after you. Why would you want to be with someone who's struggling, crawling with debt, and has more responsibilities than you should ever have to deal with?"

He chuckled and rubbed his nose along the column of my neck. "Babe, because none of those women are *you*. They don't make me want to work hard to be whole. They don't make me feel as though I'm on cloud nine even when the world is falling down around me. And they sure as hell don't make my heart squeeze tighter when I catch a tiny glimpse of their smile across a room."

His words wiggled their way into my heart and made it jackhammer against my sternum.

"And"—he bit down on my earlobe, sending a streak of hot need to settle between my thighs—"they don't make me as hard as stone thinking about a single kiss. That's what you do to me. You make me a mess of need and want. All the time. And best of all, you don't even realize how devastatingly gorgeous you are inside and out."

TRENT

Her voice cracked as she held me close, fingers digging into the muscles of my back. "I'm sorry."

"Sorry about kissing another man or sorry about assuming I wasn't all in with this relationship?"

She sniffed and wiped her nose against my hoodie. If anyone else had done that, I would have thought that was disgusting. Not with my gumdrop. I wanted to be the man who was there for her, and I had no idea when or how everything that defined who I was or the life I'd led had changed.

"Both." She sobbed into my neck, her tears warm on my skin against the Bay Area wind.

I dragged my hand up and down her back, massaging the tension I found there. "Hey, look at me."

Genevieve shook her head against my neck. "Too embarrassed," she mumbled.

I forced her back a foot, cupped both of her cheeks, and tilted her head up with my thumbs under her chin. Twin tears raced down her pale cheeks. I wiped them away before they reached the edge of her perfect pout.

"Hey, I know you're sad about your dad's car, but there's another option."

She tilted her head to the side and bit down on her bottom lip.

"Allow me to pay the taxes."

Her dark eyes went as round as silver dollars. She shook her head and tried to step back. "No way. Not at option. We'll be fine. We'll sell the car, pay two years' worth of taxes, catch up on the utilities, and have enough to buy something reliable and good on gas in the meantime. We'll be fine, but thank you for offering."

"Gumdrop..."

She placed two fingers over my lips. "No, Trent. I'm not your responsibility."

"What if I want you to be?"

And that right there was the first time in my life I'd ever felt the desire to protect and care for a woman. Money, help with Rowan and Mary, anything. I wanted to be the man who took care of things for this incredible woman.

Genevieve rolled her eyes and backed up, though she couldn't go far. I'd wedged her up against the Mustang and used my body mass for leverage to keep her there.

"No." She fiddled with the hair at the nape of my neck, swirling it around her fingers. "Neither of us is ready for that. Let's just enjoy what we have. Okay?" Her eyes pierced mine as she focused all her attention on me. As if the world around us no longer mattered.

I slid my hand down to cup a hearty amount of ass cheek. "Gumdrop, I think we just made up after our first fight." I grinned and leaned more against her body. "Are the kids home?" Cupping both of her round ass cheeks, I squeezed and ground my hardening shaft into her softness.

She mewled, bit her lip, and shook her head.

"Let's get you home then." I pulled back, walked around to the driver's side, and opened her door. "I'll follow you."

She nodded and fumbled into the seat. I slammed the door and beat feet to the Maserati.

While driving like I was Jeff Gordon, I dialed my agent and informed him I was going to be at least two hours late for my meeting. He was rightfully pissed off, but nothing would prevent me from making amends properly with Genevieve.

I slid my car right behind hers and beat feet it out so that I was opening her door before she could even turn off the engine. Luckily, she had already hit the garage door clicker, so I knew we'd be alone.

Once I tugged her out of her car, I pinned her to the hood of the vehicle and put my hands all over her. She gasped as I turned her around and pressed her front to hood. Thank God we didn't have far to go getting here from Lotus House. The top of the hood was just cool enough not to burn her sweet tits as I pressed her down. I ground my crotch against her ass while kissing the back of her neck, trailing my tongue down the white expanse.

With greedy fingers, I dug my hands under her tank, arching her upper body while pushing her sports bra up far enough to free her breasts. Her nipples instantly became erect for me. She sighed as I plucked and elongated each nub to my satisfaction.

"Love your tits, babe. When I'm done fucking you on the hood of your dad's car, I'm going to suck on them until they turn into sharp little burning points. Would you like that, gumdrop?" I bit down on the ball of her shoulder and licked the indentations I left. I loved marking her, leaving my imprint, showing any man within an arm's length that this woman was taken. Owned. Loved? I shook my head, forcing those thoughts to dissipate and be replaced with carnal desire.

"Oh, God, Trent..."

She was panting as I pulled down her tight yoga pants to her knees. Her legs were held together, and I knew it was going to be a tight fit, but that's exactly how I wanted it. Needed it. Her pretty, pale ass was stark against the royal blue of the 'Stang. I gripped her ass, leaned down, and bit into one then the other fleshy cheek.

Her body jerked, and she moaned as I licked around the bites. With both hands, I spread her ass cheeks as far as they could go and licked her from clit to anus and swirled my tongue around and around her tight pucker. She jolted and cried out while I flicked the tiny rosette, spread her wider, and fucked her hole with my tongue.

Genevieve pushed her greedy pussy against the warm hood. The wetness slipping against the metal as she ground her clit on the hard surface sent a tingle of want straight to my balls.

"You ready to be fucked, gumdrop?"

"God, yes!" she cried out, her body arching.

Yoga chicks. Hottest thing ever.

It took all of two seconds to drop my drawers and wedge my fat cock between her wet lower lips. The fit was brutal and so goddamned tight, but my girl took everything I had all the way to the hilt. Once I was all the way in, I leaned over her body and pressed my hips against her, which pushed the crown of my cock more intensely into her center.

"You like me deep inside?" Nothing felt better for me than being imbedded in her heat.

"So good..." She sighed.

"Oh, babe, this is only the beginning. You want more?"

"Yeah." Her voice was but a whisper as she planted her hands on the hood of the car.

I pulled back my hips, licked my thumb, and rested it right over her rosy hole. "Take all of me. Every. Thing. Inside." I slammed my hips into her at the same time I plunged my thumb into her backdoor.

She howled, arched, and came in one thrust. One fucking

thrust. Jesus. The woman was a goddess.

Genevieve convulsed around my cock, her lower half tightening to ball-lifting proportions. The pulses alone were enough to set me off, but I held strong, wanting nothing more than to fuck her into oblivion.

When she calmed down, her breath left her in little pants. That's when I removed my thumb, gripped both sides of her hips, pulled out, and thrust back home. So damn deep.

Heaven.

She moaned, and it spurred me on. Digging my fingers into her hips, I held on for dear life and fucked the living daylights out of my woman. Hard. Fast. Unrelenting in my desire to have her come all over my cock again.

She called out with every thrust. Every retreat made her whimper for more. My mind was in a daze. Each pore, nerve, and sensation was centered where I plowed into Genevieve's tight sheath. The wet suction of our mating echoed in the empty garage until the little nonsensical words she always said when she was lost to her pleasure started up. Christ! I loved hearing her lose her mind.

"Breathe..."

"Inside..."

"Hot..."

"Gonna..."

"Ummm..."

I wanted her with me, milking my cock when I lost it.

Leaning forward for more leverage, I clasped my hands over hers and intertwined our fingers against the hood of the car. She gripped my hands, screaming as her entire body went rigid with tension, the impending orgasm about to rock her into next week.

I growled into her ear, "Love fucking this hot body. All mine, Genevieve. Gonna fuck you forever." I breathed out harshly, my hips slamming into her ass until I lost all rhythm and finesse, focused solely on the goal of release.

"Oh, my word..."

Her pussy put the lock-down on my cock, forcing my dick to pulse and release in heated bursts deep within her.

When we both could breathe again, she groaned. I must have been heavy as shit with my weight on top of her like a sack of beans.

"Sorry, babe. Shit." I lifted up and pulled out.

The second I did, our combined release started dripping down her leg. That was new, and sexy as hell. I'd been very careful before. Here, in the spur of the moment, I'd not thought to wrap my shit. I'd always covered myself before I sank into the sweet heat of a woman, but with Genevieve, I lost myself in her.

"What the hell is that?" She moved from the car.

I watched in utter fascination, my dick getting hard, raring to go again, as I appreciated how a piece of me had been inside her and still was only now leaking out.

I plastered my back against hers and cupped her from behind. Then like an alpha asshole, I rubbed our combined essence into her lips and fingered her, wanting more of me to stay inside her. I'd never in my life had such a reaction. Hell, I'd never come in a woman before Genevieve, and now that I'd had a taste of bareback, I'd hate going back to using a rubber.

"It's us, babe, and it's fucking sexy as hell," I gritted through clenched teeth as she fucked my hand. Always wanting more, my girl. Christ. A sex goddess hid behind her quiet and calm exterior, one I loved bringing to the surface. This woman was quickly becoming my entire universe.

"What?" she screeched and pushed back, releasing my hold on her sweet pussy.

"Babe, relax. Don't be embarrassed. I think it's dead sexy."

She pulled her pants up in a hurry. "I hope you think a baby is dead sexy because I'm not on the pill!" Her voice was shrill and panicked as she ran into the house.

I stood there, glued to the spot, my hand wet, my dick air-drying, and my shorts around my ankles as the words "baby" and "I'm not on the pill" spun on repeat in my mind. Like a broken fucking record.

Baby.

Not on the Pill.

Baby.

Not on the Pill.

Holy fuck. What have I done?

CHAPTER SEVENTEEN

Upward Facing Dog

(Sanskrit: Urdhva Mukha Svanasana)

This pose is part of the Sun Salutation sequence. It is a strengthening pose that adds the additional benefit of a relatively natural backbend. Used in beginning yoga classes, this pose opens and expands the chest and heart chakra, allowing for a deep strengthening of the shoulders. Lie on your stomach, tighten your glutes, and press up into your hands until your chest is completely upright and neck straight.

TRENT

I might have well become an Olympic sprinter for how fast I hobbled up those stairs and banged on Genevieve's locked door. I turned the handle, but it didn't magically open.

"Gumdrop. You open this fucking door!" I winced at the sound of my own voice. It was the tone that screamed desperate.

"Just go away."

"The hell I will. You open this door, or I'll break the fucker down."

"You wouldn't!"

Turning, I targeted my shoulder, pivoted on one foot, pushing my weight back, and hammered forward. The wood door rattled on its hinges.

"Oh my god! No. Don't break my door! I can't afford to fix it!" She fumbled with the lock.

The second it opened, I tagged her around the waist, brought her to my chest, and walked her backward to the bed until her thighs hit. Then I plopped us both down on the comfy bed.

Genevieve wiggled until her legs were spread and my form rested snuggled between them. Funny, that's exactly where I wanted to be anyhow.

"Let me go, Trent!"

Her bravado was losing steam the longer she struggled. I held onto her hands at the wrists and planted them next to her head.

"No way. You are not running from this. I admit, I was lost in the moment. I fucked up."

She snorted and made a gurgling sound deep in her throat. "And how many times has that happened before me? Huh? Do I need to get tested?" The tears she was trying to hold back were pooled, making her eyes seem like glittering ebony rocks.

I lifted my eyebrows toward my hairline. "Are you implying that I'm a manwhore?"

She stopped struggling. "Are you admitting that you aren't?"

I thought about all the women before her. Hell, there were several I probably couldn't even name, let alone remember all the debauched things I'd done with them, but not once, not *ever*, had I gone unwrapped. It was a cardinal sin.

"No, I wouldn't lie to you like that. I've been with my fair share of women."

She pursed her lips together.

"Okay, I've been with more than my fair share, but gumdrop, none of them hold a candle to you. And not one of them had all of me. I wore a condom with every woman I've ever been with. I swear on all things holy. Hell, I swear on my career, the only thing before you that ever meant anything to me."

I crossed my heart with one hand. "May I never be able to hit another baseball if I'm lying. God strike me now!" I rose and hit my chest. "You don't have to worry about diseases. I'm clean. Just had a physical last week. The team has to get them regularly, and the coach called for testing to make sure I was keeping up with my promise of limiting the drink and not putting anything up my nose or in my veins that wasn't made straight from the man upstairs."

Genevieve closed her eyes, and the tears fell. "That doesn't prevent pregnancy. Trent, I don't know if I can handle one more mistake or life-changing event."

The tears fell, and I kissed them away, tasting her salty tears for what they were. Regret.

That feeling hit my gut hard. The last thing I ever wanted was for her to regret any of our time together. Sure, we'd been fucking around, but it didn't mean it wasn't special. Every time with Genevieve was special. Unique. The best I'd had, because it meant something. With her, it wasn't always about getting off. It was...*more.*

I rubbed her nose with mine. "Hey, no crying. We'll figure it out. Whatever happens, we'll deal with it."

She scoffed. The woman had the audacity to scoff at me. "Yeah, and what happens if I end up knocked up, and you're off to away games?"

Petting her cheek, I looked directly in her eyes. "I'm not going to deny that this possibility scares the hell out of me, but I'm also not going to stress about something we can't control. If you end up pregnant, we'll be parents. End of story."

She groaned and let her head fall into her hands. "I'll have to think about that."

"There's nothing to think about. I will take care of what's mine, and just like I intend to help with the car, I'll make sure you're provided for."

She groaned. "Not this again. You're not giving me money to pay for the house to save the car. It's over. That boat has sailed. I've got the car listed already."

"Without talking to me?" I cringed and sneered. Not my best moment, but I had a lot being thrown my direction. Her losing the house. Selling the car to save the house. Rowan and Genevieve getting screwed in the deal while losing one of their family heirlooms. The slipup with the condom, and the potential that my swimmers could be digging their way into her cervix right now. Somehow, that thought didn't scare me as much as it should.

Genevieve tried to push against my chest, but I was far stronger than she and I held her fast.

"Don't," I said.

"Don't what? Freak out? I'm freaking out. You're acting like my mate, not the man I date."

This time I scoffed. "Gumdrop, I *am* your man. The only guy in your life. Get used to it. It's not changing any time soon."

"And if I get pregnant?"

The thought of her rounded with my child made my dick hard. I knew she could feel it when she arched and pressed her hips into the steely length.

"As you can feel, the idea has possibilities."

She sighed and pouted. Seeing her pout was by far one of the highlights of my day...aside from the 'Stang fuck.

"You're a pig," she groaned.

I took that as her way of saying she'd forgiven me. She was no longer attempting to escape. If anything, she was pressing into my shaft as it came to full mast.

"I'm going to take you again. We had another fight."

"Is this how it's going to be every time we have an argument?" She moved her lips into a small smirk.

I lifted her tank, divested her of her sports bra, leaned forward, and sucked a fat pink nipple into my mouth. "God willing," I groaned and bit down on her nipple.

She moaned, shivering underneath me as I went about making her forget everything that had happened today—the fight at the yoga center, our disagreement out on the curb, our heated discussion after the condom slip. Everything. Only problem was, I had left my bag downstairs. After I made her come around my lips, I lifted her hips to fill her full of my cock once again, and I didn't even blink that I wasn't wearing a condom.

That time, I soaked up every glide, squeeze, and intense pressure of being inside my woman bare. When I gripped her hips and pushed her thighs up toward her armpits, I pressed my cock balls-deep, forcing every inch of my dick as far as possible until I bumped right up against her cervix.

Rooted deep, I let it all go.

GENEVIEVE

It had been a week since our double condom slip. If I hadn't known better, I would have believed Trent was trying to get me pregnant.

"Sweetheart, can you pass the potato casserole?" Richard, Trent's father, asked as he piled his plate full of the most succulent-looking turkey I'd ever seen.

Usually, Rowan, Mary, and I headed over to the St. James household for Thanksgiving where Amber and her grandmother, Sandra, made us dinner. It was never a traditional turkey. Last year was prime rib. They liked to change things up, so when Amber said they were going on a Mexican cruise for the holiday, I wasn't surprised. They went where the wind blew them, making their holidays more fun. Amber might have even told Mrs. St. James that I'd been invited over to the Foxes' for Thanksgiving. She was always worried that we wouldn't have somewhere to go. This year, I was officially having a family dinner with my *boyfriend's* parents.

That was definitely not something I had ever thought I'd be doing. Even so, I couldn't say I wasn't excited about it, and Rowan and Mary were even more so. Getting to spend the holiday with his idol was a high point for my brother. Over the past couple months, I'd tried to make sure they didn't get too attached, but it was useless. Idol status was reigning high for Rowan, and when Trent and his mother attended Mary's last recital, both of them bringing her flowers, he'd pretty much sealed the deal on her affection. Mary was a goner.

As for me...as much as I wanted to keep my heart to myself and protect it from breaking, I could no longer deny that I had serious feelings for the wickedly hot baseball player. He'd been nothing but committed to me and my family since day one, and his family...gah... They were unbelievably kind—loving, comforting, and most of all...inviting. Rowan, Mary, and I had felt very welcome in their home and enjoyed a few family dinners to date, this one being the biggest. In my opinion, if a woman spent a major holiday with her boyfriend, it signified a new level of their relationship. The tipping of the hourglass, so to speak.

"Here you go, Mr. Fox." I handed over the dish I'd brought.

Richard frowned. "I told you, sweetheart, to call me Rich or Dad." He waggled his eyebrows at Trent.

I laughed as Trent's eyes widened, and he looked down at his plate.

"Now, now, don't freak out, my boy. Although, we'd be delighted to expand our family." Joan Fox gave Trent her own unsubtle hint.

Trent coughed and drank a huge gulp of his beer. "Ma, Dad, really. Stop. Can we just enjoy one meal without you hinting at me marrying Genevieve and having her barefoot and pregnant by the year's end?"

A hunk of turkey caught in my throat, and I choked. Trent patted my back hard, dislodging the chunk. I hacked it into my napkin and stood.

"Um, I need a minute. If you'll excuse me." I hopped up as though my seat were on fire.

"Look, now you've done it. You choked her out," Trent

growled.

They were excited. Heck, I was too. I'd not been with anyone this long since Brian, and it felt good. Better than good. It felt real. I only hoped it would stay that way during the season. Trent was not going to leave his job, nor would I want him to give up something he loved. If we were going to continue having a relationship, we'd need to talk about the away time and everything in between. Of course, we still had the giant weight of not knowing bearing down on us. My period was due in a week. Every day that got closer, I prayed we'd dodged a bullet. However, I wasn't sure Trent was on the same page. I'd had to ask him to use a condom every time we had sex.

In the meantime, I had an appointment scheduled with the gynecologist to get on some birth control immediately. If my guy wanted to go bare, I'd have to be the one to make it a reality. He seemed unconcerned about the fact that I could very well be pregnant.

Once I freshened up and came back to the Thanksgiving meal, I felt a lot better. We ate, joked, talked about the plans for the rest of the year, and I announced that I'd sold my dad's car. According to Amber, who'd handled it for me while I worked as many hours as possible and spent my free time with Trent and the sibs, she found a buyer who willingly paid the full fifty grand. As awesome as that was, it still made me sad.

When we got back to the house, the car would be gone, and with it, another part of my father.

TRENT

Deep into the awkward push-up, I let out a long strained breath. "How much longer?" I gritted through clenched teeth.

People who thought yoga was all about being Zen and relaxed, finding their inner selves, were in for a rude awakening.

"Thirty more seconds. You can do this, Trent."

I groaned and kept my body held upright in a push-up position. The tops of my feet held my legs firm against the yoga mat while I arched my back. The upward facing dog position should have been a cakewalk, since it didn't directly force the leg into the lunges she had me doing earlier. Unfortunately, the thighs, quads, butt, and calves all had to be tightened to protect the lower back. I lifted my chin and attempted to breathe, following along with her loud breathing pattern. She did the audible inhale and exhale so I wouldn't forget to breathe, but it was damn hard to keep up when holding the upper half of my body aloft and my legs were on fire. "Okay, slowly bring the knees down, and then rest your chest between your thumbs."

In this position, I had my ass in the air and looked like an inchworm. I shook my head. "These positions get weirder and weirder, gumdrop."

Genevieve giggled. "All right, big guy, relax the belly to the mat and rest your cheek to one side. Give your body a moment. We're about to go into guided meditation."

"Thank Christ!" I scowled and turned my other cheek to the mat to relieve any fluttering tension in my neck from the seventy-five minutes of hardcore yoga she'd put me through. The woman said it was restorative, and I believed in working hard to get solid results, but today's session had kicked my ass. Probably because I'd been up all night, scouring the Internet, trying to figure out what to get her for Christmas.

"Okay, turn over onto your back."

I did so and then silently lifted my legs so she could push the bolster under the hamstrings. It felt awesome on my injury.

A few moments later, she added a scented oil to my chin and the space above my lips under my nose where I could inhale the woodsy fragrance. The next step always felt awesome. She'd place an eye pillow over my eyes, blocking out any additional light, set the music to a classical piano piece, and walk me through bliss.

The strains of one of Chopin's melodic piano pieces flitted through my consciousness.

"I want you to breathe. Let everything go. You've worked hard today, given your body a blessing. Breathe into that pride. Allow yourself to be consumed by it, for you have earned it, deserve it, worked hard for it. And relax...let it all go."

Genevieve's voice had the power to soothe all that ailed me. Not only was it soft and consistent, her voice came at a timbre that suited my senses. Her scent, touch, and everything in between just relaxed me further. When I was with her, I felt safe. It sounded strange coming from a big guy, one who had always taken care of himself, but I was being completely honest with myself. Spending time with this sprite of a woman brought me peace, joy, and a love I'd never known.

In my life, I'd been plenty blessed. My mother and father had given me all they could, raised me well, showed me what hard work and dedication could give you in life, and I'd followed that teaching all the way to the majors. Somehow, through all the glitz and glamour of fame, I lost a bit of the simpler side of life. Being with one person and loving everything she brought to my world, to my soul. With Genevieve, I'd gotten some of it back—glimpses of the life I *could* have...if I worked hard and was dedicated to being the man I should be. For her, and for me. I needed to man up, go the lengths unexplored, and give her the life that she deserved and glory in the gift of having her as part of the bigger whole.

Her voice rose and fell with the piano.

"Now imagine you're looking down on yourself. A single color fills the space around your body. What color is it?" The words were said the same as any other, yet they sounded as if they were spoken from the end of a long hallway.

Red.

A deep, dark crimson sparkled around my form as I imagined looking down on myself inside the studio. It flickered and popped as I took in the subtle hues.

"Whatever color you see is a chakra that is guiding you. It is part of your natural essence and can be open or closed, depending on where you are in your life."

The red tone shimmered and pulsed around my supine form, and I imagined it getting brighter as tiny ribbons of light swirled at the base of my body. Before my eyes, the ribbons acted like roots, burrowing into the mat below me and down into the floor and beyond. Like a tree that had taken root, my essence delved into the earth and found a home.

Just as I felt myself falling deeper into the floor, my body getting heavier with every breath, I heard her voice.

"I'm going to bring you back, counting from five. When I get to one, you will be awake and ready to take on your day."

She counted down, calling out commands that slowly woke me from that peaceful meditation, and the tethers to the roots started to break and tear apart. I frowned when she got to the number one. I sat up and faced her, the same way we did every day, only now I was completely stuck in the memory of my experience.

And just like yesterday and the day before that, she held her hands at heart center, her eyes open, and she looked at me with the most mesmerizing gaze and completed her private lesson with the words that seared right through me and burrowed pleasantly into my heart.

"The light in me, bows, to the light in you..."

"When I am in that place in me, and you are in that place in you..."

"We are one."

"*Namaste.*"

She bowed at the waist, and her head touched the floor. I mirrored the gesture. When I rose, she lifted her hands to her forehead where she pressed her thumbs and then brought them down to her mouth and touched her lips in a light kiss. I didn't know what the kiss meant, but I wanted to think she was blessing me.

And when my sweet angel opened her eyes, I knew she was, in fact, blessing me, because she already had. Her mere presence in my life had been and remained a blessing.

Only one thought controlled me in that moment. Her eyes opened, and those ebony orbs pierced straight through to my soul.

"Genevieve."

She tilted her head and smiled, which warmed me from the crown of my head straight down to my toes.

"I'm in love with you."

GENEVIEVE

I blinked a few times to make sure I hadn't imagined what he said. "Trent..."

I'd been fighting my feelings for Trent since the day we met, only realizing that the feelings had grown far too deep by the time my family spent Thanksgiving with his. When I'd given thanks to the Lord, I'd thanked him for Trent.

"I love you. I do." Trent shrugged and placed his hands on his knees, his hazel eyes never leaving mine. He didn't look away or try to avoid what he'd said. No. He was manning up and staying strong in his conviction.

We were sitting in the Lotus position, facing one another and staring helplessly. "It's too soon..." I cringed even as the words left my mouth.

Trent shook his head. "Nope. I was in deep relaxation, and I realized something."

"That you love me?" My voice cracked.

"Well, that has been weighing on me for a while. I just didn't know how to say it. But it was when you told me to imagine my color that things became so clear." His tone was awed.

"And?"

He grinned and tipped his head. "My color was red."

I nodded. "The Muladhara Chakra or the root chakra. I've known since the day we met that your root chakra was blocked. I'm actually surprised that's the color you saw." My heart was thumping double time. Seeing red went against everything that he was and had been most of his adult life. If anything, he'd always resisted being stable in one place.

"So what became clear for you?" I asked, my heart thrumming, the hairs on my neck prickling.

Trent licked his lips, and I watched that small movement. I wanted nothing more than to kiss those plump bits of flesh.

"I'll get to that. First, why did you think my root chakra was blocked?" He scrunched his eyebrows together.

I inhaled fully to give myself time to place my thoughts.

"You're always on the go, hardly ever spend time in your apartment, and even though it's top-notch, as I've mentioned before, there's really nothing personal keeping you there. You are a baseball player who travels all the time, and you've admitted that you haven't had a committed relationship since before college. Usually, people with a blocked root chakra tend to be flighty, on the go, and have very little keeping them in one place for long."

"Until now." His hazel eyes turned a startling green.

"How so?" I was afraid to hear it, but needed with all my heart for him to believe what I'd suspected.

"Now I have you. I have Rowan and Mary. My relationship with my folks has never been better, and I'm not looking forward to going back on the road. Heck, I'm not looking forward to sleeping in my bed at my cold apartment."

I swallowed, the emotions clogging my throat like a wad of cotton had been stuffed down there. "So what does that mean to you?"

I held my breath, waiting for the punch line, the end of the joke. Trent was saying everything I'd ever dreamed he'd say. Coming to the conclusion that the life he had been leading wasn't worth living any more. That beyond the glitz and glam was an honest and true life with a mate, family, and a home.

"It means I'm finally home. Wherever you are is where I want to lay down my roots."

I couldn't hold it in any longer. "I love you, too!" I squealed. I pressed forward, and sitting in Trent's lap in a private yoga room at Lotus House, I held his face and professed my love through a kiss—a single ongoing press of lips to lips that said it all.

He loved me. I loved him. This was us, committing to one

another. Laying down roots for a future together.

CHAPTER EIGHTEEN

Balancing the root chakra mentally can be an involved process. Although meditation offers the ability to connect to a higher spiritual plane that will naturally ground you, you cannot always rely on outside sources to ensure your survival. But you can always count on the connection to your higher self and/or faith in a power higher than yourself to guide you.

TRENT

Christmas Day was finally here. I'd sat on pins and needs for an entire month to drop this present on the Harper clan, and I could not wait.

Genevieve slept soundly next to me in her bed at the Berkeley home her parents had left her. For a long while, I just watched her sleep. The woman was beautiful in the daylight or nighttime hours, but in repose, her features turned angelic. A softness that wasn't there during the day came over her pale skin, making her look like the finest silk.

Snuggling up to her back, I kissed her neck, waiting for the telltale hum.

"Umm," she mumbled and pressed her perfect ass back against my morning wood.

Damn. She got me every damn time. For two weeks straight, I'd slept in her bed. And every morning her tight, sleepy body had the power to ruin me. Rolling her over, I lugged a leg over the top of her and slid over her form, holding most of my weight on my forearms. My hamstring protested as I shimmied down her body. Hovering between her breasts, I inhaled her scent. A mixture of last night's shower romp with lemon-scented body wash and my fresh breeze male soap commingled into something heady and mouth-watering.

Slowly, I inched my way down her body. I looked up at her one last time before going under the covers. Her head was tilted to the side, and her mouth was slightly open. Little puffs of air left her mouth as the last vestiges of sleep kept her under. Not for long. I planned to wake her with one helluva Christmas morning orgasm—something I was hoping to make a new tradition.

My girl only had underwear and a tank on, so I had easy access to slip my finger into the seam at the side of her lacy panties and tear the tiny edge with barely any effort. I repeated the action on the other side, and the fabric loosened and slid off. Gripping her knees, I pushed them open and up, putting her entire center on display. The covers gave little room to breathe, but who needed air when I had a juicy peach calling my name?

When her legs jolted, I knew she'd awoken, but I was ready. I held them fast, and just like a pussy-sucking ninja, I laid my lips over her core and tasted her before she could ever even utter a good morning.

"Trent..."

I licked her up and down, flicking her hardened clit with rapid jabs of my tongue.

"Baby...wow..."

I stuck my tongue in as far as it would go, wanting to taste the purest of her essence. Her hips jerked, but I didn't allow her to control the movements. No, this morning, it was all me. She was going to take every ounce of pleasure and cry out in release as I licked up every last drop. Using two fingers, I pushed into her heat. Her body trembled as I hooked them up and found that patch inside that made her go berserk.

"Oh my god..."

That was the second holy reference. A third, and I'd be tasting that sweet nectar straight from the source. I hummed and spent a few minutes fingering her deep, making her crazy. At one point, she cried out to God again, but that time, she held my head with her hands over the blankets. She tried and failed to shift her hips up and ride my mouth. Not this time. Pressing in a third finger, I went for the gusto by wrapping my lips around her clit, laying my tongue flat over it, and giving it the double rub, lapping repeatedly coupled with a firm suction.

Her pussy got so juicy, all I could hear were the labored sounds of my breathing and feel the slippery glide of my fingers in and out of her slit as she came while I was three fingers deep.

"Oh, my word..."

It was music to my ears.

I let her ride out her release, forcing it to go on and on

until her body just flat gave out. Then I licked up her cream, swirling my tongue around her swollen clit, giving it one last soft lick before kissing my way up her body. When I got to her tank top, I pushed it up so I could run my tongue over each fat nipple. They were hard little points, the size of erasers and red as raspberries, and I hadn't even touched them. I narrowed my eyes and looked at the tightened peaks.

"You played with your tits, gumdrop." The single thought that she was up here plucking at those succulent tips made my dick so hard it could cut diamonds.

She mumbled something incoherent that was a cross between a "had to" and "no choice."

Taking my time, I made my way up her body and snuggled along her side—where I enjoyed being almost as much as between her thighs—and kissed her lips. "Merry Christmas, gumdrop."

That time, she gave more effort in the return kiss.

"I'll say." She blew out a breath over her forehead and wiped the hair out of her eyes. "Merry Christmas. Shall I return the favor?" She grinned that sultry smirk.

Hmm... I thought about it for all of two seconds. That hadn't been the reason I'd gone down on her, but now that she was offering, who was I to turn down my girl's luscious lips wrapped around my cock?

"Ho, Ho, Ho on to blow she goes..." I sang, making up words to a random Christmas song.

She giggled and then rolled up and over my body. She laved each of my nipples and bit down on the flat disks until I groaned and palmed her ass. I looked down, and she winked, kissing her way over the hills and valleys of my abdomen until she reached the small thatch of hair she called the happy trail. I was all for that description because, if my woman was scratching her nails down that trail, I was a happy camper.

Just as she was about to go under the covers, I pulled them up and away, knocking that shit right onto the floor.

She pouted. "I thought you'd want me to be all incognito like you were."

"Hell, no! I want nothing in the way of me watching the most beautiful woman alive wrap her lips around my hard cock and suck me off on Christmas morning. This is how memories are made, gumdrop. The best ones. The ones we can revisit year after year—"

The second her mouth engulfed the head of my dick, I thought of nothing else but her mouth, lips, tongue, and that this was the best damn Christmas I'd ever had.

GENEVIEVE

"I can't believe you did this." I shook my head and looked down at the paper work in front of me.

Trent clasped his hands in front of his body. He sat next to me, his elbows on his knees, his head turned toward me. "Do you like it?"

I huffed. "Do I like it? Of course I like it, but it's too much. Trent, you paid off my student loans and the remainder of the semester I needed to finish my cosmetology diploma?"

"Yeah. I thought you wanted to finish and you're so close, babe. Now you can." He pointed to a line on the form. "See. I've already set you up to start the last semester in February. Same time I start spring training, provided the leg is up to par."

"It will be," I said.

Trent grinned. "With you helping, I believe it. I'm already

surprising the hell out of the coaches with how much mobility I've got. That was all you, gumdrop. Your yoga and commitment to me and my recovery got me there."

I rolled my eyes. "No, baby. That was all *you*. Your commitment to attending yoga every weekday and following your regimen. But you're changing the subject!" I knew how much that school cost, and I still owed five thousand in school loans, which apparently were now paid off.

Trent leaned forward and cupped my cheeks. "Gumdrop, look at me. Do you want to go back and get your diploma?"

I nodded.

"And do you want to one day own your own salon?"

Again, I nodded.

"Then shut up and accept the present."

That time I scowled.

"Yeah, Vivvie. This is ridiculous. Besides, I want Trent to open our gift," Rowan said, rubbing his hands together.

"Yeah, yeah! Trent, we all worked on it together!" Mary clapped and jumped up and down in her slipper-clad feet.

"All right, lead the way."

Mary pointed to a tall poster-sized present next to the Christmas tree. Trent leaned down and tore at the paper as if he were a five-year-old.

I worried about his reaction. We didn't have much money, so the present was handmade. Trent had a soft side that mostly consisted of making love to me and being kind to my siblings and his parents, but I hoped that the gift make him feel like a bigger part of a whole.

He'd told me a couple weeks ago that he finally felt like he was home with me and my family. So the three of us had covertly taken pictures over the last couple weeks, along with the random ones his mom had taken at Thanksgiving and a few we'd taken with the cell phone when we were out. I'd printed all of them, and the three of us did a scrapbooking project and made special designs around the edges. The framed collage was all pictures of him with us and his parents. One big, happy Brady Bunch style family.

Trent covered his mouth. "It's...it's...ah-mazing. I mean... wow..." His eyes were wide and his jaw slack as he fingered the different pictures. "This is one of the best presents I've ever received."

Mary squealed and jumped into his arms. He hugged her tight and petted her hair. Then he stood, and Rowan gave him the manly fist bump. Trent grabbed his hand and brought my brother into a full hug. At first, Rowan tensed but then wrapped his arms around Trent and squeezed. That was when the tears ran down my face.

Ever since Dad had died, Rowan lacked that male bonding. Trent had manned up over the past two months, giving his time to Row, which definitely helped him come out of his shell a bit, but this was the first time he'd embraced a male like that since we lost Dad.

I stood and threw myself into Trent's arms. "I'm so glad you like it," I sobbed against his warm neck.

He held me close, kissed my cheeks, and wiped at my tears. "I love it, and I love you. Now I'd like to give Row a present, but you have to promise not to be mad. This is my gift, man to man. It will hurt me deeply if you don't allow him to accept it."

Oh, no. My mind spun at the possibilities. After my gift and the Barbie dream house for Mary complete with four new Barbies, the Ken dolls, a race car, and a closet full of clothes, the options were endless. What could he have gotten a soon-to-be seventeen-year-old?

"Row, you ready for your gift?"

Rowan's eyes lit up. "Yeah, sure. Whatever, man."

He was obviously trying to be cool, which actually worked for him.

"Okay, but this present is for Christmas and your birthday. I don't want your sister killing me for going overboard."

"Um...okay." Row's voice shook. He cleared his throat and followed as Trent walked out to the front of the house.

The three of us followed Trent right out the front door and stopped on the porch. There, in the driveway, were Trent's parents standing right next to our dad's vintage Mustang.

"Holy shit! Dad's *Stang*." Row's eyes were wide as dinner plates. He ran his fingers through his hair and tugged at the layers. "No way!"

He looked at the car, to me, to the car, and then to Trent who was holding out a set of keys.

"Yes way. No man should be without the car his dad loved and wanted him to have. Right, Dad?" Trent yelled over the porch to where his dad held his mom in a tight hug in the frosty morning air.

"Damn straight, son!"

I opened my mouth and closed it at least five times. Rowan, on the other hand, grabbed the keys, hugged Trent, and ran down the steps where he laid his body over the car and gave it a welcome back hug.

Trent came over to me as Mary ran down the stairs to hug the Foxes. They wrapped her in their loving arms right away.

"Merry Christmas, sweetheart. We have tons of presents for you," Joan said.

Richard rolled his eyes and grinned. "She really does.

She went nutty on you four but especially you, little one." He petted Mary's hair.

I shook my head and sucked back a sob, watching my family happy on Christmas. Usually this day was one of the hardest without our parents. However, today, with Trent and his family, it felt like we were starting over. Making good memories with people we loved, yet never forgetting the ones we'd lost.

"Did I do okay?" Trent wrapped his arms around me from behind.

I held on to his forearms as my brother kissed the car and petted it like it was a long lost lover.

I pressed back into him. "You did more than okay. You did it all."

"What all?" he asked kissing my temple.

"You gave us back Christmas."

"And you gave me back a real life. I think we're even." He laughed and squeezed me tighter.

TRENT

"Dude, long time, no see." Clayton Hart, my private personal trainer, grabbed my hand to shake it and clapped me on the back at the same time.

I smiled wide. If I called anyone a best friend, Clay would be the one. He'd been with me since college, where we graduated together. He graduated at the top of the class in sports medicine and fitness and I went off to play for the Oakland Ports. I'd seen him several times a week for the past five years. He helped me work out and keep my weight down by giving me a menu plan.

I rubbed my gut and patted it. "Too long."

Clay grinned. "All those holiday meals, eh? I was beginning to wonder why you rescheduled our training for the last few weeks. Glad to have you back, man, and see you looking good. Actually"—he stopped, rubbed at his chin and tilted his head—"something's different."

"Yeah, the ten extra pounds of turkey, prime rib, Ma's desserts, and Genevieve's homemade meals are sticking to the ribs, making me soft." I pulled off my sweatshirt, leaving on my standard white tank and a pair of basketball shorts.

Clay shook his head. "Nah, man, it's something else. You look good. Really good. No bags under the eyes." He pulled at the skin of my forearm. "Skin seems nice and elastic, hydrated, and you don't have that scowl on your face." He chuckled and huffed out a fast breath. "Not sad to see that sour face go, that's for sure."

I got on the treadmill, and Clay set the pace. I wasn't having any trouble with the leg, so he pumped it up and raised the incline.

He assessed the machine and pressed more buttons. "Your leg is doing great, man. You're far beyond where I thought you'd be at the first part of January. I hoped, but since you'd canceled with me, I figured you were wallowing in your own self-pity. Doesn't seem that's the case."

I swished some water around my mouth and swallowed. "Nope. Everything's good, man, really good."

"Now *that* I can see. What have you been up to? Different chick every night?" He waggled his eyebrows.

I sighed and scowled.

"Ah, there's the frown. It's back. Sorry, man, didn't mean to piss you off. What's the deal?" Clay's blue eyes softened as he leaned against the treadmill.

"I'm only seeing one woman. Committed to her, actually."

Clay looked at me as if I'd just told him I quit the league. "You? In a relationship?"

"Yeah, me. What's it to ya?"

He shook his head and grinned. "Is she pregnant?"

"No!" I said too quickly, instantly remembering a couple weeks after Thanksgiving when we thought she might be. She said she'd gotten her period, and that was that. I didn't want to admit to him that a part of me wished she had been. I could definitely see a little mini Trent or Genevieve running around.

"Then what gives?"

"Genevieve is something else, man. She's beautiful, a yoga teacher." I grinned. "Takes care of her family, works hard, doesn't ask for jack shit, and for some crazy reason, she loves me."

Hitting a few buttons, I stopped the treadmill and wiped the sweat off my face and neck. Clay led me over to the weight machines. I sat down on the bench.

He rubbed at his hair and looked around. "Good for you. I'm happy for you. But is one woman really going to be enough? I mean, you've got a horde of fans and groupies, not to mention the line of broken hearts already." Clay adjusted the weights.

I pulled down the weight bar to work on my back. "Genevieve is more than enough. Seriously, she's the reason I'm doing so well. No offense."

Clay laughed. "None taken. I figured when you said yoga instructor you actually went to the classes."

I nodded. "Every last one. That shit is no joke. It's much easier to lift weights and run on a treadmill. But yoga? That is not for the weak."

"You like the class offerings?"

"I like her offering." I smirked.

He shook his head, covering a smile.

"They have tons of them, and believe it or not, most of the classes have about thirty to forty percent men, which I hadn't expected. I'd always thought yoga was for women, but there are a lot of guys teaching and taking classes. You should check it out."

Clay fiddled with the weights, adding more. "I'll do that. I've been looking for something to change things up. Personal training is great, and the money is killer with the celebrity clientele, but sometimes I just want to chill, you know? Mentally escape."

I followed Clay to the ab machine. "I totally get it. At first, I thought it was going to be easy, but yoga pushes you physically and mentally. Stretches me out good. Of course, I get private lessons from Genevieve so there is that." I grinned and licked my lips.

"You suck, man." Clay scowled this time.

"What? Have you ever thought about settling down?" I took in Clay's form.

He took care of himself and it showed. He didn't seem to have much in the way of fat, and women gravitated toward him naturally. Usually, that meant a guy had a nice face, too, but I'd never thought much about it either way. I typically had the same response from the opposite sex. When the two of us were out, step back. The ladies came in droves.

"Is that what you're doing?" He smirked.

I tipped my chin. "Yeah, man, I am. Genevieve is it for me. No bullshit. I just gotta get through the away games and keep my shit in check. You?"

Clay shrugged and flipped a towel over his broad shoulders. The black Chinese letters that ran down the outside of his left arm were slick with a mist of sweat that glinted off the overhead lights. He'd probably worked out before I arrived.

He inhaled and let out a slow breath. "I'd love to settle down, start a family, but I've been there once before, and look how shitty that turned out. Not sure I could trust so easily for a second round in the love department." He ran his hand through his spiked blond hair.

"I hear ya." I stood and gripped him on the shoulder. "If you do want to give it a shot, let me know. Genevieve works with a host of hotties over at Lotus House Yoga Center. Seriously man, they are bangin', and all of them are sweet as cherry pie."

Clay groaned. "Now you just sound like an asshole again. Come on, let's work off that layer of cake over your gut and get you ready for spring training. We still on for personal training in between?"

"Hell, yes. I need to stay in prime shape. I've got a contract to secure and a woman to keep satisfied."

CHAPTER NINETEEN

Child's Pose

(Sanskrit: Balasana)

Child's pose in yoga is the primary resting pose. It is used in almost every single yoga class to give the body and mind a moment of peace. Typically, the position has the arms on the mat, stretched out in front of you, but you can modify by tucking the arms. Kneel with your knees wide. Lay your chest down between your bent legs, resting your forehead on the mat. Stretch your arms out wide or tuck them in.

GENEVIEVE

The nurse practitioner entered the all-white room and shook my hand. "I'm Tammy, and I'll be giving you your annual exam." The tall brunette smiled and washed her hands. She was taller than I, around five feet eight. Her hair was brown and cropped close to the nape. A cool pair of blown-glass earrings dangled from her ears. The hues and tones in the glass perfectly matched the purple-rimmed glasses she had perched on her small button nose. "You mentioned on your form that you were interested in some contraception? Are you using anything now?"

"Just condoms. I haven't had the need for anything consistent until recently."

"And you're looking at the birth control pill?"

I nodded and swung my bare legs. Sitting naked in the doctor's office with only a weird paper vest and a paper drape over my lower half while the nurse and I communicated about contraception was uncomfortable. I wish she'd chatted about this before or after my exam. I could hardly focus on anything but the fact that she was going to be up close and personal with my hoo-hah.

"When was your last period?"

"I should be due anytime." I glanced at the calendar across the room. "Actually, I'm normally pretty regular. I should have gotten it two days ago, but that's not unusual right? I was a week late last month, which was scary because my boyfriend and I had been reckless."

The woman narrowed her eyes. "So you were a week late last month and are late again? Do you normally have unprotected sex?"

My entire body got tight. "No. Not at all. I've actually only recently started having sex again after a three-year dry spell. My boyfriend and I only had a day of slipups, but it worked out. I had a light period, even though it was late."

"Did you take a pregnancy test?"

I held the vest together more tightly against my chest, shook my head, and bit my lip. "No, because I had my period."

"Hmmm. Well, let's take a look."

After about five minutes of a most annoying experience, the nurse finally pulled off her gloves and tapped my knee.

"Just as I thought." She bit her lip and stood.

I looked around the room while she washed her hands and leaned against the counter.

"Genevieve, you are most definitely pregnant. If what you say is true about your period, I'm going to guess around eight weeks, but we'll need to take you over to the other room to be sure. I'll give you a moment to gather yourself, and I'll meet you over in room two. Okay?" Her eyes were kind as she patted my knee once more.

"Pregnant," I whispered.

She stopped with her hand on the door.

"But I had my period. It doesn't make sense." The edges of my vision started to darken and narrow. My heart became a steady throb banging against my chest like a bass drum. A fine mist of sweat broke out across my hairline, and I worried I'd faint. It couldn't be. It just couldn't. I shook my head, tears distorting my vision and then falling down my cheeks.

"A lot of women have a period the first month or two. It could also have been implantation taking place. We'll know more when we do the ultrasound."

Tears ran down my face. I wasn't sure if they were happy tears or sad tears. They were definitely freaked-the-heck-out tears. What would Trent say? Last month was the first time we'd admitted our feelings. We'd had all of three months together, and now a life growing was inside me—a piece of him and a piece of me. Oh God. I held my hand over my mouth as the sobs released.

★ ★ ★

Armed with a handful of ultrasound pictures of my six-week-and-four-day-old baby, a bag full of pamphlets for a new expectant mother, and the first month of prenatal vitamins, I walked down the chilly Berkeley street. Aimless. I didn't know what to do or where to go. The only thing I could think about was how Trent was going to take this information. Would he be happy? Angry? When it had happened, he said we'd deal with the outcome together and that we'd be parents, but that was what any guy would say when he just put a woman at risk. Did he really mean it?

My phone beeped in my pocket.

To: Genevieve Harper
From: Baseball Hotness
Gonna hit the Albatross Pub with my buddy Clay to catch up and have a few brews. Don't hold dinner. See you tonight, gumdrop. Be naked. ;-)

Albatross. Boy, did that name fit the current problem in our lives, even though he was none the wiser. Picking up the pace, I made my way home to cook dinner for the family and figure out what and how I was going to tell Trent about the baby.

TRENT

The table swayed as Clay and I slammed down our third shot of Patrón Silver. Empty beer mugs littered the booth where we sat. So far, we were head-to-head with the drink even though he'd sworn he could drink me under the table any day of the week. I accepted that challenge and upped it by betting cash on it. A Benjamin each, and the loser owned the title of lightweight.

Several of the guys from the team sauntered in. We played pool, drank a beer, took a shot, and repeated. We were four beers and four shots apiece in, and I was feeling mighty fine.

"Hey, Foxy, been a while since I've seen you out and about," a husky voice said from behind me.

Before I could turn, DawnMarie had her arm around my shoulders and her hand on my thigh creeping up my leg.

DawnMarie was tall and thin with a giant pair of fake titties that looked mighty fine on her. I'm sure she'd paid a pretty penny getting those suckers to look so good. I'd seen a few in my day, and hers were solid. DawnMarie—all one word, all one name. I knew this because she'd made me write it across my abs in black marker one night when we'd had some fun. As a matter of fact, we'd had several nights of fun over the years. She was a team groupie. Followed us from place to place, bedding whichever player suited her fancy at the time. She was a damn good lay, very attentive, and her dick sucking skills were top-notch.

"Hi, DawnMarie, mind moving that hand?" I slurred and frowned.

"Why would I do a silly think like that? If I remember correctly, you loved the things this hand could do."

I snickered drunkenly and looked down. Her bright red nails were like talons digging into the meat of my thigh, reminding me that they were not the soft lily-white hands of my gumdrop—the woman who would be right pissed if she saw this chick hanging all over her man.

"Sorry, darlin', I'm a one-woman man, and I'm keeping it that way."

DawnMarie scoffed, leaned her fake tits against my chest, and licked up the side of my neck. I couldn't help it. My dick responded, hardening painfully in my jeans.

She nibbled on my ear. "Betcha I could change that one woman rule to one woman at a time." She bit down and tugged.

It felt good, but not as good as the way my girl touched and kissed me there.

The liquor swirled heavily in my gut as I blinked.

Just as I was about to tell DawnMarie to take a hike, I turned my head and zeroed in on the most beautiful woman in the world. And then I couldn't see her anymore because a sticky pair of lips covered mine, and I was being kissed by a woman who tasted like apple beer. I tried to shove her away, but DawnMarie held on tight. Damn, the bitch was strong. I shook my head, but she took that as her opportunity to swing a leg over mine and hop into my lap.

"I can't believe you!"

Genevieve's words hit my ears right before a deluge of ice-cold beer slithered right over my head and down into the collar of my shirt, my chest, and all over DawnMarie, who jumped off me so quick, I could barely catch the blur of color as she screamed.

"You lying, cheating piece of work! And here I was worried about you! I waited up all night, needing to talk to you even though I have to teach in the morning. And here you are at a quarter to two with your mouth on this...this...bimbo!"

"Gumdrop, please. Listen." My words sounded strange and came out of my mouth like I had to speak around a mouthful of marbles.

"No, don't you call me that. I'm nothing to you. Nothing but the woman whose heart you broke. The woman whose life you tore apart. And the woman who's pregnant with your baby!" Her voice cracked.

Another cold bucket of liquid sprayed all over me as her words hit their target. Chills rippled up my arms, and my stomach tightened painfully.

"I'm going to throw up," I mumbled, not able to move. I couldn't even form the words to reply to what she said. The beers and tequila I'd pounded back on an empty stomach after working out were vying for attention.

The last thing I saw was Clay holding up his hands toward my fiery little blond goddess.

"You don't understand. DawnMarie was just playing around..."

Clay tried but failed to get Genevieve to see reason. Probably because he was as drunk as I was, only he'd tossed back a full meal when we arrived, and I'd forgone the meal to shoot the shit with my teammates. Bad decision. Coming here instead of going home to my woman was bad. Fuck. I was fucking everything up.

"Get your hands off me. And you"—Genevieve pointed at DawnMarie—"can have him!" She sucked in a breath as tears poured down her face, and she turned and stormed out of the bar.

I tried to go after her, but my shoes were filled with concrete. Every step felt heavier and harder than the next.

"Genevieve!" I roared as I fell forward, knocking into the table and hitting something hard and wet that smelled like stale beer.

GENEVIEVE

"Genevieve, I'm coming in!"

At first, I flinched, thinking it would be Trent banging down my door, but it wasn't. It was Amber, my best friend in the whole world. Thank God. She entered the room and scrunched up her nose. I sat up and ran my forearm under my nose to wipe up any remaining snot.

She sat next to me, her face solemn and kind.

The last time I'd been this far gone into an emotional tailspin was when my parents died. This wasn't like that, but it was a death. The death of a relationship and a future I'd wanted more than anything. And worse, I had the proof of that potential future nestled safely within my womb.

I tried to be strong. Tried to look at her like it was just another day, one where I hadn't spent the evening crying my eyes out so hard my nose burned and my throat was raw, but I couldn't be that person. Not now. Not with what I knew, and definitely not in front of my best friend.

My body shook and my lip trembled. The tears raced down my cheeks and coated Trent's hoodie I'd wrapped myself in last night for my cryfest.

"Jesus, Viv, what's wrong? Is it Trent?"

I choked out a garbled version of yes.

"Yes, it's about Trent?"

I could barely breathe, so I just nodded and let the tears fall. My nose ran, and I sopped up the tears and snot once again as I tried to suck in air. Sorrow and anger were two walls crumbling in on me as I tried to take a breath.

"Oh, no, did he break up with you?"

I shook my head and cried harder, the sobs turning

into full-body heaves. I pulled my legs up to my chest and hugged them, planting my head on my knees where I'd have a cubbyhole to hide in.

Amber petted my head, running her fingers through the dingy strands of my hair. "Did you break up with him?" Her tone was soft and lilting—the most comforting voice in all the world now that my mother was gone.

I nodded. "Yeah." I coughed and cried some more, planting my head down and letting it all out.

For a few minutes, she let me cry, continuing to comfort me and whisper soft words of encouragement. Eventually, she needed more information.

"Okay. So then, why are you like this?" Slowly she lifted a hand and covered her mouth. "Oh, no!"

My bottom lip puffed out almost as if programmed. I nodded.

"He cheated?" she gasped.

I nodded again. My lip trembled, and I swallowed profusely, trying not to lose it, the "it" being my mind and my meager lunch from yesterday. As it was, my stomach churned and revolted against the lack of food.

"That low-down dirty dog! I can't believe he did that. I'm sorry. Thank God you found out now, only a few months in, and not a year down the road. Or worse, after you married and had kids with the loser." She shook her head and frowned.

I didn't respond. Couldn't. Just stared at her sweet face, her long brown hair and kind green eyes.

A knowing glint hit her eyes and she tilted her head. "Is there something you're not telling me?"

Licking my lips, I sat up and pushed my dirty hair out of my eyes. "I found out yesterday that..." I couldn't even form the words. God, this was harder than I thought it would be.

Amber grabbed both of my hands and held them between us. "Anything. You know you can tell me anything. We've been best friends our whole lives. No matter what. Promise." She leaned down and kissed the top of both of my hands. "Now tell me. You're scaring the bejeezus out of me."

I inhaled deep, two full breaths, and then ripped off the Band-Aid. "Amber, I'm pregnant."

"Oh, that's not so bad...see... You'll bounce back. Wait... *what*?" She crushed my hands in a fierce grip.

"You're hurting me!" I yanked my hands back.

Emotions surged over Amber's face like a tsunami wave crashing against a barren shore. Shock. Happiness. Confusion. Fear. And then...anger. She stood, put her hands on her hips, and started pacing. "That low-down, rotten, dirty, filthy mongrel! I can*not* believe this. He got you pregnant and then cheated! What a jerk. Well, you know what?" She turned around, hands on her hips in a girl-next-door version of the Wonder Woman stance. "You're going to take his booty to the cleaners. You said he's über rich right?"

"Yeah, but..."

She shook her head and sliced the air with her hand. "I'm so tired of men taking advantage of kind women. If we have to, we'll get a paternity test. Show them exactly who fathered this angel baby. My God..." She ran her hands through her hair. "This is crazy. Are you okay? What did the doctor say?"

I shrugged. "I'm fine. The baby is six weeks and four days... well, five days now. The heartbeat looked good. Was really fast." I swallowed. "Would you like to see?" I wanted to show someone the little peanut inside of me.

"Heck, yeah, I want to see. I've got best auntie status no

matter what. And just think, down the road, I'll be able to take care of the little guy or girl." She smiled.

I pulled her into my arms. "Thank you. Thank you for loving me. For not judging me." I sniffed. I didn't want the tears to come back again.

Amber held me tight. "Honey, I'd never judge you. Just because I'm a virgin doesn't mean I judge those who choose to have sex. And I definitely don't judge you for getting pregnant. Things happen in the spur of the moment. I get that. I'm just worried about you."

I let out the breath I was holding. "I'm worried about me, too. This is a huge wrench in the five-year plan. And I'd just gotten back into the swing of things with the house, bills, and my coursework I'm supposed to start next month. I can't do that now. Using his money...ugh."

Lying back down on the bed, I rubbed at my stomach. The tension in my limbs made my entire body feel like a bundle of exposed nerve endings. Everything hurt.

Amber lay down beside me. "I promise to be there for you and the little one," she said and crossed her heart.

The tears came back with a vengeance and slipped down my cheeks. "I promise to let you be there, and to ask for help when I need it." I crossed my own heart.

"I love you, Vivvie. You're the sister I never had."

"You're the sister from a different mister, Amber."

She snorted and giggled. Lying there with my best friend, I accepted that this was part of my fate, part of God's plan. Why he had to be so cruel, I didn't know. At least, through all of it, I had the love of my sister and brother and my best friend. I had thought at one point that Trent and his family would be part of that, and I guessed they would be eventually, only in a different capacity.

I rubbed my belly, settling the ache deep inside that stemmed more from the fissure in my heart than from the little life growing inside me.

CHAPTER TWENTY

ROOT CHAKRA

When your root chakra is open and balanced properly, you will feel secure in your world. Average daily tasks will seem effortless, and you will go about your day fully at peace. You should have no doubt or concerns about your place in the world. You will feel protected in your relationships and secure in your finances, career, and future.

TRENT

"Wake up, you sorry piece of shit!" came a booming voice directly over my face. Raindrops sprinkled against my skin, droplets pooling at the corner of each eye.

Was I outside?

I blinked a few times, attempting to open my eyes. The room was so bright, as if a flashlight shining were directly into my eyes. Shading the light with my hand, I tried to sit up. The room spun, and my head ached like I'd been in a fight and lost. Big time.

"Dude, get up. It's three in the afternoon. Someone has some serious groveling to do."

I recognized that voice.

"Clay?" My voice sounded thin and hoarse, like my vocal cords had been put through a meat grinder.

"Yeah, man, get up." The bed shook around me. "Jesus, you are a lightweight!"

He continued to move the bed, and if he kept it up, I'd hurl all over him. Serve him right for waking my ass up when I felt like garbage.

"Dude, fuck off! I need sleep. Shit, where's Genevieve? My gumdrop will make it all better," I mumbled, turned over, and rubbed my face into a pillow that smelled of Tide, not like lemon body wash. If I could have coordinated my brain cells enough to move the muscles in my face, I'd have pouted. "Have my girl make me something to soak up the shit rolling in my stomach, will ya?"

No answer came.

"Where is she anyway?" I opened an eye and glanced at the room.

Clay's face appeared sideways and level with the bed. "She's not here. You're at your apartment. We cabbed it here and crashed on the couch. Don't you remember anything about last night?"

The act of thinking made my head pound like a drum in a marching band. Flashes of the night before started to stream into my conscious state.

DawnMarie leaning her fake tits into my chest and licking

up the side of my neck.

Genevieve screaming.

I can't believe you.

You lying, cheating piece of work!

Liquid pouring over my head.

I'm nothing to you. Nothing but the woman whose heart you broke.

Pregnant with your baby.

The world spinning and going black.

"Shit, Clay. I am so screwed." I rubbed a hand over my face, desperately trying to clear the fog.

Clay sat down on the bed and clapped me on the shoulder. "Yes. Yes, you are. Shall we go grovel?"

"Fuck, yeah." I rubbed my fists into my eye sockets and down my face again, the night's scruff prickling against my palm. A foul odor reached my nostrils as I lifted my arm. Turning my head, I sniffed my underarm and got a rank whiff of beer and tequila. "First, I need to shower."

★ ★ ★

"Open up! I know you're in there," I hollered at the heavy wooden door to Genevieve's Berkeley home.

Finally, the door opened, and I was face-to-face with a tall brunette. Pretty, but plain, nothing like my blond fireball.

"Didn't you get the hint after the first twenty knocks that your presence is unwanted?" She blinked and smiled snidely.

"No. I need to talk to Genevieve."

The brunette shook her head. "So you're the two-timing baseball-playing rich guy who got my best friend pregnant and cheated on her at the first opportunity. Yeah, she's got absolutely nothing to say to you. Take a hike."

I groaned and shuffled my feet, itching to bust through the door. My gumdrop was hurting and in that house, and I needed to fix it.

"But I need to talk to her. And I didn't cheat!"

She jerked her head back. "Really? Kissing some bimbo and allowing her to grind all up on your junk while sitting in your lap, in a public place, while your pregnant girlfriend frets at home waiting to tell you she's having your baby may not be considered cheating to you"—she pointed an accusing finger—"but to the rest of the world, I assure you, it's cheating. Now"—this time, she waved at me in dismissal—"carry on with your day. We'll have our lawyers get in touch with you about child support and the like when the time is right."

"Child support? Fuck that!" I growled through clenched teeth, anger spiking fiery hot down my spine.

"Oh, you're not gonna pay? We'll see about that." Her innocence seemed to slip right off her face as quickly as I could snap my finger. "Paternity tests will prove..."

"I'm not denying the baby is mine!" I snarled. "I'm denying that she'll need an attorney. I'm going to be there, right next to her for every second of this pregnancy, and lying in her bed." I pointed up at the top floor of the house.

The woman in the doorway huffed and put a hand to her chest. "You're delusional if you think you're going to get her to see you as anything other than a lying cheater." Her words held such disdain they almost burned the edges of my skin.

I groaned and took a harsh breath. "Look, lady..."

"Amber." Bitter contempt filled every letter of her name when she spoke.

"Amber, right. The best friend. Yeah, she told me about

you. I'd looked forward to meeting you, but we always missed each other, you being away at your internship and all the last couple months. Anyway, I need to talk to her. There are things I need to say."

Amber smiled a placating smile that didn't show her teeth—a gesture someone gave a person who was spoiling his day with a load of bullshit. And I was that guy. The guy who'd earned that gesture. Fuck. There was no way I was going to get through to her best friend. I'd have to try something else.

"Afraid that's not going to happen any time soon. Genevieve needs some time. She's got a lot on her plate, as you know, and this new development? Well, that's going to take some getting used to. I suggest you give it a bit. Wait for her to contact you."

"Yeah, okay. Fine. Just tell her I stopped by and to call me." I gave her the most pleading puppy-dog look in my arsenal.

★ ★ ★

Two weeks went by. Two long, fucking weeks of absolutely no contact with Genevieve. I'd called, texted, stopped by every day. The yoga studio wouldn't even allow me to enter past the main door. This angelic woman around my mother's age named Crystal came out after I'd yelled the house down. Yogis didn't like people raising their voices and screeching in their lobby when people were trying to find their Zen spot. Crystal, who apparently owned the joint, offered me a full refund. Turned out that when a person screwed over one of their own, they did not react kindly to that and made it clear I was not welcome in their establishment at that time.

Out of ideas, I went to her house and sat on her stoop. Two

hours passed before the Mustang pulled up and into the drive. I rushed over to the garage and waited as Rowan came out.

The second he saw me, he scowled. That was not a good sign.

"What do you want, Trent?" He tried to pass by me quickly, a backpack slung over his shoulder.

"I need to talk to your sister, man."

He made a noise between a scoff and a gag. "For what reason? To make her cry some more? Because that's all she does. That and vomit. Whatever you did to her broke her heart. Usually, when a guy breaks a girl's heart and still wants her back, it's because he cheated. Is that what happened?" His eyes were hard.

"It wasn't like that..."

He pushed past me, shaking his head. "I used to think you were the best thing that ever happened to us. The great Trent Fox." He held his hands out wide. "Best hitter in all of baseball. Now you're just a prick who ruined my sister. Leave us alone. And better yet"—he walked back over to me and slammed a set of keys into my hand—"take the car on your way out. I don't want anything from someone who'd hurt my sister just to get in her panties. I hope the next woman you bed gives you an STD."

Then he was gone through the garage and into the house, the metal door rolling down to the concrete.

My heart squeezed tight, and my knees shook. Man, I'd hurt this family and was beginning to wonder if I'd ever get through to them. A sharp pain shot through my heart, and I doubled over. I took a few breaths and rubbed at my chest. A tinkling sound reminded me of what was in my hands. The keys. And dangling right next to the car key was the key that would give me my in.

The key to the front door.

Later that night, around midnight, I walked around the house, checking it out. Everything was dark and quiet. Circling back to the front, I used the key and opened the door. The alarm beeped once. I typed in the death date of the Harper parents. It beeped once more and turned off.

I couldn't believe I'd resorted to breaking and entering. Well, technically I didn't break in since I had the key, but still... If they wanted to press charges, I could get into some serious trouble. Worth it. The woman upstairs held my heart and my unborn child.

I had to react. Risk it all. That's what my mother told me when I explained the shit storm that had happened at the bar. At first, she reamed me to kingdom come. Then she ran around the house, planning out her future grandchild's life and how she'd be a prominent player in it.

Slowly, I made my way up the staircase. Music flowed from Rowan's room, but that was not unusual. The kid slept with it on.

Holding my breath, I walked up the small flight of stairs and listened at Genevieve's door. Nothing but silence. I took one small breath and turned the knob. I looked at the bed, but she wasn't there. The bathroom light was on. On quiet feet, I walked over, and there, lying on the floor, was my worst nightmare. Genevieve's lifeless body was sprawled on her pink fringe bathroom mats.

I ran over, hit the tile on my knees, and yanked her into my arms. "Babe, oh my God, Genevieve!" I smacked at her face. Her eyelids fluttered. I pulled her head into my chest and thanked the good Lord she hadn't left me. "Genevieve, what happened?"

Her eyes rolled back as she blinked, her gaze unfocused. “So sick.” She started to heave again.

I rolled her over, and she vomited nothing but thick green bile.

“Rowan!” I roared at the top of my lungs.

His door slammed against the wall. Then I heard the pounding of his feet on the stairs, up the landing, and into the room. He skidded across the wood floor in his socks.

“What did you do?” he yelled.

“Nothing! I found her passed out. She’s really sick.”

“Yeah, I know, dumbass. She’s been throwing up nonstop for two weeks.” He stepped over us, got a washcloth, wet it, and laid it over her forehead. “She’s burning up. What do we do?” He winced, and his face paled.

I made a quick decision and lifted her body into a cradle hold. “Watch your sister. I’m taking Genevieve to the emergency room.”

“She’s not dressed!” Rowan said, pulling on his hair.

I looked down. Genevieve was in a tiny tank and a pair of panties and nothing else.

“Give me that throw blanket. Hurry!”

Rowan tossed it over Genevieve’s unconscious form.

“Gumdrop, you’re gonna be fine. Just fine. Row, call my mom. Get her to come here to watch Mary. I’ll meet you at Summit Medical.”

“Okay. Okay.” He stopped, took in a deep breath, lifted his shoulders, and pushed them back. A man stood in Rowan’s place. Somehow, he’d gotten older in the span of the ten seconds it took him to pull himself together.

GENEVIEVE

I woke to the sound of angry whispering but kept my eyes shut, not certain I wanted anyone to know I was awake. One of them sounded like Trent and the other my friend Amber.

"I'll say it one more time. I. Did. Not. Cheat. On. Genevieve. That broad is a groupie. Screws anything that moves. I was drunk, and she was all over me." Trent ground out the whispered words staccato style.

"Oh, sure. Convenient excuse." Even whispering, Amber's voice was tight, strained. She was in full mama bear mode.

"Amber, I swear to you. I swear on all things holy, on my mother's life, my job, I would never cheat on Genevieve. I love her. More than anything in this world."

She scoffed. "You say that now, but what happens when she gets all big with her pregnancy? Hmm?"

"More of her to love," he said instantly.

I almost laughed because that was such a Trent reply.

"And when you go on the road? You won't have the comforts of home keeping you warm at night. What happens then?"

He sighed, and it sounded heavy, as though the weight of his future teetered on the edge of this question.

"I don't know, Amber. Tons of guys are married and have girlfriends. Hopefully, Genevieve will be able to come to some, Rowan to others. I'll hang out with the guys who have WAGs. Whatever it takes."

"WAGs?"

"Wives and girlfriends. And I'll swear to Genevieve if she'll have me back, I'll stay far away from any groupies. Especially DawnMarie. She feels really bad, by the way. She had been drinking too, and usually, when a player tells her he's committed to a woman, she backs right off."

"Now you're defending your hookup?"

Amber's words were scathing, and I wanted to reach out and defend Trent, because I knew what he meant, even though it still hurt to hear it.

"No. Not at all. I just want it clear that I did not hit on her. She took advantage of me. I've got three people, including Clay, who will tell you exactly how it went down."

"Well, good for you. A bunch of liars are willing to back you up."

"Jesus, Mary, and Joseph, woman! You'd cut off your nose to spite your own face," Trent growled.

A throaty scoff rang louder in the room than before. "Don't you dare take the Lord's name in vain."

"Christ on a cross!" Trent hummed.

This was the time I needed to make my presence known and break it up before it got even uglier. "Anyone want to hear what I've got to say?" My voice came out as barely a whisper.

Amber and Trent both rushed to opposite sides of the hospital bed.

Trent leaned forward, kissed my hand, palm, and wrist before holding my hand to his cheek. "Thank God, you're okay. You had me so scared." His eyes filled with unshed tears.

Amber held out a pink cup with a straw, and I sipped the water. It felt like straight razor blades going down my throat. I coughed a few times but was surprised when I didn't vomit the water back up.

"What happened?" I glanced up at the IV bag pumping fluids into my body.

"You're severely dehydrated. You've lost a significant

amount of weight in the past couple weeks due to being so ill. They did a vaginal ultrasound while you were out, and the baby is fine. Heartbeat still going strong." Trent smiled. "They've got you on some pretty strong anti-nausea meds." He rubbed his face into my hand. "Gumdrop..."

I closed my eyes and turned my head to my friend. "Amber, thank you for being here."

"There's is no place I'd rather be," she said.

"I need a few minutes with Trent. Okay?"

She nodded, glared at Trent, and then walked to the door. "I'll just be right outside if you need me to kick out some cocky baseball player who breaks hearts."

I smiled. "Thank you, Amber. I'll be fine."

When the door closed, Trent leaned forward and pressed his forehead to my belly. That's when the tears started. The man I'd come to love—the flawed, beautiful, kind, cocky, overconfident male—clutched at my body and cried. Each word was a balm to my aching soul.

"I didn't cheat," he choked out. "I wouldn't. You have to believe me. Please, Genevieve. I need you. I need us. I'll do anything to make it right."

He lifted his face. Deep purple smudges were halos around his hazel eyes. "I love you. I love this baby. I want to be with you. Always. Genevieve, I want to marry you. Build our life together. Me, you"—he put his hand over my belly—"our baby, Rowan, and Mary. One big happy family. Please don't take that away over a misunderstanding. It will never happen again. I swear it."

Trent placed kisses over my belly and gripped my hand. I'd been miserable, unfeeling for two weeks. Completely and utterly lost without him. I didn't know how to be just me anymore. And since I was carrying his child, I didn't want to be just me. I wanted to be part of an us—him, me, and our baby. Of course, Rowan and Mary would be there too, but this was the start of my own family.

"I believe you and..."

"And?" More tears were pooled in his eyes.

"I love you. I'll always love you, Trent, and I don't want to live another day without you."

"Oh, thank God." His shoulders slumped, and the tightness he held seemed to seep right out of his pores as he closed his eyes and allowed the tears to slip down his cheeks.

I tugged his hand and brought him close. He kissed my forehead, each cheek, the tears I didn't realize I'd cried, and finally my lips. A life-changing, simple press of lips to lips said everything we needed to say and more.

EPILOGUE

"Gumdrop, wake up!" Trent nuzzled my neck and grated his chin along the column.

A sensation of a thousand butterfly wings tingled down my neck and throughout my body as he laid kisses on every available surface.

"Mmm, that's nice."

He nudged his scratchy chin down between my breasts. In seconds, he had my camisole top pushed below my breasts, and the cool air kissed the tips of my erect nipples. They weren't cold for long. Trent laved each tip and sucked one into the heat of his mouth. He swirled his tongue around the tip, mesmerizing me before biting down gently on the sensitive peak. A lightning bolt of desire rippled down my chest to land right between my thighs. My clit ached and throbbed, needing him somewhere else.

I opened my legs wide so he could wrangle his bigger body between them and I could shamelessly rub my center against his thick erection. God, I loved his big body. Everything about him screamed male, sex, and ecstasy all rolled into one fine package that was all mine for the taking.

"Babe, I got it."

He pulled at the tight peak, and I arched.

"Yeah, you did." I sighed, allowing him to work me up good.

He chuckled against my breast, kissed it, and then ground his lower half into my sex.

"No, gumdrop. I got the contract. They renewed." He slipped his hand down between our bodies where he tunneled under the slip of panties I wore to bed. In seconds, he pushed two fingers deep inside. I gasped and lifted up, wanting him deeper. Always deeper so I lost where he ended and I began.

He fingered me, pressing deep, tickling that spot inside that I loved, and pulled out. He repeated the process until my lower half was so wet he could have drunk from me. That's the way he liked it. Trent always made me insane with lust before he put me out of my misery and doled out the orgasms like he was serving up a platter of decadent desserts.

"Baby..." I tilted my hips, reaching for that inner tickle that would send me over the edge.

"If I let you come, will you listen to me?" He pushed his fingers in and held them there, high and deep.

I moaned and arched, almost there. "Yeah, please..."

I was not past begging. Ever since hitting the second trimester in my pregnancy I wanted him all the time. Day and night, and sometimes in between. He obliged willingly.

Considered it his manly duty to take care of his pregnant girlfriend.

"All right, gumdrop, you ready for it?"

I nodded, incapable of speech when he was rubbing that inner heaven. With a wicked glint in his eyes and a targeted thumb, he pressed hard against my clit. My entire body jolted, pleasure rippling through every limb, sparking a sensation so intense I lost my breath. He swirled his thumb around my hot button, pressed those deliciously thick fingers high and deep once more, and then sucked my erect nipple into his mouth. When he bit down, I lost my mind, my body, and my heart to the only man who could bring me such extreme bliss.

For several moments, he fingered me slow and shallow before removing his hand, pulling off my panties, and tonguing my center.

"Pure honey. Just like candy," he growled, stuck his tongue in as far as it would go, swirled it around as my insides quivered against his mouth.

Once I'd calmed down, he kissed his way back up my body, rose to a kneeling position, and pulled my legs up, placing my ankles on each muscular shoulder so my feet were boxed around his ears. Then he entered me nice and slow, careful not to bend me in half where his child rested. When he was planted deep, he ground in, swirled his hips in a circle, and stopped.

I opened my eyes and pouted. "Why did you stop? I was just getting into it."

He laughed and kissed my ankle. "Because you weren't listening before. I was trying to tell you that I just got off the phone. My contract has been renewed for five years. You'll never believe for how much, either." He grinned and thrust into me.

I gasped. "A lot?"

He bit down on my ankle. "Pay attention."

I lifted my hips so he'd get the hint that I needed movement. "I am paying attention."

"Not to my dick. To my words. Gumdrop, they renewed my contract for seventy-five million for the next five years. That's fifteen mil a year!" He pulled out and thrust back in hard. He gripped my hips, lifted me, and started thrusting in and out.

I moaned and tightened the muscles inside to give him that extra squeeze I knew made him nutso. He groaned and clenched his teeth, his jaw hard and stoic as he took his pleasure from my body.

"Why on earth would someone pay that much money for anything?" I arched, wrapping my legs around his waist. The new position put his length directly in line for my G-spot. Every jab of his cock was a press of sheer bliss.

He pressed his thumb down on the crux of my sex and swirled it in mind-numbing circles. "Because...I'm damn good at my job."

"Oh, God..." I cried out, my legs tightening around his waist.

He held my hips and pounded into me.

"I'm gonna..."

"Yeah, you are. Come all over my dick. Fuck, I love it when your muscles squeeze me like that. Nothing better than being in you, Genevieve. Nothing in this world."

My entire body went ramrod straight, every muscle tightening, toes curling. I gripped the sheets, held on for dear life, and exploded around the man I loved. He was not far behind. Trent dug his fingers into my hips where he thrust once, twice, three times, and finally, rooted deep, letting it all go.

TRENT

"Are you having fun?" Genevieve asked over the speakerphone in my laptop. Her blond hair was back in a tight bun, and she rocked the red lips today. Jesus Christ, I missed those red lips.

"Vivvie, you have no idea what Trent showed me today. I got to hang out in the locker room. Naked dudes were roaming around, others were getting their uniform on, and they joked around like brothers. Trent even got me my own jersey to wear that matches the team's for each game we do in a different city."

I grinned as the most beautiful smile spread across my girl's face. "That's so great, Row. Did you thank Trent for bringing you along?"

"He did!" I hollered, finishing up in the bathroom. "More times that I can count. He's more excited about the trips later in the summer, though."

It was June, and Rowan was out for the summer. Instead of hooking him up with summer ball, I got the coach to agree to let him come along to my away games with me. Take the summer off. He'd practice with the majors on the sidelines, catch some balls, get water, towels, play ball runner during the games, and make a little money. And I got peace of mind that my girl wasn't worried about me playing another kind of field.

"Row, why don't you go down and hit the pool for a bit? I'll meet you there. Want to talk with your sister alone. Yeah?"

"Sure. There are some serious hotties here in Vegas."

I laughed and whacked the kid on the back of the head only hard enough for him to know I was playing around. "Behave."

He rubbed at his dome and pretended to be offended. "Always." He grinned. "Love you, Vivvie!" Rowan got up and headed to the hotel room door.

"Love you more, Row!"

"Hey, you." I sat down in front of the laptop, looking at the most beautiful woman alive. "Do it. You know I want to see." I smiled and licked my lips, waiting for her to move.

She frowned. "Do I have to?" Her red lip puffed out.

"Come on, gumdrop. It's just me."

"But I feel fat." She pouted more deeply than before.

"You are not fat. You are pregnant with my baby, and I want to see. It's been a whole day." This time, I pouted. The woman I loved couldn't resist a Trent Fox original pout. I'd perfected the damn thing the second I knew it affected her so deeply.

She rolled her eyes. "Fine!" Then in all her yoga gear glory, she stood, backed away from the camera, turned sideways, pulled up her tank to below her ginormous breasts, and showed me her bump.

My baby. Her pregnant belly was getting bigger every day. Since she was due at the end of August, I repeatedly checked my schedule to make sure I could fly out at a moment's notice. I had the travel agent on speed dial just in case. Now, in June, she was perfectly rounded. The entire world definitely knew she was pregnant, and I loved it.

"God, you're stunning, gumdrop."

She huffed and tugged down her tank. The yellow cotton fabric stretched across her bump. Pretty soon, she'd need another size up, but I wouldn't be the one to recommend it. That was one of those things a man never tells a woman. Anything involving size or clothing was off limits, especially when she was worried about her body image. Truly, I had no idea why she worried. I loved seeing her rounded with my child growing inside her. It gave me an incredible sense of male pride. My child was changing her, turning her into a mother. Now if I could just get her to marry me, we'd be set.

"Shut up. You say that every day."

"How about this? Marry me."

She groaned again. "Same answer as yesterday. I need more time."

"Time for what? To decide you don't want to have me in your life?"

That made her laugh. "Goodness, no. I don't want our married lives to be about me getting knocked up. Let's discuss it when he's born."

"He?" A fluttering sensation lit across my skin.

Genevieve's smile widened, and she picked up an image and placed it near the camera. It was the image from yesterday's ultrasound. I hated that I hadn't been there for that, but I'd thought we were going to wait to find out the sex until we could both be there. I touched the screen, tracing the shape of my child's face and head. Then she lifted another picture.

"It was supposed to be a surprise, but this picture was a spread-eagle shot. When I asked what that little blob was between the legs, the tech laughed and said it was the baby's penis and testicles. She didn't realize she'd blown the surprise, but really, it was my fault. I'm sorry. Are you mad?" Her smile immediately turned into a frown.

I shook my head. "Mad that I'm going to have a son? Hell, no. I'm fucking stoked. This is the best day of my life. I'm going to have a son..." I leaned on the table, staring at the beautiful woman who had given me more than I ever thought I'd want in life.

I was finally settled. Soon we'd have our baby boy, William

Richard Fox—William after her dad and Richard after mine. Then I'd convince her to be my wife, and life would be perfect.

"No longer feeling the need to resist those roots? Still seeing the Muladhara chakra red tones when you close your eyes and meditate like I taught you?" She winked, lifted her hand, and propped her head in her palm.

"Absolutely. We're digging in, Genevieve. From here on out, I'm home, secure in the fact that I'm exactly where I'm supposed to be. With you and our son. I've laid down my roots, and they are there to stay."

THE END

Want more of the Lotus House clan? Continue on with Amber St. James and Dash Alexander's story in: ***Sacred Serenity***, Book Two in the ***Lotus House Series.***

EXCERPT FROM *SACRED SERENITY*

A LOTUS HOUSE NOVEL (BOOK #2)

I grinned at the sinfully sexy brunette as I stood there silently, arms crossed over my chest. She said I was beautiful. Interesting.

I'd seen Genevieve's best friend roaming around Lotus House. Watched her in action, taking the classes here. Her body was long and lean, perfect for the more complex *asanas*—or yoga poses as the Westerners said.

While I stood there quietly, her green eyes shone like emeralds. The catlike shape added to her allure. But that wasn't what made my knees quake. It was the thick, long dark chestnut-brown hair. She wore it plainly, straight and parted down the middle, the length covering her ample breasts. The best part was the natural hue that glinted off it in the sunlight streaming in from an open window Genevieve had yet to close before class. My guess was it wasn't dyed either. It had never changed color in the two years I'd caught a visual of her. What I wouldn't give to bind it in a fist and wrap it around my wrist, tugging it softly back as I feasted on her exposed neck.

She kept her look simple, yet she had an earthiness that called to the deepest part of a man. The instinct to hold and protect this woman was a powerful aphrodisiac. Those feelings plowing to the surface were rare for me, but I'd learned long ago through my Tantric practice not to deny or hide how I reacted to those around me. In this case, a desire born of aesthetics wasn't the only thing sending a flushed excitement through my veins. It was her energy. The magnetic field around her sizzled and threaded with mine in the most sensual of caresses. I wanted to wrap my arms around her and keep her close, bathe in her true spirit.

My cock thickened and stirred, awakening after a too long repose. I let my hands drop into a clasped ease in front of my groin. No need to scare off the little bird. As it was, her form fluttered as she covered under the weight of my appreciative gaze, readying to fly away. I wanted her to do the opposite. Respond to me instead, the way a proud peacock would, opening its feathers, fanning them out for premium viewing. I wanted to set my gaze upon not only her bare body, but her unhindered soul.

Though the woman stood tall, at least five-foot-ten, her shoulders curved in within my presence, as though she were silently submitting to me, or worse, afraid. I held out my hand and plastered a calming smile over my features.

"Dash Alexander. I don't believe we've been formally introduced."

She looked at my hand, and as if readying for battle, straightened her shoulders, firmed her spine, and clasped my hand in a steady grip. Grinning, I yanked on her hand and caught her off guard, which was my intent. When she bumbled into my chest, I wrapped a hand around her waist, kissed one cheek quickly, and then the other, though I couldn't help allowing my lips to softly skim along her silky skin to her temple, where I laid another soft press of lips. She gasped, and that soft intake of air, the tightening of her fingers at my pecs spoke wonders to my senses.

This scared little bird wanted me. She didn't just think I

was handsome. No, her attraction sparkled along her body like a fine gossamer mist. The scent of strawberries entered my nose and weaved around my senses. I squeezed her body to me in the smallest of embraces before grudgingly stepping back, putting a more appropriate distance between us.

Her eyes seemed glassy and unfocused when I let her go.

She shook her head and blinked several times. "Amber... Amber St. James."

I smiled and cupped her cheek. She leaned into it. A swell of male pride rushed through my chest. I caressed the high cheekbone with my thumb, appreciating the blush that pinked them. Her face was free of makeup, just the way I preferred a woman. Raw beauty.

"Happy to meet you, Amber."

For a few moments we stared at one another, our bodies' energy reaching for one another in a cosmic way I was used to experiencing in my classes, but not privately.

"Dash, glad you're here." Genevieve interrupted our eye-fucking of one another. "Amber is in medical school and needs to learn all she can about the practice of Tantric sex for her Human Sexualities coursework. As our resident guru, I thought you could help her out."

I cast my gaze to Genevieve. She pouted and put her hand up over her rounded belly, reminding me of the debacle I'd caused between her and her mate half a year ago. Payback could sometimes be a pain in the neck. Then an idea formed. An absolutely brilliant one, and not only would it help Amber with her schoolwork, it would solve a major issue for me.

I stared at Amber and looked over to Genevieve. Her hands came up to her chest in a prayer pose at heart center, only this was no prayer. She was downright begging. Her lips moved in a "Please, please, please" silent request.

"All right. On one condition."

Amber's green gaze brightened, her lips tipping up into a shy smile. "Name it."

Her voice was filled to the brim with gratitude, and I loved it. In fact, I wanted far more of it and looked forward to the time where I'd feel it surrounding me in a far more primitive and primal connection.

Flashes of her in myriad tantric sexual poses zipped across my subconscious. Her in Yap Yum position where she would sit in my lap, face to face with me until I'd tip her head back, allowing all that hair to dangle and tickle my thighs. I'd worship her breasts, plucking them into tight little berries. Our sacral and root chakras would meld in perfect alignment as I plunged into her, awakening the lioness hiding under the lambswool she wore.

"How better to observe the class than through participating?"

Two simultaneous gasps rang through the cavernous room until Genevieve spoke.

"Dash...there's probably something you should know about..."

"In what manner are you suggesting I participate exactly?" Amber squinted and crossed her arms over her chest.

Classic defensive pose. I hadn't expected that. A woman who just admitted to being attracted to me and responded instantly when in my arms didn't seem altogether eager to physically bond. Perhaps she had a significant other? A trail of prickling heat built at my chest and expanded out.

Jealousy. Now that was a new one for me. I couldn't recall the last time I'd been jealous, especially of a woman I didn't even know or a partner of hers that may or may not exist.

I lowered my voice so as to not sound too forceful or demanding. "My assistant bailed again. It seems I can't keep a single one for more than an eight week session,"

Amber pinched her brows together. "Is that how long a normal couples course is? Eight weeks?"

I nodded. "Yes, though some like to repeat it and work in detail on specific sections of the workshops."

"Would I have to assist you naked?"

I found it impossible not to laugh. So much so that both Genevieve and I burst out into raucous laughter at the delicate woman before us. She was beyond the pale. Her innocence positively leaked from every pore.

"Hardly, though I definitely wouldn't deny that the concept appeals to me...greatly."

Continue reading in:

Sacred Serenity
A Lotus House Novel: Book Two
(Coming Soon)

ALSO BY AUDREY CARLAN

The Calendar Girl Series

January (Book 1)
February (Book 2)
March (Book 3)
April (Book 4)
May (Book 5)
June (Book 6)
July (Book 7)
August (Book 8)
September (Book 9)
October (Book 10)
November (Book 11)
December (Book 12)

The Falling Series

Angel Falling
London Falling
Justice Falling

The Trinity Trilogy

Body (Book 1)
Mind (Book 2)
Soul (Book 3)

The Lotus House Series

Resisting Roots (Book 1)
Sacred Serenity (Book 2)

ACKNOWLEDGEMENTS

To **Debbie Wolski,** my yoga guru, for teaching me everything I know about the art of yoga. I can only dream that this book will help give my readers a positive connection to the practice so that they seek out their own experience. Thank you for always opening your doors and inviting me into your world. I adore you.

To my husband, **Eric**, for sticking by my side through fifteen months of yoga instructor school, months of lost weekends writing and learning more about my connection to the beauty that is yoga, and loving this new facet of me as you have for the last nineteen years. I feel like every day I love you more than I did the day before and go to bed with the knowledge that I will again awake with even more love filling my life.

To my editor **Ekatarina Sayanova** with **Red Quill Editing, LLC**...you understand me and my characters almost as much as I do. Every edit you help to bring a new piece of my writing alive I didn't know I had. Thank you for making me sparkle.

Helen Hardt, thank you for teaching me about expletive construction and how to make my sentences stronger without them.

To my extraordinarily talented personal assistant, **Heather White (aka PA Goddess)**, you help keep me focused and centered on what's important in life. That, my lovely, is priceless.

Jeananna Goodall, Ginelle Blanch, Anita Shofner—Thank you for being incredible betas but more than that, even better friends.

Gotta thank my super awesome, fantabulous publisher, **Waterhouse Press**. Thank you for being the non-traditional traditional publisher!

To the Audrey Carlan Street Team of wicked hot Angels—together we change the world. One book at a time. BESOS-4-LIFE lovely ladies.

ABOUT AUDREY CARLAN

Audrey Carlan is a #1 New York Times, USA Today, and Wall Street Journal bestselling author. She writes wicked hot love stories that are designed to give the reader a romantic experience that's sexy, sweet, and so hot your ereader might melt. Some of her works include the wildly successful Calendar Girl Serial, Falling Series, and the Trinity Trilogy.

She lives in the California Valley where she enjoys her two children and the love of her life. When she's not writing, you can find her teaching yoga, sipping wine with her "soul sisters" or with her nose stuck in a wicked hot romance novel.

Any and all feedback is greatly appreciated and feeds the soul. You can contact Audrey below:

E-mail: carlan.audrey@gmail.com
Facebook: facebook.com/AudreyCarlan
Website: www.audreycarlan.com

ALSO AVAILABLE FROM

WATERHOUSE PRESS

ON MY KNEES

THE BRIDGE SERIES: BOOK ONE

Haunted by the responsibility of caring for her troubled family, Maya Jacobs gave the only answer she could when Cameron asked her to marry him. Years later, entrenched in a soulless professional routine, she distracts herself from the lingering regret of her decision with a "work hard, play hard" lifestyle that guarantees no man will ever find his way into her heart again.

Cameron Bridge has spent the past five years married to the military, trying to escape the painful memory of losing Maya. After fighting his own war in the desert, he starts a new life in New York City, with his siblings, Olivia and Darren, by his side. When fate brings Maya back to him in the heart of a city filled with its own hopes and shadows, can Cameron find the girl he once loved in the woman she's become?

Visit MeredithWild.com for more information!

CRAVING

THE STEEL BROTHERS SAGA: BOOK ONE

After being left at the altar, Jade Roberts seeks solace at her best friend's ranch on the Colorado western slope. Her humiliation still ripe, she doesn't expect to be attracted to her friend's reticent brother, but when the gorgeous cowboy kisses her, all bets are off.

Talon Steel is broken. Having never fully healed from a horrific childhood trauma, he simply exists, taking from women what is offered and giving nothing in return...until Jade Roberts catapults into his life. She is beautiful, sweet, and giving, and his desire for her becomes a craving he fears he'll never be able to satisfy.

Passion sizzles between the two lovers...but long-buried secrets haunt them both and may eventually tear them apart.

Visit HelenHardt.com for more information!